TREATY OF WAR

TREATY OF WAR

A Jackson Crow Thriller

JAY BRADFORD

This book is a work of fiction. Names, characters, places, and incidents are the product of the author's imagination or are used fictitiously. Any resemblance to actual events, locales, or persons, living or dead, is entirely coincidental.

Copyright © 2022 by Jay Bradford.

All rights reserved. No part of this book may be used or reproduced in any manner whatsoever without written permission except in the case of brief quotations embodied in critical articles and reviews. For more information or rights inquiries, contact info@jaybradfordbooks.com.

Published by Peacemaker Press. Printed in the United States of America.

ISBN 979-8-433895-15-7

ACTUAL TREATY TEXT

Treaty of Mutual Cooperation and Security Between the United States and Japan, signed on January 19, 1960

Article V: "Each Party recognizes that an armed attack against either Party in the territories *under the administration of Japan* would be dangerous to its own peace and safety and declares that it would act to meet the common danger…"

1

THE ASSASSIN BLENDED into the crowd as he watched Ambassador Steven Blair thumb through heavy bond paper on an antique table in the Treaty Room. The flags of the United States and Japan flanked the ambassador like quiet sentinels. Behind him, Thomas Jefferson observed from a portrait on the powder blue wall. Blair and Jefferson wore the same wry smile—the hallmark of diplomacy. It almost amused the assassin, because the country's first secretary of state would not have been smiling if he knew what Blair knew.

Seated before the signing table, the honored guests expected the ceremony to be a formality. The terms of the agreement had been set for weeks, vetted by the lawyers, cleared by the White House.

"Are we ready?" the ambassador asked the young woman to his left.

She nodded, lips pressed tight. She looked nervous.

The assassin did not like that. She should not be nervous. Only three people in this room needed to be nervous, and two of them would be dead soon enough.

"Your first time amending a treaty between two world powers?" Ambassador Blair asked, with a relaxed Southern drawl. "You've done excellent work, Ms. Sun."

"Thank you, Ambassador Blair." She spoke softly, her shoulders loosening.

Not my problem, the assassin reminded himself. If she knew something, someone could handle it after he was gone. His beard had turned white long ago. He had only two bullets to fulfill his final duty, and then his grandchildren could live well—maybe even afford a move to Beijing.

Ambassador Blair turned to Ambassador Sora Tanaka, the Japanese statesman next to him who'd been reviewing his copy of the treaty in Japanese. Blair put his hand gently on Tanaka's back. "Shall we sign?"

Tanaka went through the same exercise. He whispered with a young Japanese lawyer on his other side. Her long, elegant hair bobbed up and down, giving the confirmation. It was a pity, the assassin thought, to spoil such porcelain skin. But this was business.

The two silver-haired ambassadors held up their fountain pens. The press cameras flashed as they signed the treaty, one copy in English, the other in Japanese.

When it was done, Ambassador Blair stepped forward and addressed the cameras. "This is a momentous day for our countries, and for the Japanese and American people. In 1960, the United States signed the historic treaty that committed our country to defend Japan, and in return gave us bases for our armed forces in the Pacific. Our treaty endured half a century—through the Vietnam War and the collapse of the Soviet Union—longer than any other alliance between two great powers since the 1648 Peace of Westphalia." Ambassador Blair paused, smiling, as if proud of his own remark. "Our treaty provided peace and stability in Asia, and now we renew it to ensure another century of peace."

Ambassador Blair talked on and on about the history of the U.S.-Japan alliance and the strategic importance of their joint security against rising threats.

Rising threats, the assassin thought. *That's us.* His chest puffed with pride as he snapped a picture, along with the rest of the press, and waited.

In his closing remarks Ambassador Blair invited the guests to stay for a reception. The politicians, diplomats, and journalists began to mingle. Ambassador Blair led his staff to stand beside the Japanese delegation. They formed a line, like sitting ducks, before a half dozen photographers.

"Take a few," Ambassador Blair said. "Let's get a good one."

The assassin stood to the far left of the row of photographers. He snapped another picture. Then, in one smooth motion, he lowered his camera, drew his gun, and leveled it at the target.

Her smile was serene. He didn't hesitate.

The gunshot exploded over the sound of camera clicks. A round hole appeared on the Japanese woman's forehead, blood on the powder blue wall behind her. No sound escaped her lips as she collapsed.

"No!" Someone screamed. "Hina!"

The assassin had one, final bullet. He pointed the gun up to his own chin, caught Ambassador Blair's calm blue eyes, and pulled the trigger.

2

JACKSON CROW COULDN'T quite hear the two gunshots from his office. He was downing coffee and trying to stay awake during a meeting about endangered turtles in the Galapagos. Alarms started going off, vibrating the devices that kept diplomacy humming. Eyes went to phones just as the State Department's intercoms came to life. The announcement sounded urgent:

EMERGENCY HIGH ALERT.
SHOOTING ON THE SEVENTH FLOOR.
IMMEDIATE LOCKDOWN IN EFFECT.

Jackson had lived through enough emergencies to know that this wasn't a drill. The other five lawyers in the meeting weren't looking so sure. All eyes slowly shifted from their screens to him. They were on the sixth floor, only one below the shooting.

"We should be safe here," he said, assuring them. The last thing he needed was a bunch of panicked lawyers running around like wet cats. "They don't lock down if there's danger inside. Otherwise we'd be evacuating." He felt his phone vibrate in his pocket. "We'll finish our meeting later. Head back to your offices for now. This will probably be over soon."

As the group left, he checked the encrypted text on his phone. It was from Reagan Murphy. She worked in the White House now. She also happened to be his ex-girlfriend, not that it mattered anymore.

Murder in the Treaty Room, her text said. *Get up there. Report holes.*
OK.

A rush of adrenaline brought him to his feet, like a former addict taking another hit. His mind shifted immediately to Lily Sun. She was his young associate, a Chinese American fresh out of law school and one of the lucky few who landed a job at the State Department. She'd gone to the Treaty Room for the signing ceremony with the American and Japanese delegations. Jackson had entrusted this treaty's details to her. He'd never seen someone so excited to watch a piece of paper get scribbled on. Surely Lily was okay...

He started to dash out, but hesitated. He opened the locked drawer of his desk. He took out his pencil-thin weapon and blew away a layer of dust. He rolled up his sleeve and fastened the discrete holder and tranquilizer darts onto his lower arm. He still missed his real gun, but it felt better to have this weapon on than he cared to admit.

He left his office, his leather wingtips tapping as he hurried through the bureaucratic maze of fluorescent lights. It wasn't hard to piece together the basics from the emergency announcement and Reagan's text. *Report holes.* "Holes" was an old inside joke with Reagan from college, back when they'd read philosophy books, eaten donut holes, and talked about the meaning of life. Nothing beat fresh donut holes, with their crispy glazed sugar exterior and warm breaded inside. They could make you happy even while reading Albert Camus. He and Reagan had decided that whatever's missing in life could be readily filled with delicious donut holes. Now Reagan was some Deputy-blah-blah, tight with the President. Jackson refused to care. But she *had* helped him when he'd wanted out of intelligence work. She'd landed him this nice cushy job to keep him out of trouble and closer to her. So much for staying out of trouble.

Part of him had hoped that this diplomatic business—agreements between nations, instruments of peace, for God's sake—might mean fewer corpses. But he had to admit this treaty worried him. It wasn't every day the Americans and the Japanese renegotiated their joint security while China was trying to take over every cubic inch of its surrounding seas—islands, whales, oil fields, and all.

On the seventh floor Jackson found a crowd lining the hall outside the Treaty Room. Four Diplomatic Security guards had guns raised. It wasn't clear whether they were protecting the crowd or keeping them under surveillance. Maybe both.

Jackson held up his office badge and walked past the guards. An appearance of authority went a long way during an emergency. No one tried to stop him until he got to the door, where two other men blocked the way.

"We're on lockdown," one guard said, face stern, hand on his gun.

"I have orders from the White House," Jackson said.

"I don't care if Mother Teresa sent you," the guard said. "Orders are, don't let anyone in."

Not good. A Diplomatic Security guard with an attitude. Jackson didn't hold it against him. DS agents were highly trained law enforcement, responsible for keeping the State Department and all U.S. embassies safe. This guy was doing his job, but so was Jackson.

"Sir, my name is Jackson Crow," he said. "I'm from the legal adviser's office. I'll give you ten seconds. Then I'm calling the NSC. Then the President will find out about this." Jackson held up his phone. "One. Two…"

The other guard's eyes opened wider. He started whispering urgently to his partner. Whatever he said—while Jackson counted out loud—must have been enough. He was on "nine" when the guards moved out of his way.

Jackson rushed into the room. Small crowds surrounded two fallen bodies. DS agents were maintaining order, no doubt preserving the crime scene until the FBI showed up.

A sigh of relief escaped from Jackson when he spotted Lily. She stood with her arms crossed, swaying like a slender willow and staring down at a motionless Japanese woman. A dark pool had spread from the woman's head and over the golden parquet floor.

Jackson moved quietly to Lily's side. "You okay?"

Lily turned slowly to him. Her crisp shoulder-cut hair hung like a helmet of black silk. There were streaks of tears on her ashen face. "She's dead. She was shot."

Jackson knew it sometimes helped to say it out loud. He put an arm around Lily's shoulder.

The Japanese Ambassador, Sora Tanaka, was kneeling beside the young woman's body, ignoring the blood that soaked the knees of his pants. "Hina, Hina," he whispered. The back of his hand pressed gently against her pale cheek.

"Hina Himura," Lily said. "We were just talking. She was…"

"*Korosareta*," Jackson said. He stepped forward and helped the Japanese Ambassador to his feet. The others in the group backed away instinctively.

"Yes," Ambassador Tanaka said. "She was murdered."

Jackson turned to Ambassador Blair, who had been watching quietly, expressionless. "What do we know about the killer?"

Blair pointed to a DS agent who stood beside the other dead body. "Ask him. They've been running checks."

"I would like to see the man again," Tanaka said, his Japanese accent faint.

The group moved to the other figure sprawled out on the floor. He was an older man wearing a suit and a press badge. A gun was on the floor by his hand. It looked like plastic—a green-light through a metal detector. But it was real. The puddle by the man's head proved it.

"I am certain," Tanaka said. "I have never seen him before."

"Bao Li." A DS agent held up an identification card in his gloved hand. "He had press credentials. Dual US-Chinese citizen, with Chinese media. We are sweeping the building, pulling all the footage, anything we can find."

The dead man unnerved Jackson. He was too old to be an assassin, with snow-white hair and a hollow face. Someone had groomed this man for a job like this, maybe for years. Jackson could already see the headlines taking form, about two dead foreigners in the State Department. *Beautiful Japanese lawyer murdered…by octogenarian Chinese assassin…*

Ambassador Tanaka turned to one of his staffers. "Find everything you can on Bao Li. This is no coincidence. The Chinese know the importance of this treaty." He glanced down at the dead body, then met Ambassador Blair's eyes. "How did you let him into this room?"

"We'll get to the bottom of it," Blair said, steady but with an edge in his voice. "We're on the same side. We mourn with you."

The Japanese statesman's face was blank.

"It's a terrible tragedy," Ambassador Blair added. "We'll do everything we can to make this right."

Tanaka didn't respond. He turned to his assistant again. "Have our people ready the plane. We will bring her back to our people, to her family." He stepped back from the dead man, but paused and glanced at Jackson. "I don't know who you are, but if you know *korosareta*, you will know we expect more than just words as apology."

"We will find who is responsible," Jackson said, bowing slightly. "And they will pay."

3

LI ZHANG CHECKED his watch again. It was an old watch with a cracking leather band and a bland white face—a gift from his father before he'd become a general in the People's Liberation Army, rich and powerful enough to buy Rolexes and even have a second son. Now the old watch showed four o'clock. Something should have happened by now.

Zhang went back to reading his copy of the Washington Post and sipping his coffee. It was from Dunkin' Donuts. Too much sugar and cream, but nothing was more American. He'd reached the Sports section when he heard the first sign of action.

A door closed too hard.

He slid on his sunglasses and glanced up. Diplomatic security was shutting down the main entrance of the State Department. This was not usual. This was good.

Zhang raised his hand to adjust his glasses, pressing the undetectable button by his ear. A green dot blinked twice at the margins of his vision. The recording was on.

He calmly put down the Post and the coffee and stepped out of his white Ford Taurus with the blue license plate that read DIPLOMAT at the top. The sun was bright and the clouds billowed high above. It was a glorious April day.

He held a slim notebook in his hand as he approached the huge concrete rectangle known as the Harry S. Truman building. The Americans had made their home of diplomacy look like a grey domino laid on its side—a one-dimensional version of the Pentagon. Zhang found the building to be yet another sign of American arrogance, as if they didn't need to impress anyone. Except now they did need to impress, and they failed. Zhang and his people had been running circles around them for a decade, and soon it was going to start paying off.

He was forty feet from the building's entrance when one of the guards stepped forward, blocking his way. "Sorry, sir, this entrance is closed."

Zhang smiled and nodded. "I see." He slowly lifted his press credentials before the guard. "I'm with the Beijing press."

"No one can enter," the guard said.

"But I'm scheduled for an interview."

"Sorry, sir."

"What happened?"

"There was a shooting."

"Oh no." Zhang put his hand over his mouth, more to cover his faint smile than to feign surprise. "Was anyone hurt?"

"There was a shooting. That's all I can say."

Zhang nodded, keeping his voice serious. "I understand. Thank you, sir."

As he turned to go, he tapped his glasses to relay the message to his father, General Li—the only other person who knew who had paid for this assassination. The two of them now had the leverage to use that information. Zhang wasn't above calling it what it was: blackmail.

He returned to his car and drove away, past trees full of pink-and-white blossoms lining the road. *Yes*, he thought, *Father will be most pleased.* For once, even more pleased with Zhang than with his brother who wore a Rolex and commanded an aircraft carrier in the East China Sea.

A glorious day indeed.

4

JACKSON FELL INTO an old habit as he walked with a group to Ambassador Blair's office: humming the Battle Hymn of the Republic in his head. He'd started it years ago, the first time someone had shot at him. The song's steady cadence had a way of steeling the nerves and focusing the mind. He considered humming aloud, if only to calm Ambassador Blair, Lily Sun, and the four DS agents who escorted them in silence. The agents had their guns drawn, looking around like another killer was waiting. Jackson doubted it. The Chinese had wanted this murder to be public, to make a statement. It was a targeted assassination. It was not an attack on America. Not yet, anyway.

As they rounded a corner, Ambassador Blair interrupted Jackson's silent humming. "Jackson, why did you come to the Treaty Room?"

Jackson shrugged, keeping up his pace. "I was nearby, in my office. So when DS sent out the lockdown alert, I came up as soon as I could."

"But why?" Blair asked.

Jackson couldn't answer that fully. He knew it would look odd, because most people didn't force their way into the scene of a shooting during a lockdown. He glanced to Lily. "When someone from my office is involved, it's my job to help."

"I'm glad you came." Lily shook her head, breathing out heavily. "I still can't believe…I've never seen so much blood."

"Such a mess," Blair muttered.

The group reached the door to the Ambassador's office suite in Asian-Pacific Affairs. The DS agents stationed themselves outside as Blair, Lily, and Jackson entered.

The woman at the front desk, Linda Jones, had short, curly grey hair and the settled look of a secretary who has spent her career in an office chair. She gave them a long up-and-down stare. "What happened?"

"We signed the treaty," Blair said, matter of fact. "Then there was a murder. A murder-suicide. The victim was a Japanese woman. The killer was Chinese. Our people are still tracking his details. "

Linda's hand covered her mouth. "Oh my God…"

"The lockdown should lift soon," Blair said, beginning to move toward his office. "Get me a line to the White House. ASAP."

Jackson found that interesting. Blair's first report should have been to the Secretary of State, but it was no secret that the Ambassador and the President were old friends. The press had a field day when the President had nominated his rich hunting buddy from Georgia for this post.

Linda didn't hesitate. "I'm on it," she said, turning to her computer. "You taking the call from your office?"

Blair paused and glanced back. "No, the cafeteria."

Linda's face flushed, but Jackson couldn't tell whether it was embarrassment or anger at Blair's sarcasm. She might be a useful asset. *No, Crow, stop thinking like that.*

"I'll have it set up now," she said.

Blair looked to Lily. "After the lockdown's over, go home and get some rest. You saw it happen, and you know this treaty. I have a feeling we'll be flying to Tokyo soon."

"We?" Lily hesitated. "I mean, okay, but I have a meeting on Thursday, and…"

The Ambassador held up his hand. "Don't worry about whatever else is on your plate. This takes priority now. Jackson, you can find someone to back her up, right?"

"We'll manage," Jackson said. "What do you expect our role to be?"

"Lily's my lawyer on this," Blair said, with a flash of annoyance. "I want her with me in Japan. She worked on the treaty, with the Japanese woman."

The woman who was shot. No wonder the Ambassador was on edge. Jackson's office usually had to push to get the attorneys involved, but they'd never faced a situation like this. He glanced at

Lily. She was as smart as they came, but she was green—a lawyer in her late twenties who had just dipped her toe into the swamp of Washington, D.C. The Ambassador was a different animal. He had a family fortune and decades of political games under his belt. Jackson doubted Lily could manage him on her own. Not to mention that the killing of the Japanese lawyer meant Lily's life could also be at risk. It could have something to do with the treaty.

Jackson didn't wanted to say anything so bluntly in front of Lily, but he saw little choice. He tried to keep his voice gentle as he met Lily's gaze. "If Hina Himura was a target, we have to assume you are, too. It's safer for you to stay here. I'll go instead."

"No, I'll go," she said, standing up straighter. "I'm not afraid."

"See? I knew she could handle it." Blair smiled wryly at Jackson. "And come on, you—of all people—know we take risks with this line of work."

"No," Jackson said. "Lawyers don't usually get shot."

"Who said this was *usual?*" Blair snapped, before smoothing his tie and calming his voice. "Anyway, now we've been warned. We'll have security on high."

That much was true, Jackson thought, but more security wouldn't be enough. The assassin might have been Chinese, but he'd flown in like a Japanese kamikaze. Someone wanted to be sure the attack hit hard, with no evidence left behind. Chinese intelligence was probably involved, and that meant Jackson's old colleagues would be watching as well.

"Fine," Jackson breathed out, in disbelief at what he was about to say. "We'll both join you in Tokyo."

Blair was quiet, studying Jackson. "Why you?"

"Lily is still at risk," Jackson said. "She may have firsthand knowledge, but she reports to me. I'm responsible for her. My office will fund the travel."

"Okay." Blair's voice became gentle as he looked to Lily, the Southern charmer resurfacing. "We don't do this because it's easy, do we?"

"That's right," Lily agreed. "This treaty is about peace. It's like you said, we need these alliances against China. They can't shatter everything just by…" She looked down, biting her lip, no doubt thinking of the puddle of blood on the parquet floor.

"I know you worked closely with Hina," Blair said. "She died serving her country. That's a great honor for her, you know?"

"I know," Lily said.

"And I'm serious, get some rest. Things are going to be heating up in Japan." Blair turned to Jackson. "I don't know why you're getting involved, but remember who's in charge of our affairs in Japan."

The President, Jackson thought, but he kept his face blank as he nodded. He could let the Ambassador think he was still calling the shots. He'd talk to Reagan about that.

"Good," Blair said. "And neither of you say anything to anyone. Not yet. Let's meet back here tomorrow morning. Linda will be in touch."

Linda looked up at the mention of her name. "I should have the White House in just a minute."

"Thanks," Blair said, turning toward his office. "I'll be ready."

5

REAGAN MURPHY LOVED the West Wing with all her heart, mind, and soul. She loved the tall windows, the gilded frames, and the American flags stationed around her standard-issue government desk. She loved sitting at the center of power, with the world order balanced like a spinning top above her. Maybe the Imperial Palace in Beijing thought it was on the rise, but all it took was a single phone call from the Oval Office, a few doors down the hall, to make the Chinese President jump.

There would be no calls from the Oval Office today. President Wallace had just arrived from Europe and had an important campaign rally in Ohio tonight. They needed to win Ohio again in seven months. The President's numbers had been sliding there, and everywhere, in lockstep with the dipping stock market. His challenger was Sarah Matheson, the Governor of New Hampshire, and a firecracker on stage. She'd caught the nation by storm, and people were excited about her "unusual" mix of policies—legalize pot, tax it to pay for a mandatory military service program, and privatize Social Security. The latest poll was the first real crisis, with Wallace at 42% and Matheson at 43%. The campaign director said it was a good sign. Being down a point or two in the polls often led to victory, he claimed.

Reagan disagreed. Her boss was an incumbent with every political gift under the sun and a billion-dollar war chest for the race. He had navigated almost four years without any major blunders. There was peace with Russia and China, a drawdown of troops in the Middle East, and even a growing economy…until a couple months ago. He should have been crushing Matheson.

The last thing the President needed was an international crisis on his hands, months before election day. He'd given Reagan clear orders: *Keep things quiet. No wars, no bombs. If somebody pushes, give a little.*

Well, she'd been giving and giving to the Chinese, but now they might have pushed too far. If they were behind this shooting, all her plans could blow up. And why on earth would they do it? Hadn't Reagan given them enough already?

As the Deputy National Security Adviser, she not only wrote the President's speeches, she also created content for those speeches. That's why she'd been talking, off the record, to the Chinese. Their President had his own speeches to write. Not that he had to worry about re-election, lucky guy, but even his Communist Party leaders slept better when the people had bowls full of rice and screens full of games. Trouble was, the rice bowls had been getting dirty, and the country's billion-plus people were grumbling. They were crowded in their cities. They wanted more space and more respect, even if that meant taking it from someone else. The Chinese government, naturally, needed to relieve domestic pressures.

"We need a military victory," they'd told her, "but we don't want a war."

Easier said than done. Hawks in both countries were clamoring for a show of force, anything to be the alpha country. But Reagan was not going to let World War III start on her watch. She glanced up at her PhD diploma framed on the wall—military history, with highest honors for a thesis on Thucydides. She'd spent her most precious youthful decade staring at words on a page for precisely this moment. She knew why Sparta and Athens had waged war for decades and destroyed a Greek empire, why England and Germany had barreled into World War I, and why every dominant world power suddenly found itself with a potential for war when it started losing its dominance. But not on *her* watch. The Americans could tolerate China as a world power, as a friendly equal. They had a vast ocean between them and plenty to keep themselves busy in their own hemispheres.

Like dealing with Japan.

Reagan thought she was done with this issue. She'd pushed for the last-minute revision to the treaty with Japan, just like the

Chinese wanted. The Japanese had resisted at first, but they agreed once they got the drawdown of American troops on Okinawa, like they'd been requesting for years. If they wanted to start defending themselves, so be it.

But how was America going to deal with an assassination on its own soil?

This was why Reagan had planted Jackson in his position. It was assets like him that helped her rise to where she was. And now he owed her.

She lifted her purse from under her desk. She took out her guilty pleasure: a picture from college, when they'd been dating six months. His hair had been long then. He called himself a Native American mut, but she loved his copper skin and high cheekbones. The sharp lines of his face made him look more like a hawk than a crow. She liked to imagine him turning eyes in his new lawyer job. In another life they would have married and had a few Crow children. But they both had different priorities. He had chosen to keep his secrets, and she had chosen her career. They were nothing more than friends with a backstory. For now.

She sent him another encrypted text. *Find any holes?*

His reply came within seconds. *Lots of blood. Old Chinese man killed a Japanese lawyer, then himself. Fake press credentials. No evidence. Guessing PRC.*

Just as she'd feared. *Why?*

Will find out. Flying to Tokyo tomorrow with Blair and Lily Sun, our lawyer who witnessed.

Suspects?

No. Potential targets.

Not good. Find out why.

On it.

Reagan shook her head and started pacing her office. This was a PR disaster. She'd have to write a new speech for the President.

She glanced down at the picture again. Could she fully trust Jackson? It still drove her crazy that he'd never opened up to her about his intelligence work. He'd kept his lips sealed even after she'd gotten a security clearance high enough to see everything that crossed the President's desk. His secrecy meant Reagan needed to take extra precautions—and from her perch, she could do almost anything. Maybe she'd enlist the CIA to trail both him and this Lily Sun—for their own protection, of course. Reagan could imagine Jackson's thoughts: *I have to protect Lily. Must protect the girl. Must protect the girl.* He could be such a caveman. Not that she held it against him after what happened to his sister.

She put the picture away. She had another move to make.

She had cultivated a key contact within the Chinese government, Li Zhang. He was undercover with the Beijing press, and his father was China's top-ranking general—next in line for the presidency, according to her reports. She and Zhang had worked out a handshake deal for their leaders. Even now, sitting alone in her office, she found it as exhilarating as sex—not that she was well qualified to make the comparison; her strict Catholic upbringing had left her with prudishness outstripped only by ambition. She shaped the world even if no one outside the West Wing and the Imperial Palace knew about it. The whole thing would make the Chinese *and* the Americans look strong, without anyone dying. No wars, no bombs, and a near-guarantee for President Wallace to win a second term.

It was set to happen within a week. But this murder complicated things.

Reagan picked up the phone and dialed.

"Hello." Zhang's voice on the other line was distorted by some technology that kept it from being recognizable. It sounded like he was talking underwater, with an onion in his mouth.

"It's me," Reagan said.

"Code?"

"Whale."

"Code?"

Reagan stayed silent. This was the normal routine. She'd stay silent for a few seconds while the guy undoubtedly tried to track the number that had called him, and to pinpoint its location. But he would fail, as usual, which would give him the confidence to proceed.

"What is it?" he asked, his voice now sounding normal, with flawless English.

"We did our part. The treaty was signed."

"Yes, I have seen. This is very good."

Reagan forced her voice to remain calm. "Why was there a murder?"

"It's only a distraction."

"Did you know it would happen?"

Silence.

At least he wasn't lying. "You should have told me," Reagan said. "The last thing we need is another wildcard. It will be delicate enough to preserve our deal."

"Our deal stands. Nothing will come of this…event. We will manage it."

"Why was she killed?"

"I cannot say, but you should know we weren't the ones who wanted it done."

"Then who did?"

"Ask around your government. You'll find out sooner or later. But it needs to stay quiet for a week, until our deal is executed."

Around our government? That suggested someone with authority, but not President's level. Not the White House, or Reagan would know. "Tell me why it happened," she insisted.

"That's irrelevant," Zhang said. "It's a distraction. All of this is a distraction, which will only help. Soon pressure will release on both sides. We both win, as agreed."

"Yes, we both win," Reagan said, fuming about Zhang's veiled clues. It took some nerve for him to hide what he knew from her. She was the one who controlled their deal. She was the one who held peace in balance.

But she decided not to press further yet. That would be Jackson's job.

6

LILY SUN FELT numb, and angry with herself for feeling numb. Hina had been shot in the head. Cold-blooded murder, body on the floor, skin chalk white. Why wasn't she terrified or furious or out of control? Sure, she valued control right up there with water and air, she had to admit that. But weren't there times when control was meant to slip away? Like when a friend gets shot?

All she could do was keep moving, numbly. She walked with Jackson Crow back to his office. He'd showed up for her. Not that she needed his help, but she never minded having him around. He was quiet and funny and smart. She knew he had some kind of baggage, with those premature flecks of gray at the temples of his black hair and the rumors that he was some kind of spy. But he was a good boss. Their routine meetings had become her favorite part of the job.

Lily shook her head. *Don't think about him like that. Not now. Not after my friend was shot...*

Even if she'd known Hina only a couple months, they'd gotten pretty close. They'd bonded first over sushi, talking about international law. That was early in the US-Japan negotiations, when the two of them, as the junior lawyers, had learned the treaty inside and out. Later they'd discovered that they both played Camelot. It was the latest online game starting in China and taking the internet by storm. She and Hina even played together once, logging into the same virtual world from opposite hemispheres. They'd slayed a dragon and earned two BitStones—enough of the cryptocurrency to buy a fine sushi dinner in Tokyo. "Now we're dragon sisters," Lily had said, and Hina had laughed.

My dragon sister. A grip of sadness broke through the numbness, like a hand reaching through the shock and taking hold of her. The world needed more like Hina. Now she was gone. Why had that old man shot her? It made no sense. Hina did everything with grace and elegance. She had no enemies. Everyone loved Hina.

They entered Jackson's office, with its neat stacks of paper and ever-present smell of coffee. Late afternoon sun streamed through the window. The walls had a couple generic pictures from a tropical island. There were no personal touches. No photos, diplomas, or awards. It looked like the home of a serious lawyer, or of someone trying to act like one.

Lily took the familiar seat across from his desk. Jackson sat, glanced at his phone, and typed something quickly. Lily noticed the corners of his eyes tensing—rare for his usual mask of calm. She reported to him, so this was now his responsibility, too.

He brushed back his dark bangs and let out a faint sigh as he pocketed his phone. Then he met Lily's eyes. He smiled gently. "Sorry. You doing okay?"

She nodded and tried to smile back. She still felt numb.

"That was brave back there," he said. "After what happened, I certainly don't expect you to go to Tokyo. You're free to change your mind."

"No, the Ambassador's right," she said. "I've been the lawyer on this, and I want to see it through. For Hina."

"I understand."

"I'm glad you're coming." The words carried more weight than Lily expected, calming her nerves. She felt caught up in something far bigger than this treaty, and Jackson's steady gaze and voice were like a life raft in the storm. If nothing else, Lily thought, this would save her from having to dine alone with the Ambassador. It was no secret that Blair, the wealthy perpetual bachelor, liked pretty women. Hina had joined him for dinner once as a professional courtesy. She'd told Lily it was no big deal. Hina never lacked for courtesy.

Jackson's secretary brought in a folder of forms and placed it in front of Lily.

"I'm so sorry," the secretary said. "These are from the investigators. They said it was a priority."

"Thanks," Jackson said. "That's fine. Lily, you can fill them out here, if you'd like. Maybe we can go through the questions together."

Lily said she'd like that. In fact, given the events of the past hour, there was no place she'd rather be right now.

7

KATHY SULLIVAN FOUND herself back in the good ole U.S.A.—in her office, no less—when her red desk phone rang. Number unknown, like usual. She stood and gazed out the window at the most clandestine forest in the world, basked in the day's fading light and tucked just inside the beltway in Langley, Virginia. She took a deep breath, then lifted the phone to her ear.

"Hello?"

"Kathy Sullivan?"

So it was official business. And not from her Agency, where anyone wanting her would have come by to talk in person. That was still the safest form of communication.

"Speaking," Kathy said.

"This is Reagan Murphy, Deputy National Security Adviser."

"Hello, Ms. Murphy." Kathy knew who Reagan Murphy was. Every American knew who Reagan Murphy was. The National Security Council, or NSC, was full of stodgy suits who trailed the President with briefcases and wrote memos about stopping terrorists or bombing places or both. Reagan probably wrote memos, too, but she was the opposite of stodgy. She was beautiful in a way that Kathy instantly hated, though Kathy had long ago accepted that her own perfectly average looks were ideal for a career that required avoiding attention. It wasn't just that Reagan was stunning. The tabloid headlines made it worse. They claimed the President had a relationship with his fiery red-headed aide with the long legs and the runway walk. Nothing substantiated, but enough to keep the airwaves humming for a while. The First Lady had no comment, and neither did Kathy.

"What can I do for you?" Kathy asked.

"This is very sensitive."

When Reagan paused, Kathy resisted the urge to say: *duh, why else would you call me?* Instead she studied the bright new leaves of the

Langley trees. They were beautiful, almost fluorescent green, this time of year. Kathy had a feeling from Reagan's tone that she'd be leaving again soon and might not see this view for a while.

"The Director gave me your number," Reagan said. "He told me you were the right person."

"He knows me well." *Too well, really.* The CIA Director, David Strassitch, had been Kathy's handler years ago in Lebanon, where he'd taken a bullet for her. He was the closest thing to a father she'd ever had. So why hadn't he called her himself?

"We have an international emergency," Reagan said, with the emotion of a dental assistant calling a patient about an appointment. "There's been a murder at the State Department. The assassin killed himself. The victim was a Japanese lawyer. The killer was Chinese."

Kathy had learned this a couple hours ago, along with the rest of the world. It was shocking, but she'd dealt with a lot of shocks in her career. And this one was on U.S. territory—not her domain—so she didn't expect to be dragged into it, much less by the White House.

"Sounds messy," Kathy said, deadpan.

"Yes, many moving parts," Reagan agreed. "For now I need you to monitor two lawyers from State. Jackson Crow and Lily Sun. Don't let either get hurt…or know you're watching."

Kathy had never heard of Lily Sun, but the name Jackson Crow made her swallow. Not even the gently rustling trees could slow her quickening heartbeat. She'd helped train Jackson when he'd arrived at the CIA, before he moved to a more encrypted black box—the National Security Agency. She'd heard that he left intelligence for law school…allegedly. It was no secret at Langley that Jackson had gained unique access to information that made him a perpetual source of mystery. Even to Kathy. He also remained one of the few field agents she'd ever lost to anything other than a bullet. His departure still stung, because he'd been one of the most promising talents she'd ever seen.

"The Director told me you knew him," Reagan said.

"Yes."

"I know him, too. We're old friends."

Old friends? The tiny hairs on Kathy's arms stood up. This was not one of those silly small world coincidences. This had to be a deliberate collision of forces. The Director didn't make decisions without thinking fifty moves ahead, and he'd told Reagan to call Kathy. He knew she'd trained Jackson. She needed to be careful.

"Anything more than monitoring?" Kathy asked.

"That's all for now. The situation will evolve."

"Always does."

"The Director said your partner will be Grant."

"Understood." No surprise there. Two targets to be monitored. Two agents. Logan Grant was competent enough, especially in a fist fight, but he stood out too much. She'd been complaining for years about the CIA's love affair with former All-American lacrosse stars.

"I have to warn you about Jackson," Reagan said.

"Okay…"

"He probably feels protective of his associate, Lily Sun."

"I see."

"He might do anything to protect her," Reagan said, as if it was personal. "Don't let him get himself killed, okay?"

"Understood." So Jackson now had a savior complex. Kathy could deal with that.

"Any questions?" Reagan asked.

"No." But Kathy had been at this long enough to know that she should repeat back the orders one last time. "We'll watch Jackson Crow and Lily Sun. We won't let them see us. And we won't let them get killed."

"Good. Report anything important to me immediately. And report every morning, no matter what. Use this number." She read out the ten digits.

"10-4."

Reagan hung up and Kathy sat at her desk, staring at a small chessboard on the corner. The board had been a gift from the Director, a reward for surviving Lebanon. She wondered if he had rigged this game somehow, like giving one side an extra piece. Jackson was not just a rook. Neither was she.

The mission had three rules. Pretty standard:

1. Watch.
2. Stay hidden.
3. Protect.

That was all fine until rules 2 and 3 conflicted, and if that happened, Kathy might have to let Jackson see her to save him. The Director knew she would follow the rules to the letter, until they needed to be broken.

8

JACKSON LEANED BACK in his chair, trying to ignore the uneasy churning in his gut. His personal kryptonite sat across the desk from him. He'd been working with Lily for six months now. They'd become friends in the professional way, which meant he knew plenty of superficial facts about her. She liked to run during lunch and order Chicken Lo Mein when working late. She signed her emails, "All the best, Lily," and she loved the Oxford comma almost as much as the Vienna Convention on the Law of Treaties. You could get pretty close in six months, in the professional way.

But none of that prepared him for this.

He'd spent the afternoon gently prying into what Lily knew about Hina, but hadn't uncovered much. Lily was too shaken up to talk through the details—no wonder after she'd seen two people shot right in front of her. She had no clue why anyone would want to hurt her Japanese friend, a lawyer like her. Ambassador Blair was wrong. This was not a job risk at the State Department, much less for lawyers. No one got into the legal business expecting bullets. Even Jackson had come here hoping to get away from them.

He figured the killing probably wasn't personal, but that made it all the more disturbing. The questions tumbled through his mind. What was the point of an assassination—sow chaos, put people on edge, create political strife? If it was some kind of political statement, why kill the young Japanese lawyer instead of the Japanese ambassador? And why now, in the Treaty Room? Jackson worried it was related to the treaty itself. He and a dozen others had cleared it, but Lily was the one who knew all the details and got the paperwork done. Did Hina and Lily know something about the treaty that he didn't?

For now Jackson kept his thoughts to himself—they wouldn't be much comfort to Lily. She was reading over a report for the FBI, making sure it was consistent with what she'd seen. She acted tough.

Maybe she was tough. But her eyes were soft, and her lower lip had traces of a quiver, like a bowstring.

The thing about kryptonite is that it comes from the past, because it's the past that reveals weakness. So the glowing green rock was from Superman's home planet. So the terrified girl sitting across from Jackson might as well be in Manila. That's where he'd lost his little sister, Julia. Twenty years had passed, but it didn't matter. Time couldn't diminish kryptonite. Time was only a lockbox that kept the kryptonite fresh for a moment like this.

They're going to kill Mom, Julia had said, sitting across from him at a plastic kitchen table in a two-room flat in Manila. She had the cutest brown eyes.

Mom's done this before, Jules. Jackson had replayed the memory more times than he could count. He'd wanted to be assuring. It was true, after all. Mom had done this so many times. She'd get inside the system, whatever it took, and she'd find what she needed to know to report the trafficking crimes and bring the bad guys down. If anyone got spooked, she'd run and take Jackson and Julia with her, just like she'd done a dozen times before, from West Africa to the Middle East, from Southeast Asia to the Philippines. *No one's going to hurt her*, Jackson had said. *We'll be fine.*

But Julia hadn't believed him. Her lips quivered as she stood from the plastic table and told him she was going to warn the cops. The police station was only a couple blocks away. It was 3 pm when she left.

Jackson had gone out looking for her half an hour later. He asked the police but they said she never came by. He asked around the neighborhood. No one had seen her.

When his mom got back that night, she feared the worst. She knew the types who could make a pretty 14-year-old disappear in Manila. She was right. The cops found Julia's body three days later. Jackson still shuddered at the pictures in his mind. It sent a terrible, terrible message. The kind of message that worked in a lawless world. They'd left Manila and gone back to the U.S. five weeks later, just Jackson and his mom.

Jackson forced himself to look at the quivering-lipped young lawyer across the desk. This was not Manila. This was Washington. And she was not Julia. She was Lily Sun. But rationalize all he wanted, he'd never let another girl walk out alone with a quivering lip. That was his kryptonite. Superman could never stay away from it. Neither could Jackson.

When Lily finally finished her review, Jackson insisted on walking her back to her apartment. Most of the State Department had already left the building.

"It's five blocks," Lily said. "I'll be fine."

"Long enough to get hounded by the press." *Or foreign intelligence*, Jackson thought, as he felt the weapon hidden at his wrist.

Her large, innocent eyes blinked. "Alright, if you insist."

She told him her address as they headed out. Once they reached ground floor, Jackson saw yellow tape and police holding back the reporters at the main entrance. The press probably thought anyone leaving this long after the shooting knew something about it.

"Let's try another way," Jackson said.

They turned around and went down to the basement. They passed the odd little stores designed for diplomats with temporary stays in Washington—the post office, the dry cleaner, and the bank—before winding through the underground corridors to a door on the east side of the building. It was known as "the runner's entrance."

Jackson nudged the door open and heard a crowd. If this entrance was being watched, they all were. He stepped out and faced at least a dozen reporters. Cop cars lined the street.

Jackson told Lily to keep her head down and follow. He pushed his way through the crowd, Lily close behind. The press called out questions. *Any comment on the murder? What happened in the Treaty Room?*

One aggressive reporter with a blond buzz cut managed to grab Jackson's arm, the one without the weapon, and stop him. "Hey, I know you," the guy said. "You're with the legal adviser's office. What happened in there?"

Jackson stared down at the man's hand on his arm. He didn't want to start a fight. "No comment."

Their eyes locked.

The reporter let go.

Jackson hurried off with Lily, refusing to say another word to the reporters. After walking a block, they'd gotten clear of the commotion and began winding their way through the historic neighborhood of Foggy Bottom. The sun hung just above the horizon in the clear April sky. The streets were crowded with cherry blossom petals and students from George Washington University. The students seemed oblivious to the murder-suicide that had happened just blocks away, but they still made fine props for enemy agents to hide behind. Nothing made a spy more invisible than a hoody and headphones in a pack of students. Jackson glanced back before each new turn. He felt uneasy but couldn't see any signs of a tail, so he made the final turn to Lily's place.

She lived in a large brick apartment building, probably half full of graduate students. Jackson stopped with her at the entrance.

"Thanks for walking with me." She stood close, with her hands stiffly at her sides, looking up into his eyes. "I really appreciate it."

"My pleasure," Jackson said, trying to keep it light. "Can't believe you've lived this close to the office all this time."

"I know. Sorry." She looked down. "Guess I should have invited you over, or something."

"No, that was my job. I just didn't..." Jackson suddenly felt awkward. He was her supervisor, so of course he couldn't have invited her over.

She laughed. "Oh well, better late than never. I've been wondering, by the way, about what Ambassador Blair asked. Why did you really come up to the Treaty Room?"

Lily was smart, maybe too smart. She knew that Jackson hadn't come just because he was a senior lawyer and her supervisor. For now, it was safer for her not to know much more. He needed to understand the danger better. "A friend told me to check it out since I was close," he said. "Just to have eyes at the scene."

"Your friend called you right after it happened?"

"Basically."

"I just figured they'd call an investigator first...or the CIA or something."

"Maybe they did." Jackson shrugged. "I bet lots of people are getting involved in this. Probably more than we know."

"Makes sense. Well..." Lily turned to go. "Thanks again, Jackson. See you tomorrow."

"Try to get some sleep tonight. It's a long flight to Tokyo."

She nodded and slipped inside. Jackson watched until she was in the elevator, going up. Then he walked back the way they'd come, hands in pockets. He'd survived kryptonite another day. Now it was time to figure out who was watching.

9

"ALL CLEAR," LOGAN **Grant** said. "He's gone, and she's inside."

Kathy moved away from the video monitors and climbed forward into the passenger seat of their white Channel 9 news van. She had hidden in the back while Jackson walked by—not even he should suspect vans like this after a shooting just a few blocks away, but they couldn't risk him recognizing her. Now she glanced up at the young lawyer's window, where a light had blinked on. The sky was growing dark.

"Did he see you?" Kathy asked, turning to her partner. He really was far too noticeable with his model jaw line and flop of brown hair. He reminded her of Hans Solo.

"Don't think so." **Grant** sipped his coffee, eyes still studying the street.

"Good. Our orders came from the highest level. We have to keep them in sight, but not be seen."

"Why not use a drone?" **Grant** asked.

Oh, my pupil, Kathy thought. *Must you be so naive?* The reasons began flooding through her mind. You don't use a drone because: any spy worth her salt knows a drone means someone's watching; any reporter worth her salt knows a drone means a story; and any professional spook knows a drone is a job threat. She could go on. But for now she answered, "Nothing beats eyes on the ground. That's why we'll be on her flight to Tokyo."

"Why? We already have people there."

"Those are the orders. The analysts believe that this girl knew the victim best. She could be the next target."

"That's a shame," **Grant** said. "I read the file. She seems like a grade-A American. Daughter of Chinese immigrants, concert pianist, Harvard, Yale Law. And she moves like a ballet dancer."

"She sounds too clean cut. Did the analysts find anything interesting yet?"

"Not yet. Her work was standard State Department stuff. Lots of bowing, signing things." Grant's square jaw yawned, as if flaunting its squareness, before he took another sip of coffee. "They didn't find anything about the treaty, either. It was just renewing an old joint security agreement with Japan. The delegations from both sides were in the room for the ceremony, and so was the press. Turned out the press included a killer."

None of it added up for Kathy. "Have the analysts run a comparison of the new treaty with the old one?"

"Sure, but no surprise there," Grant said. "A couple little word changes. Ambassador Blair already said what was different in his statement. We are drawing down some of our military in Japanese territory. More of the same political stuff…"

"It can't be that simple. Think about it. The Chinese just assassinated a Japanese lawyer on our territory. Maybe she knew something we don't about the treaty."

"You think this is about a piece of paper?"

"It's a treaty, not just a piece of paper," Kathy said. "Treaties have stopped wars. And they've started them."

"Fine," Grant mumbled. "But we can't be sure they killed the lawyer over this treaty. Maybe she was caught up in something else."

"Maybe." Kathy hated not knowing the reasons for her orders. Before heading out on the mission, she'd asked the Director but he'd been tight-lipped. He claimed to know nothing more than she did. Were they just trying to protect Jackson and this other lawyer, Lily Sun, or were they monitoring them for some other reason?

"Let's get more analysts on this." Kathy looked to the apartment above. "I want to know everything about Lily Sun. Everything."

"Will do." Grant stared down at his coffee, quiet for a moment. "What do you know about the guy, Jackson Crow? I heard he used to work for us."

"Yeah, he was in Kabul a while. But he left the Agency…"

"So why's he caught up in this? The analysts couldn't find anything."

"He went to the NSA, then law school..." Kathy failed to hide the contempt in her voice. "Now he's some top lawyer at State."

"Was he good?" Grant asked.

A small grin, arising from deep within Kathy's memory, tugged the corners of her lips. "Last time, in Afghanistan, he was assigned to gather intelligence on a particularly vicious warlord. He got caught somehow, and everyone gave him up for dead. A few months later the SEALs found him in a cave near a village in Kashmir, with six dead Taliban, including the target."

"So he was good."

Never had anyone like him. It wasn't brute strength, though Jackson's lithe frame could hold its own. His talent was knowing the bad guys. He managed to get more information than anyone else. No one had figured out his sources. "He could be an asset, or a liability. We need to figure it out soon. People are watching this from high places."

"The White House?"

Kathy didn't answer. She noticed the light in the target's apartment window blink out. "A lot of people are going to be watching her. We need to figure out who they are."

"And then what?"

"Then we report on it and let someone else decide what to do." Kathy took a deep breath, then her words came through gritted teeth. "We're not paid enough for politics."

10

JACKSON HAD TO change his normal commute. He'd seen the square-jawed guy in the white news van. Hard to be sure, but old instincts told him it was an agent. He figured they were just monitoring Lily, and he was okay with an extra level of protection.

But then, a few blocks from her apartment, he'd spotted another guy trailing him. The guy looked Asian and wore headphones and a backpack. He hadn't looked away or turned around or done anything stupid like that. He could have passed for a normal college student, except for his walk. That was the hardest thing for a spy to hide. His stride had too much purpose and precision, like former military.

Jackson used his phone to hail an Uber, then he ducked inside a coffee shop. The place was almost empty; not many people needed a caffeine fix at sundown.

Jackson came out—paper cup and newspaper in hand—and confirmed that the same guy with the headphones was on a bench in a park across the street, studying his phone, maybe snapping a picture.

Jackson didn't like that.

He leaned against the coffee shop's brick wall and unfolded the newspaper in front of him, waiting for his ride. The map on his phone showed his Uber arriving. He lowered the newspaper and watched it come to a stop across the street, in the perfect location on the opposite curb to block the other guy's view. The street was mostly quiet, with only a few pedestrians around.

As he lifted his coffee cup for a sip, Jackson released the clasp that held his slim weapon inside his shirtsleeve. He hadn't used it in a long, long time. He could never bring himself to put it away for good, and now he was glad for that. The CIA chemist who had supplied the tranquilizer for the darts had assured Jackson that the unique concoction of ketamine and etorphine would never go bad, and would work in seconds to knock someone out for an hour or two. If only Jackson could still hit a target...

He tossed the newspaper and his cup into the trash before starting to cross the street. The gun was about the size of a pen, so he had no trouble hiding it in his palm. While keeping the guy on the bench in his sights, he stopped by the Uber driver's open window.

"Jackson?" the driver asked.

Jackson nodded and began moving around the front of the car.

The guy on the bench watched him. It was almost dark outside, but the streetlights gave Jackson a clear view of the target areas—exposed skin at the neck and face.

Their eyes met when Jackson was only ten feet away. Jackson smiled casually, as if he suspected nothing.

The guy reached toward his backpack on the bench. Jackson opened his mouth in a wide yawn, raising his hand to his lips. In a fluid motion, his lips closed around one end of the gun, he blew, and the dart fired out.

Direct hit.

A small red feather was all that showed, but the man's face went blank as his hands went to his neck. No sound escaped his lips.

Jackson rushed to the man's side and lifted him to his feet, with one arm draped over Jackson's shoulder. He grabbed the backpack and slung it over his other shoulder. Jackson shuffled as quickly as he could under the dead weight. It had been a while since he'd hauled a body. He suddenly missed the twenty pounds of muscle he'd shed since the Agency.

They reached the back of the Uber. Jackson opened the door and set the bag and body inside, resting the man's head against the window.

He glanced around outside. No one seemed to have noticed.

Jackson sat beside the motionless man in the back, then caught the driver's surprised eyes in the rearview mirror. He was young, and looked scared.

"My friend's sick," Jackson said. "Can you get us to the GW

hospital, stat?"

"Sick? Man, he looks dead." The driver swallowed. "What'd you do to him?"

Jackson spoke calmly. "He's epileptic. I gave him his medicine, but he needs a doctor right away. He could die if you don't hurry. It's only a few blocks."

"Alright man, but I got nothing to do with this."

The driver floored it.

Once his eyes were on the road, Jackson wasted no time. He searched the body and found a wallet with a student ID and a couple credit cards with a matching name. He opened the guy's bag and saw only a few textbooks.

What if I was wrong? What if he isn't a spy?

Jackson's nerves were getting to him. He looked closer at the books. Most were thick tomes for science classes, but one was slim: *The Art of War* by Sun Tzu, in Mandarin. An American student might read it. A Chinese spy would memorize it.

He reached into the guy's pocket, took his phone, and used the guy's thumb to unlock it. There was nothing suspicious. He had an app for encrypted texting, but those were fairly common. Two apps on the home page were for the U.S. Army. One was for ROTC at George Washington University. It could be a good cover. Or it could be authentic.

At least I'm right about the military, Jackson thought.

The Uber skidded to a stop in front of the hospital. The driver looked back at the motionless body. "We're here, man. Take your *friend* and get out."

"Thanks for the ride," Jackson said.

He stepped over the young man's body and dragged him out, again with an arm draped over his shoulder. The Uber sped away.

Jackson spotted a bench within sight of the hospital entrance, but not too close. He moved calmly—no emergency, nothing to see—and set the body down on the bench in a sitting position, with his hood up and the backpack by his side. He could pass for a college kid who drank too much. Jackson resigned himself to not knowing for sure whether the guy was a spook or not. The guy would be fine, but just in case he was innocent, Jackson stuffed a hundred dollar bill in his pocket for his troubles. Then he turned and walked off without looking back.

The metro station was fifty feet away. Was he being watched? Or was he being paranoid?

Either way, Jackson forced himself to maintain counter-surveillance tactics as he moved into the metro station. He rode two stops east and got off in the heart of Washington. Once on the street he hailed another Uber, with a different account.

The car came in three minutes. They drove south and crossed the bridge over the Potomac River, where the lights of monuments reflected in the dark water. Jackson kept his eyes behind them, toward the gleaming Lincoln Memorial. No sign of a tail. He told the driver to stop by the first metro station in Virginia, Rosslyn, where he hopped out and hurried down and caught the next train. He stood at the back of the metro car, newspaper covering his face again. Two stops later he got off at the Pentagon stop.

He waited on the platform for everyone to leave. No one waited for him. The way seemed clear, but that depended on who was following. Maybe it was more old friends from Langley. If they were watching Lily, they might also watch him. Reagan sent him the text, after all. She would expect to hear from him. And she might have information.

He decided to call her from the train platform, cell service faint.

"Jackson?" she answered.

"Hey," he whispered. "Can't talk long, but I'm checking things out like you asked."

"Good. So who's behind this?"

"Not sure yet. Could be the treaty. Could be more. I bet we'll learn in Japan."

"You going in your legal capacity?" She had a mocking tone in her voice.

"I'm going as me, Reagan." Jackson glanced around the platform and confirmed no one was paying any attention. He needed to temper his mood. He'd been trying to put his past behind him, and he was not happy about drawing lines between his identities again. But that was his problem, not hers. "I'll learn whatever I can," he said.

"This is very important to the boss." She had taken on her impatient, professional tone. "When you're back, let's talk again."

"One other thing," Jackson said. "I'm being followed. So is the other attorney, Lily Sun. Is the Agency involved?"

"Itching for your old work?"

"No, I'm just worried for Lily. She could be a target."

"Okay, yeah, they're keeping an eye on her. That's all." Reagan paused. "Stay safe, okay?"

"I can handle it."

"You always do. Talk soon." She hung up.

He made his way out of the metro station, thinking about Reagan more than he wanted to. When they'd broken up years ago, she'd told him that she'd give him a second chance if he would be honest with her about everything. He'd made his choice then. He didn't regret it, not much, but Reagan was not the type to easily fade from his mind.

He walked the final stretch in the dark to the high-rise apartment buildings that overlooked the Pentagon. He stopped a few times, pretending to check his phone. The nighttime reflection showed blue against black, and worked well enough as a mirror as long as he didn't press his thumb down to turn the screen's light on. He let the screen stay dark so he could check his surroundings. All was clear.

At the busy corner one block from his apartment, he saw the familiar homeless guy who tended to stand there with a cup, hoping for a dollar from a commuter waiting at the red light. When Jackson passed, he said good evening.

"Nice night, eh?" The homeless guy's breath smelled like malt liquor.

"Like always," Jackson said, passing him.

It was their normal routine. Jackson paid the guy twenty bucks a week to keep an eye out, and he promised to pay an extra hundred whenever the guy had credible information that something unusual was happening. It was probably overkill, but Jackson couldn't shake the habit.

He was glad for it now, because it meant all should be secure in his regular apartment, one floor directly above the apartment he kept for emergencies. This was not an emergency, not yet. He reached his building and went up to the ninth floor, unlocked the door to his place, and shut it quickly behind him.

He locked the deadbolt and the chain, then hung his keys on the rack by the door. He surveyed the spartan room—desk with a large computer screen, solitary chair, and a couple bookshelves. Everything was in order. He was slipping his shoes off when he first noticed the plain, unmarked manila folder.

Jackson stood still, staring at it between his feet like a man who'd stumbled upon a rattlesnake. Someone must have found out where he lived, gotten here before he did, and slid it under the door.

He considered turning around and walking out. He felt like if he picked up the folder it would be Afghanistan all over again. An envelope had started that whole mess. He'd barely gotten out alive and he'd sworn he wouldn't do it again. But…

He had to protect Lily. He wouldn't let her become another Julia.

He stepped over the folder and went to the little table by the window. He usually had no need for a couch, but for once he wished he had one.

The lights of the Pentagon were mostly off. A few windows gleamed on the higher floors. The senior staff would be there, thinking about past wars and future wars. They would always be there. No treaty could stop it. No secret agent. The most they could do was to slow the wars down, spread them out, and make them hurt less.

Jackson turned away from the window and found the folder in his hands before he could stop himself.

He opened it.

There was a single picture inside. It was a glossy, high-resolution image showing the Treaty Room, with its elegant parquet floors, powder blue walls, and crystal chandeliers. The white Corinthian columns bore the golden seal of the United States at the top. The American and Japanese flags framed the group smiling in the center.

Jackson studied the ten people. Five Americans and five Japanese. The smiles were mostly genuine, if a little tired. This was a celebration of months of work. They'd negotiated an important treaty.

Something about the picture suddenly struck Jackson. Eight of the ten people were looking away at a slight angle, probably at another photographer's camera. Only two people were looking straight at the photographer of this picture. One was the victim, Hina Himura, and the other was Ambassador Blair. Blair's face was dignified as ever, his silver hair coiffed. The high resolution showed fine little wrinkles around Blair's strained eyes. He stood between the Japanese Ambassador and the young woman who was shot.

Jackson remembered that the killer had press credentials. Had he been the one to take this picture? And if so, why would they have been looking right at the killer? It could be coincidence. Maybe Hina had a supernatural premonition of her fate. But Blair?

Whoever brought him this picture must have wanted him to see this. He flipped it over. The words on the back, scrawled in red ink, made him sit in the room's solitary chair.

To Jackson, from Japan.
Follow the BitStones.

No, no, no, Jackson thought, staring blankly at his reflection in the dark computer screen. His face looked hollow and tired. He was done with BitStones—the cryptocurrency that had made his career without anyone knowing it. He'd managed to avoid them and the Agency for years now. His life was almost normal. Protecting Lily was one thing, but this? No, he wasn't going back, couldn't go back.

But what if someone in Japan knew about him and BitStones? Impossible. Only a handful in the world knew that, and not even his old employer. And yet, what if BitStones had something to do with the murder in the Treaty Room?

Jackson did not have answers.

All he had was a photo and a few words.

Unless…he went back to his old network.

Follow the BitStones…

He stretched his tense body and went to the small twin bed in the bedroom. Lying down, he held the picture up again and found himself looking straight into the pale blue eyes of Ambassador Blair.

11

"Want another?" the bartender asked.

Zhang looked down at his near-empty pint of craft beer. The bartender had recommended it. He felt the faint Asian flush coming on—despite his elite intestinal constitution, a few strong American drinks could do that—but, what the hell, this was a celebration. The job had been done well.

He lifted his glass, finished it off, and tapped it down on the well-worn bar. "What's your best cocktail?"

The bartender smiled as he took Zhang's empty glass. "Old Fashioned it is."

Eight televisions were on behind the bar. Seven of them showed the same boring baseball game, which meant the dozen patrons at the bar had nearly half a TV each as they clutched their drinks, clueless about Zhang and the threat he represented to their exceptionally comfortable existence. He'd wanted to watch the news in a place where real Americans would see it. He wanted to see their reactions to a Chinese assassin killing a foreigner in their own Treaty Room. He wanted to see fear.

But none of them cared. They were glued to baseball. He alone watched the sole TV showing news about the shooting.

After a while a press release from the State Department flashed on the screen:

We can confirm that there was a shooting, and two people are dead: Hina Himura from a Japanese delegation, and Bao Li, who took his own life. He had credentials with a Chinese media station.

We express our deepest condolences to our friends from Japan. The treaty signed today shows the strength of our alliance.

We are investigating all leads and will report on any further developments.

Two talking heads wore serious expressions as they discussed the shooting. *Such a tragedy*, the newswoman said. *Who do you think is behind it?* the newsman asked. They blabbered on, speculating that it had something to do with intelligence operations, how covert operatives could be expected with high tensions between China and Japan, or maybe it was some romantic vendetta—the victim was gorgeous, after all.

Zhang could not help but laugh. The newscasters were clueless but they'd come closer to the truth than most.

Hina *was* too attractive, Zhang thought. That's why she had learned too much. She had been so effective, so quick, in seducing the ambassador. The Americans and the Japanese were alike in their vulnerability to desire. Zhang had not hesitated to take advantage of their weakness. The ambassadors knew they couldn't talk now, not when he had evidence of their affairs with a woman who had just been murdered. Not a single person had said anything about the change in the treaty. He'd even sowed a little distrust in the White House. He could not have planned it any better.

"What's got you cracked up?" the bartender asked, as he placed a glass of amber liquid with an orange slice and a red cherry in front of Zhang.

"The news." Zhang tried a sip. A bit sour, a bit sweet. "Hey, not bad."

"Best in town." The bartender shrugged. "Let me know if you want another."

Zhang smiled as the bartender attended the next patron. Americans always wanted another. Then another. They would never learn. Still, he had an odd affection for them, the way a guy loves a senile old dog. Even though it's blind in one eye, grey hair matted, and sleeps half the day, the creature's unquestioning loyalty deserves respect. The problem with the Americans was that, as they'd gotten long in the tooth, they'd begun to serve a new master, a worse master. Zhang's job was to know his enemy, so he'd studied the country's founders. He'd read Alexis de Tocqueville. He knew this country had once been great, almost as great as his country, with strong communities, hard workers, and courageous fighters. Success had been their master. Now they served sports, hard drinks, and anything else that dulled an old dog's pain.

A vibration at his thigh made Zhang's fist clench his drink tighter. It was his encrypted phone, securely running from secret servers wholly owned by China at a telecommunications help center in West Virginia. He glanced around to ensure no one was watching—which of course they weren't because it was the seventh inning and the Nationals were down one and at bat. He pulled out the phone and unlocked the message in Mandarin on the screen.

A member of the Japanese delegation departed from his hotel at 7 pm, carrying an envelope, which we believe had pictures from the camera that he took from the body of the killer. The building where he delivered the envelope has only one relevant match: Jackson Crow. We believe this is the same person who escorted Lily Sun to her apartment, and managed to lose one of our agents.

Zhang had sent out two agents to watch the CIA spooks who were monitoring Lily Sun. One of Zhang's men had learned about the Japanese man taking the camera. Zhang had no reason for concern. A single picture couldn't reveal any connection between the killer and anyone else, but he didn't like the Japanese guy digging like this, especially now that he was trying to get another American involved, and apparently one who was not a bumbling idiot.

He typed back: *What do we have on Crow?*
Here's the file.

Zhang opened an attached file and scanned the familiar report. His government had hit the motherload not long ago, taking every single security clearance file from the U.S. government. That meant he had, at his fingertips, every biographical detail of every important U.S. employee—and their families and friends. The Chinese Government never publicized their knowledge, but oh, how they used the data. Sometimes they sold it. Sometimes they hacked with it. But mostly they compiled, processed, and analyzed the information, deploying it daily to their advantage.

But this report on Crow was strange. Zhang had seen hundreds of these, and they always painted a complete picture of who a person was, where they'd lived, what they'd done. This Jackson Crow was different. Born, raised, and educated in North Carolina, then ten years of consulting with "EFP Inc." before law school and taking his current job at the State Department. No criminal record. No international travel. No organizations. No publications. No debt. Nothing that made him qualified for his position. He looked like the most one-dimensional simpleton you could make up. Which meant he had to be made up.

Zhang needed another agent to watch this guy. He might even do a little monitoring himself. He typed: *Put Xun on him. And dig harder. Check with the Iranians.*

On it.

He put the phone away and picked up his drink again, thinking. In seven days none of this would matter. His father would order the first shot and take back what belonged to China. The American military would sit back and watch, thinking this was only about a few barren islands and never expecting the surprise takeover of a far, far more important island.

By then it would be too late. They would brandish words about "violations of international law" and "acts of aggression." Zhang and his people would laugh behind their Great Wall, caring about as much as the Russians cared after taking Crimea. The Americans had once understood the order of things: the strong take what they can, the weak suffer what they must. But now the Americans were old dogs, asleep on the watch. Little skirmishes like these—about an ambassador, a murdered Japanese woman, or pictures delivered to an American spy—wouldn't wake them up.

As long as this stayed quiet for seven days. No uproar about the treaty—even the White House had promised that—and no revelation about the ambassador's role. He needed to make sure neither Jackson Crow nor anyone else learned anything about that.

"Need another?" The bartender leaned over the bar, pulling Zhang out of his thoughts. "Great game, right?"

The patrons were still drinking. The baseball game was tied in the ninth inning. And Zhang's glass was empty.

But he was no American.

He knew when it was time to stop playing and start fighting.

"I'm all set. You take BitStones?"

"It's the twenty-first century, ain't it?"

Zhang held out his phone, and the bartender scanned his unique BitStones code. Zhang signed his English name, *Patrick Li*, and tipped fifty percent. "Good luck to your Nationals."

12

KATHY LEFT HER partner Grant in the news van while she took an evening stroll down to the State Department. She passed a quaint bar with smiling patrons watching a baseball game. It was the kind of thing that used to make her happy, knowing that she protected peaceful lives like this.

She thought about the young lawyer Jackson had escorted to her apartment. Why did Jackson think she needed protecting? What did she know? Whatever it was, Lily Sun would be fine under Grant's watch. And Jackson could take care of himself. But if Kathy was going to do her job well—and no one did it better—she needed more information.

One missing piece was Ambassador Steven Blair. He'd been in the room with Lily when the murder happened. He'd signed this treaty. But he never even came up in the call from the White House or the analyst reports. The press had plenty to say about this, though. He'd long been personal friends with the President. He came from family money, but turned from millionaire to billionaire through his investments in a major construction conglomerate in China. He lived as a perpetual bachelor, but that didn't stop the tabloids from speculating about who was angling to marry him. Kathy didn't want to doubt the guy, but she knew that ambassadors didn't get plum posts like Tokyo without baggage. No harm in listening to his world for a while.

Everyone knew Foggy Bottom and Langley had links. The link was personal for Kathy. She'd gotten her start as a diplomatic security officer in Cairo, and she'd never given up the title or the badge. "I'm with DS" worked at most embassies around the world. And it made getting into the State Department a breeze. Kathy swiped her badge at the side door and walked straight to the sixth floor without anyone asking a question. She found the Asia-Pacific affairs suite and knocked. It was after hours, but it had been a big day.

The door opened and a tired assistant behind the nameplate Linda Jones greeted her. "Can I help you?"

Kathy held up her badge. "I'm Kathy Sullivan from diplomatic security. Is Ambassador Blair still here?"

"Are you guys ever going to stop with the questions?"

"Sorry," Kathy said, with every trace of empathy she could muster. "I know it's been a long day. This won't take long."

"He told me not to let anyone disturb him."

"This will take one minute, tops. It's about Tokyo."

Linda sighed. "Fine, but I'm not getting blamed for it." She stood slowly and pointed down the hall. "I'm going to the restroom. I never saw you. That's his office."

Kathy suppressed her annoyance as Linda shuffled away. It seemed like no one could take responsibility anymore. At least this time it worked in her favor. She went to the ambassador's office, knocked three times, and barged in.

Steven Blair was standing by the window, pouring golden liquid into a low crystal glass. His head snapped to her. "Who are you?"

She held up her badge. "I'm so sorry to intrude, Ambassador. I'm with DS."

"Again?" He set down the bottle, as if reluctant to leave it, and went to a leather chair in the room's sitting area. His loafers were already off. His red and blue argyle socks settled on the coffee table. "What now?"

"We just wanted to follow up on one thing for tomorrow." Kathy leaned against the doorway with her arms crossed. With her left hand hidden underneath her right arm, she pressed the small sensor behind the edge of the wooden doorframe. It was almost the exact same color as the wood. "We've added an extra DS agent for your team. His name's Logan Grant. You probably won't even notice him. But you can imagine why we want to keep your delegation as safe as possible."

"Fine." He studied her. "I don't recognize you."

She smiled. "I just got back from a tour in Lagos."

"Tough post. You didn't get much of a tan."

Kathy restrained her grimace. So what if she was pale? Just once she'd like to get through a conversation with a man without him saying something about how she looked. "I mostly stayed inside."

"Fair enough. Anything else?"

"That's it. Safe travels."

Moments later she was out the door and out of the building and walking again past the quaint little bar with the baseball game on its TVs. She was back in the van when she checked the microphone. The signal ran through a covert satellite and, with complete encryption, fed the sound straight into her ear buds.

It was an hour later when she and Grant heard the first words feeding from the Ambassador's office.

"Not again, Linda." Blair sounded annoyed. "This better be important."

"It's the President." Linda's voice was louder. She was probably standing right where Kathy had been standing, by the microphone.

"About time. Put him through."

There was a slight pause. Then came a familiar, calm voice: "Steve?"

"Hey Mike," Blair said. "Thanks for calling."

"I just got back from Europe," the President replied, "but I got the read out. Sounds bloody awful. You okay?"

"Yeah, like a bird dog with a little blood in his mouth. I'm fine."

The President laughed lightly. "Everything set for tomorrow?"

"All set. We leave for Tokyo in the morning."

"You'll have company, of course. Dave is sending some of his best."

Dave? Kathy figured that had to be her boss, David Strassitch, Director of the CIA. So "his best" was her and Grant. She couldn't resist a smile.

"I figured as much," Blair said. "DS keeps telling me about the protection we will have. Anything I should keep an eye out for?"

"My office is working up the talking points. Stick to them."

"Right."

"The Japanese are up in arms about this."

"I know." Blair paused. "You see China's statement? Deepest condolences and all that BS. They didn't say anything about whether they were involved."

"It doesn't take a genius to figure that out."

"Our friends in Japan will want some sort of revenge."

The President sighed. "It won't change anything…"

"You're expecting the Chinese to move soon?" Blair asked.

There was a long pause. "Yes, gotta let it happen. My generals say we have little choice. But we need more to sell it. Maybe more from our friends in Japan…"

"So that's my job?"

"You got it. Just follow the talking points and grease the gears behind closed doors."

"That's why you gave me this job, right?"

"You know how to grease, Steve."

"Sure do."

"Take it easy on the sake, okay?"

"I can handle my sake."

"That's what I'm afraid of. Keep the reports coming. Safe travels."

"Thanks, Mike. Anything else I should know?"

"You'll be watched."

Blair laughed. "Aren't we all?"

13

CAPTAIN LI DONGHAI loved mornings on the East China Sea. The windows of his control tower were open and the air fresh and cool as he sipped his tea. He watched the approach to the Diaoyu Islands. Three of the five islands were visible, heaps of rock rising from the vast ocean. Birds soared in the sky above the islands. Here they could find a bite of fish and nest safely. That would not change. The rocky islets had withstood millennia of ocean assaults. Like China, they would withstand millennia more.

"Starboard side," Donghai commanded in Mandarin. "Maintain this cruising distance."

The sailors sitting before him executed the command, bringing the massive aircraft carrier around in a wide arcing turn. He had five thousand men on board. He could take these islands now if he wanted. And he did want that. He'd planned every angle to win before a fight began. He'd been waiting twenty years. His people had waited far longer. But Donghai was ever-obedient, and so he waited for the order from his father, General Li.

This morning's message had his spirits up. The treaty had been signed in Washington. His father had not told him everything, and his brother Zhang—as usual—had told him nothing, but Donghai knew enough to understand that the American's protection over these islands might finally be lifted. He had no idea how his father had arranged such a thing. He was not one for politics. That was for his brother and his father. It seemed the way of things, that a father of two sons would have to have his gifts divided between them. There was much reason in the one-child policy. Or, at least, a one-son policy.

Donghai left his perch in the Captain's seat, high in the control tower, and went down to the deck. He liked to see his men. He liked to hear from them. He passed the fighter jets and came to the side of a man leaning on the railing, gazing out at the islands.

He was a young sailor, maybe twenty. He had the look of a rural boy. A mainland farmer looking for opportunity on the sea, as Donghai's father had been many years ago.

"What do you see?" Donghai asked.

The man bowed hurriedly, no doubt surprised to find himself face to face with the Captain. "Sir, I see the islands, sir."

Donghai smiled, recognizing the accent. "You are from Gansa Province?"

"Sir, yes, sir."

"My family is also from Gansa. I have not been back in thirty years. I once thought I'd never want to return to dry land after living on the water. But I would like to see Gansa again."

"It is very dry. Sir."

Donghai motioned to the islands again. "These rocks rise from the ocean but have no fresh water to drink. Why do you think they are important to us?"

"Because they are ours, not Japan's, sir."

"Precisely. They are ours." Donghai breathed deep of the ocean air. He'd patrolled these waters for so long, restrained himself as a lower officer, and then restrained the ships under his command. But soon restraint would come to an end. He would lead this warship and the five others awaiting command to surround the islands and seize them, by any force necessary.

"Permission to speak freely, sir?" the sailor asked.

Donghai liked the sailor's energy. "Yes, speak."

"Why do we still wait, sir?"

"We have no concern of Japan," Donghai said. "They could not stop us if they tried. They know this, and so they will not try. But the Americans are still strong. They hold the shield the Japanese could not hold by themselves. When the Americans lower their shield, then we will move." Donghai did not mention that his attack would be a first move, timed perfectly for the much larger battle to come.

"This will happen?" the sailor asked.

Donghai noted the failure to address him properly, but he

would take men of zeal over men of decorum. He, too, was from Gansa. He clasped the young sailor's arm. "It will happen, and we must be ready any moment."

"Yes, sir." The man nodded and turned again to the islands. The two of them stood side by side, gazing at the rocks glowing in the light of the rising sun.

14

IT WAS DAWN in Washington when Jackson rode his motorcycle past the tidal basin, watching the rain batter cherry blossoms to the ground. They reminded him of Japan. He'd be flying there in a few hours. He hadn't slept much, thinking about the lawyer who had been shot, the photo, and the message. His best guess was that the victim knew something. Maybe she'd even tipped off Lily. He hoped not. Sometimes it was better not to know something, but Jackson had already learned more than he wanted. He'd locked the photo in his briefcase.

When he arrived at the State Department, Jackson headed straight to his office. It was still early, so only the European bureaus had arrived. His suite was quiet. His footsteps were the only sounds.

But when he opened the door to his office, he froze in shock.

Ambassador Blair was sitting at Jackson's desk, reading the morning paper. The front headline said, *Murder in the Treaty Room*, with the subtitle *Unknown Chinese killer dead*. Blair looked up and spotted Jackson. He calmly set the paper down as he stood, then smoothed his pinstripe suit and blood red tie.

"Good morning, Jackson." The Ambassador glanced around the office, then looked back at Jackson with a smile. "We've gotta get you a better view. This courtyard can't be very exciting to watch. I don't know how you survive."

"Why are you here?"

"I just wanted to talk before we fly out. Come to my office?"

"You lead the way," Jackson said, forcing his voice to stay even. He hated being caught off guard like this.

They walked out of the Legal Adviser's office and through the quiet corridors. Along the way Blair talked about the prior night's Nationals' game. "Great comeback even if they lost," Blair said. Jackson agreed politely but wondered how it could be a comeback when you lose. They soon reached the Ambassador's office, with its wood-paneled walls and windows looking out over the Washington Monument. There was an unmistakable scent of bourbon.

"When I first started my career," the Ambassador said as he sat behind his desk, "would you believe I didn't even have a computer in my office? Not a window, either."

Jackson sank into a leather chair opposite the Ambassador. "You wanted to talk?"

"All our materials—the briefing papers, the talking points—we have to get them right. The team on the ground in Tokyo is helping, too. I need something different from you."

"I'm listening."

The Ambassador leaned back in his chair and folded his hands behind his silver hair. "We must keep the positive messages flowing. But there's more. I talked to the President last night."

"And?"

"Look, I know you're Lily's supervisor. But I'm not an idiot. You're getting involved in this awfully fast. Like someone higher up called you in. Why?"

Jackson toyed with different answers. This would go easier if Blair thought he was just another Department lawyer. Jackson doubted the President would have known about him, much less mentioned him to Ambassador Blair. But Reagan could have said something. "If there was a murder at the Embassy in Tokyo, wouldn't you get called in?"

"Of course."

"This was like that. Part of my responsibility is to look out for Lily. Make sure everything is done right, legally."

"Legally," Blair smiled. "I'm sure it will be. I've sent you the list of everyone who was in the Treaty Room. Mostly Americans and Japanese. A few Chinese and Koreans, too. This wasn't some one-off killing. Everyone knows that. But our friends in China aren't going to like the media speculation."

"Friends?"

The Ambassador smiled. "Don't tell me you're more cynical

than I am. The President wants a report. He wants to know whether politics are wrapped up in this."

"American politics?"

"There's no such thing anymore. People used to say all politics is local. That must have been nice, before Facebook, Twitter, and whatever kids use these days. Now all politics is global."

"So you want to figure out why someone would have wanted to kill the Japanese lawyer?" Jackson knew there had to be another reason for Blair's request. "I have no doubt the FBI's investigators are looking into that."

Blair leaned forward, with his elbows on the huge oak desk. "It's not me who wants this. It's the President."

"How can I help?"

"I left some materials in your office."

"Thanks. I'll take a look."

"Good. I'm counting on you, and Lily." The Ambassador turned to his computer screen.

Jackson took the cue and stood to leave.

"Wait," the Ambassador said, "one more thing."

"Yes?"

"There are a few press pictures in the materials I gave you. Most of them cover the front pages today. But we're missing something."

"Oh?" Jackson kept his voice steady.

"We have video footage showing the shooting. You can't see the killer or the victim very well, but it looks like the killer took a few pictures before he drew his gun."

"I remember he had press credentials." Jackson held Blair's gaze. "Anything interesting from his pictures?"

"Yes, they're missing."

"Really? How?"

"Come here. Watch this."

Jackson moved to the Blair's side. He could hear his uneasy breathing. He noticed a picture by the computer monitor—Blair and the President wearing bright orange hats and camouflage, with rifles over their shoulders.

Blair pointed to the still image on the screen. "This is the guy to keep an eye on."

Jackson took in every detail. Blair was pointing to a middle-aged Japanese man wearing a suit and staring at the killer on the ground a few feet away. Blair had his arm over the Japanese ambassador's shoulder as they stared down at the victim. Lily had her hands over her mouth. Her face was ashen, terrified.

"Now, watch this." Blair clicked, and the still image sprang into motion. Most of the crowd was running for the exits. The Japanese man moved forward deliberately and knelt beside the killer. In one smooth motion, the man took the killer's camera, ejected the memory card, and tucked it inside his jacket before turning for the exit. The pool of blood by the killer's head was still spreading, and everyone else moved away from the body.

Blair stopped the video. "You see?"

"Who is he?"

"So far we have only a name and a title. Moto Tachibana, deputy legal adviser in the Japanese Foreign Affairs ministry."

"I thought he looked familiar. He's my equivalent."

"Exactly. You might get a chance to talk with him in Tokyo. Try to learn anything you can, but be subtle about it. Can you do that?"

"Absolutely," Jackson said, expressionless but amazed. This Japanese man had somehow sent him the picture without the Ambassador knowing it. Why?

"Good. The President wants a report on whatever you find." Blair stood and walked with Jackson to the door. "It's going to be a whirlwind in Tokyo."

15

GENERAL LI SHENG sipped Longjing tea in his Beijing corner office. The sun had begun its descent through the dense brown clouds that hung low over the city. He would never call the clouds smog. He considered the clouds more like dust rising behind an army on the march, heralding power on the move, heralding victory.

General Li did not usually require tea in the afternoon, but had found it difficult to sleep the night before, knowing that—on the opposite end of the earth—years of planning were nearing their conclusion. Now the baton had come into his hands, with all the power that entailed as a general of the People's Liberation Army and Vice-Chairman of the Central Military Commission. He would lead the PLA to an effortless victory for his President. His fame would grow. His people would take a step closer to the proper world order, with China reigning in the space between heaven and earth.

But not all had gone as General Li had hoped. His oldest son, Zhang, had disappointed again. While Donghai commanded a naval fleet like a maestro conducting an orchestra, ready to be the PLA's fist, Zhang could hardly seem to command his own temper. General Li had long accepted that Donghai alone had the abilities to follow in his father's footsteps, but there had always been hope that Zhang would prove himself worthy in other ways. This killing of the Japanese lawyer was another of the boy's reckless ideas. Zhang had said it was a way to blackmail an American leader, an ambassador no less.

Very well, Li had said. He could appreciate the benefits of such an asset. But now he'd heard the report of American agents becoming involved. This would not have happened if the woman had not been killed. General Li had expected it, of course, but Zhang had assured him this could be controlled. Except it hadn't been—a package had been delivered by the Japanese. China's eastern neighbors would not go down without a fight, even if the

Americans were willing to back away.

It was time to check with his team.

General Li left his office, bodyguards falling into step beside him, and made his way to the underground tunnels of the Central Military Commission. These tunnels had been built decades ago as an elaborate bomb shelter when tensions were high with the Soviets. Chairman Mao, in his infinite wisdom, had them designed large enough to protect millions of Beijing's people, with all the functions required to maintain community life. Now, as General Li peered down one of the hallways stretching a mile into the distance, he smiled at the brilliance of these facilities. They served perfectly as the PLA's nerve center. The barracks meant his soldiers—of the digital variety—could live and work completely down here, without any risk of losing the secrecy that their missions required.

He wiped a speck of dust off the stars on his shoulder and entered a room with over one hundred computer stations and hackers hunched over at them. There were four rooms just like it. This first room was the training ground, and the best would move on, room by room. The second room looked like a group of people playing a computer game. General Li did not need to know the details of a silly game, but he understood that this allowed his government to convert their hordes of U.S. dollars into a cryptocurrency that China could monitor. They called it BitStones. The BitStones were used in the third room, where hackers moved and tracked the cryptocurrency, funding whatever actions the government needed to keep hidden.

The hackers who did well in the first three rooms made it to the elite, fourth room. That was where they managed the most sensitive operations. Their next project was nearly complete. It would be a world wonder, making their military bases in the South China Sea look like child's play. It would, as Sun Tzu said, fall like a thunderbolt against their enemies. It would change everything. Only General Li, the President of China, and a few select others knew what all four rooms were doing. It was General Li's responsibility to keep it that way.

He strolled the aisles between the stations, studying the screens. These men had been ordered to report anything they found involving certain individuals.

General Li caught sight of an email on a computer screen. It made him stop beside the hacker. "What is that?"

The hacker looked up, eyes bloodshot. He'd been at this station for many hours, and he had another hour before his shift was over. It was the worst time possible to receive the general's attention. "An email."

"It is an email from Moto Tachibana."

"Yes. He has sent many. I have not seen anything unusual."

The General leaned over, putting his hand on the hacker's shoulder, and studying the intercepted message on the screen. It was from Moto Tachibana to Oda Kobayashi, 10:36 pm, Eastern Standard Time. The words were simple.

I'm very sorry. We have found nothing. But he has the picture.

The general's grip tightened on the hacker's shoulder. "Were you not going to bring this to our attention?"

"Yes, sir, but I..."

"You see this email is from only a few hours ago." General Li's voice had risen to nearly a shout. "Do you know who Moto Tachibana is?"

"He is on the list."

"Yes, and what do we do," General Li scanned over the room of hackers, finding all eyes were on him, "when we find an email involving someone on the list?"

"We report it, I know, I just—"

Li yanked the hacker from his chair and pointed to the center of the room, where a man was stuffed inside a clear glass box.

"No, please, no," the hacker stammered.

Li raised a gun to the hacker's head. "Your turn."

The man moved forward with leaden feet. He reached the glass box, gun still pressed to his head, and released the latch that could only be opened from the outside.

The man who had been inside crawled out, like a caterpillar

miraculously escaping from a jar.

"Get in," General Li ordered. "Now."

The hacker did as commanded, curling up to fit inside.

"You," Li said, pointing his gun at the man who had just escaped. "Seal it."

The man shook his head.

"Seal it!"

The man's voice, parched from dehydration and near-suffocation in the box, croaked out, "No."

The gunshot sounded like an explosion as its sound echoed off the metal floor and walls and dozens of computers. General Li sealed the box himself as its former occupant collapsed.

Li straightened his uniform and clasped his hands behind his back as he turned to face the room of hackers. "This is war," he said calmly. "If you want our nation, our families, our friends to live, you will follow my orders. Am I understood?"

"Yes, General Li," the hackers answered in unison.

"I said, am I understood?"

"Yes! General Li!"

General Li left the room and, as he walked, he thought again of Sun Tzu. The ancient master had understood war, and the human soul. *Engage people with what they expect; it is what they are able to discern and confirms their projections*, Sun Tzu had written. *It settles them into predictable patterns of response, occupying their minds while you wait for the extraordinary moment—that which they cannot anticipate.*

This was as true of the enemy as it was of General Li's own men. He did not enjoy cruelty to these men toiling at their computers. But they expected it of him. They expected to fear him. Their extraordinary moment would be his blessing, bestowed bountifully on them when they prevailed, because it was their work—without even their own full knowledge—that ensured the enemy did not anticipate what he planned. No one could trace their immense project. No one knew of the troops ready to march. Not even the Chinese people dared hope for the victory he would bring.

When he reached his office, General Li issued three commands to be delivered immediately and with utmost secrecy. First he ordered Donghai to make a pass of Okinawa, to test the reaction, and to wait for the order to move on the Diaoyu Islands. Second he ordered Zhang to ensure that whatever package the Japanese had delivered to the Americans was obtained and evaluated. Maybe Zhang would redeem himself and his reckless actions. Third General Li ordered the American ambassador—who now had no option but to comply—to ensure the Japanese still expected the Americans to come to their defense, regardless of the treaty, and to report on any intelligence assets he believed to be involved. General Li did not expect the ambassador to carry out the second command, but it would provide an adequate reason, when he failed, to eliminate him and the vulnerability he posed. As he gazed out at the sun nearing the murky brown horizon, the general peered through the clouds of war and saw himself, like the skyscrapers of Beijing, on the rise.

16

LEAVING AN AIRPLANE'S coach seat, row 36, after sixteen hours of crammed legs, salted peanuts, and in-flight entertainment made Jackson feel like Houdini escaping chains and a locked box. So much for government perks. At least he'd enjoyed the constant surveillance of the same square-jawed spook, sitting at the back of the plane and trying not to be noticed.

Jackson stretched his arms high as he retrieved his bag and briefcase. Then he stood in the center aisle, waiting to exit the plane.

Someone tapped his shoulder. "Hey, you like steak?"

Jackson instantly recognized the man, with his pepper-grey hair and face worn with worried wrinkles. He was the senior Japanese lawyer who had been in the Treaty Room and had taken the killer's camera card—Moto Tachibana. And, unlike the American agent, he'd somehow managed to avoid Jackson's detection on the flight.

"Yes," Jackson said. "I like steak."

Moto handed Jackson a tourist magazine. "Here, page 17 shows a restaurant you must try. It is near the Embassy."

"Thanks," Jackson said, thinking of the envelope that had been slid under his door in DC, the one with the picture of Ambassador Blair staring at the murderer. This man must have given it to him. And now he was a taking a major risk talking with Jackson here. "Why do you recommend it?"

"They serve only the best. Many watch for reservations." There was fear in Moto's eyes. "Do not wait."

Jackson held the magazine in plain view. "Thank you. I will."

Moto smiled and nodded and said no more.

Jackson exited the plane and joined Lily as they passed through customs. Blair was waiting on the other side—perks of flying first class as an ambassador. There was no other sign of Moto.

A fleet of black cars picked them up outside the airport. Jackson, Lily, and two security personnel rode in the vehicle behind

Ambassador Blair's. The city's skyscrapers rose around the caravan of black cars as it wound its way into downtown, heading straight to the Mandarin Oriental, where Blair had insisted they all stay.

Jackson watched the steel lines and neon lights blur past. This city felt more alive than Washington. Lily and the others were gazing out as well.

Jackson pulled out the magazine that Moto had given him on the plane. He turned to page 17, where a small yellow post-it note was stuck, with the carefully written words: *Review the signed version. See the change. Hina knew. I knew. Lily knew. Protect the islands. They are the tip of the iceberg.*

"What's that?" Lily asked, staring down at the magazine.

Jackson slid his hand away, taking the note with it, so that the magazine showed only a picture of an extravagant steakhouse. "A man on the plane recommended this restaurant. He was one of the Japanese lawyers, Moto Tachibana."

"Moto is very kind," Lily said. "Hina…respected him greatly." She was quiet a moment. "Why was he recommending a restaurant?"

"Just being nice, I think. He said it was good, and close to the Embassy. Maybe we can try it?"

"I'd love that."

Jackson smiled. She sounded genuine. If Hina had been killed for knowing something that Lily and Moto knew, they were obviously at risk. That must be what Moto was trying to tell him.

"Good," Jackson said. "Tomorrow then, after our meeting."

When they arrived at the Mandarin Oriental, the staff hurried to open the doors of the black SUVs as a security detail swept out. Jackson and the others followed Ambassador Blair into the lobby. It had the rectangular frames, matted rugs, and white paper thin walls of a Japanese ryokan. The mahogany floor gleamed like a mirror.

After Blair had been swept away like the dignitary he was, Jackson stepped up to registration beside Lily.

A Japanese man in a black suit smiled and bowed. "Hello, Ms.

Sun, Mr. Crow. We are so very glad to have you with us."

"Thank you," Lily said.

The man nodded. "Our country is honored by your delegation's visit. We have received the instructions. Your upgrade is complete." He looked past them and nodded to someone. "Shoji will show you to your suite."

Jackson turned as a woman approached in a silk geisha's dress. She bowed before Jackson and Lily, then rose with a delicate smile. "Please, follow me."

She led Jackson to the black marble elevator bank. The doors opened and she pressed the PH button. Penthouse. Jackson's stomach sank as the elevator soared up.

"Will the Ambassador be on the top floor, too?" Lily asked.

The woman nodded. "The floor has been reserved for your party."

Jackson noticed Lily yawn widely in the elevator mirror. It would be early morning back in DC, and they'd hardly slept on the flight over. "Jet lag?" Jackson asked.

"A bit." Lily met his eyes in the reflection. "You don't look so bad. What's your secret?"

"Green tea?" Jackson shrugged. "I've been drinking it nonstop. I'll probably crash soon."

The elevator opened. The escort stopped in front of a door halfway down the hall. "This one is for you, Ms. Sun. Here is your key."

Lily took the key and opened the door. She glanced back at Jackson. "What's next?"

"Try to get some sleep," Jackson said. "Maybe we can grab dinner in a couple hours."

Lily agreed and entered her room. The woman led Jackson to the end of the hall.

"This is your room, Mr. Crow."

She opened the door and stood to the side as Jackson entered. The suite was a cavern of glass and marble. The floor-to-ceiling windows opened to the city below and beyond, as if inviting all of

Tokyo inside. The bedroom to the side had an immense white bed with a dozen pillows.

"The champagne is on us," the woman said, pointing to an iced bottle on a low table in the main room. She popped the top, and poured a glass. "You've traveled far today," she said, handing the glass to him.

To be polite, he took a small sip.

"And if you need anything, please call the desk. We are here to serve you."

"I'll do that."

"Good evening, Mr. Crow." She bowed and left.

Jackson completed his tour of the suite and pulled a chair up to the window. He gazed out as the sun fell over Mt. Fuji in the distance. It wasn't long before the drugged champagne put him to sleep, so deeply that he didn't hear the door to his suite open.

17

KATHY SULLIVAN AND Logan Grant had set up surveillance across the hall from Lily's room. They could have relied on microphones alone, but hotels were often double-booked by spies. Kathy assumed the Chinese would also have the rooms tapped, so she had arrived in Tokyo a few hours before the delegation. She set up cameras, mics, and heat sensors. It was best to have a presence on the ground in case anything went wrong.

Grant had reported nothing unusual about the travel. He'd been at the back of the plane and watched Jackson and Lily read briefing papers. "Another action-packed day," he'd yawned.

She assured him the action would come, but she had not expected it so soon. Jackson had been asleep about half an hour when a Chinese man arrived at his door, wearing the white pants and shirt of hotel room service. He pushed a cart with a silver-plated tray on top. His round body and bald head sort of matched the tray—without edge, without distinction. The problem was: Jackson hadn't ordered anything.

She rushed to Grant and woke him. "We have a visitor."

She turned back to the screen, where the hallway camera showed the man enter without knocking.

"We have to stop him," Grant whispered.

Kathy ignored Grant. Jackson could always handle himself. But still her pulse raced as she waited, and watched.

Another camera perched like a spot of dust on a lampshade in Jackson's room. Its live feed showed the room service guy push the cart quietly to Jackson, then stand silently in front of him.

"Now!" Grant whispered as he stood.

Kathy grabbed Grant's arm. If the guy was trying to kill Jackson, he would have already shot him. "We're not to interfere. Our job is to protect, but not to be seen."

"I know, but—"

She shook her head, though she didn't like it. "Those are the orders. Jackson will have to take care of himself."

18

JACKSON'S BAD DREAM ended with a jolt. His arm was swinging wildly as he woke, trying to shake off the ants that were swarming over it in his nightmare.

But then something caught his arm, held it firm. "Careful."

His breath froze. Even Tokyo's city lights were not enough to see the face in front of his.

"I mean you no harm."

Soft voice, Jackson thought, *Chinese accent*.

"I bring you opportunity."

"Who are you?"

"Listen now."

Jackson nodded. He glanced down at his right arm. No ants, but it still felt odd. How long had this man been in here? Had he injected him with something?

"Someone gave you an important thing." The man's voice was calm and serious, but not threatening. "It is of little value to you. It may be of great value to others."

The only things Jackson had been given in the past day—aside from a meager airplane dinner and this room upgrade—were Moto's note and the high-resolution photo. But even in a stupor he knew better than to give anything away.

"What are you talking about?" Jackson asked.

"Time is short now. I will be plain. Others want the picture, and will pay steeply for it."

Jackson's eyes began to adjust. The man was wearing all white—room service garb. He was neither smiling nor frowning. This was not personal for him.

"What picture?" Jackson asked.

"This is no game, Mr. Crow. Name your price."

"How will you use it?"

"It will be destroyed," the man said. "Right here, right now.

That is all."

"And in return…?"

"I will transfer funds."

"I don't need funds."

"How about ten thousand *BitStones*?" The guy emphasized the last word like a dirty secret.

Jackson forced himself to remain calm, but all the old memories of his former life came crashing down like an avalanche. First was the Japanese message—*follow the BitStones*. And now this? It had been years since he'd even accessed his accounts. And Vin, his only remaining friend from those days, had been off his radar for three years. Jackson had handed over control of his accounts to Vin and sealed their bargain with a Mai Tai at a dive bar in Mauritius. So how could this guy know anything about Jackson and BitStones? Maybe he didn't. But why a million dollars worth of Stone just to destroy a single picture?

He knew this wasn't just about the picture; they wanted to track him. China had created BitStones to compete with cryptocurrencies like Bitcoin and a dozen others like it. Chinese gaming companies awarded BitStones to gamers who won competitions. These were not little events just for nerds. People packed stadiums to watch gamers compete, and BitStones were doled out in millions. Some of those millions had gone to Jackson and Vin and their friends. And where millions of encrypted BitStones went, the criminals followed. There was no better way to launder money. Everyone suspected that the Chinese monitored BitStones for their own purposes, but there were no known instances of anyone going to prison in China because of BitStones. If a dragon sleeps long enough, people start to think it's harmless. In some games, pointy-eared elves joined guilds that killed dragons to earn BitStones that funded terrorist attacks. Drug dealers formed teams of gamers to win BitStones and then trade them for kilos of cocaine.

This all made BitStones a constant threat to America. Not only were the Stones allegedly untraceable, but they also rivaled the dollar. The exchange rate had been guaranteed to never change—

one hundred U.S. dollars to a single digital Stone. Gamers bragged that it made BitStones a hundred times more important than dollars. Jackson doubted it. The United States had real bombs. But now the average video-gaming Joe bought groceries with Stones more than he did with dollars. The U.S. Government could not stop BitStones, so it did everything in its power to track them. Including hiring Jackson.

"A lot to take in, right?" the guy said. "What's your answer?"

Jackson leaned forward calmly. "Why not dollars?"

"Too easy to trace."

Ironic, Jackson thought. The Chinese government thought only it could track BitStones. But Vin—and years ago, Jackson, too—had hacked into the exact same information. That made this deal worth the risk. "So a million dollars worth?" he asked.

The man smiled. "Yes, ten thousand Stones."

"Show me the Stones," Jackson said.

"You first."

Jackson stood slowly, hands up, and went to his briefcase. He unlocked it and pulled out the picture. He took one last glance, then handed it over to the guy. Jackson could see him better now. Shaved head, definitely Chinese. His room service cover wasn't bad.

"The Stones?" Jackson said.

The guy studied the picture without expression, then pulled his own phone and logged into a BitStone account. "What's your account?"

Jackson still had a dozen inactive accounts. He chose one he'd used solely for one-time transfers like this. He pulled it up on the phone.

The man tapped the screen and the Stones transferred. Then he pulled a lighter and lit the picture on fire, dropping it in a blaze into a golden hotel trashcan.

"If there is another copy of the picture," the man said, "we will find you, and we will kill you. Understood?"

As Jackson nodded, he heard a knock at the door.

"Don't move," the man demanded. He rushed quietly to the

door and looked through the peephole. He came back to Jackson. "Say a word of this," the man whispered. "And she will suffer."

The knocking came again. Louder.

"Go ahead," the man said.

Jackson rose and went to the door. He opened it and saw Lily outside. He let her in.

"Hey!" she said, stepping past him and admiring the room. "You ordered room service?"

Jackson glanced back into the room. The Chinese man was rolling his cart towards him and walked past them. "Good evening, Mr. Crow."

After the man had left, Lily turned to Jackson. "You look kind of awful. What did you order?"

Jackson looked again to where he'd been sitting. A glass bottle of Coca-Cola sat on the table. "Just a coke," he said.

"I'm starving. Want to head out for sushi? We're in Tokyo, after all."

"Yeah, I could use some fresh air."

19

ZHANG HATED TOKYO, but for once he wished he were there, in the middle of the action instead of logging in for another videoconference with his father, General Li. He respected his father, maybe even loved him, as duty required. His father reminded of him of Mao. Many soldiers had loved Mao before they'd been executed for disobedience.

The screen came alive. His father's stern face greeted him, without a smile. He wore his usual green uniform with military stars of honor. Behind him was a room packed full of computers and hackers toiling away. Zhang figured they were mining BitStones, or tracking them. They were probably hacking into dormant accounts like they usually did. It amused him that his father oversaw a bunch of gamers.

"Zhang, you have news for me?"

"Yes, Father." Zhang bowed. He always bowed. "My agent has confirmed that the package was a picture from the Treaty Room. It has been destroyed."

"And the man who delivered the picture?"

"Moto Tachibana departed the airport and did not arrive home. His driver had a fatal crash on the highway. Head-on collision. No survivors."

"Good, my son. Very good. Who has seen this picture?"

"Jackson Crow, and maybe his associate, Lily Sun." Zhang had already briefed him about Lily. He didn't think she knew anything, and if she did, she was a world-class actress for hiding it. But Zhang also knew his father didn't like taking risks. "Ms. Sun was friends with Hina Himura, who could have told her what she learned about our plans, and about the American ambassador's role. And Ms. Sun may have told Mr. Crow. I suggest we eliminate both of them."

General Li studied Zhang silently, intensely, through the screen. "This is becoming messy. More deaths now would mean more mess.

Can you keep it quiet four more days? That is all we need. Donghai has maneuvered excellently to position."

My brother, Zhang fumed, *always maneuvers excellently*. He knew his father liked to pit them against each other, to make them compete and improve. He hated the constant games; he had little choice but to try to win.

"Yes, of course," Zhang said, remembering one of his father's favorite tactics. "I have another idea. Sun Tzu teaches that the way is to avoid what is strong and to strike at what is weak."

"What do you propose?" His father sounded interested.

"We kidnap Ms. Sun. That way we keep her silent, and we gain leverage against the Americans in case something goes wrong. We may even learn something from her. We will kill only if necessary."

"Very well. But do it quietly. Anything else?"

"No," Zhang said, but he was not satisfied with it. He hated these all-business calls. He wanted to see his father smile. He deployed an old inside joke between them. "We're just leaving the world a better place than we found it, right?"

His father's face softened, smiled, then laughed—the deep belly laugh of a tyrant who knows no fear but enjoys little true humor. He had taught Zhang, when he was a young boy, that the phrase "leaving the world a better place" was one of the most naive statements of mankind. People were deluded to think they had some duty to "the world." Such nonsense. Duty spread so thin had no flavor. Make China a better place? Yes. Make your family and yourself better? Absolutely. But the world? No, the world is the arena, and anyone hoping to make the arena a better place didn't understand the game.

"You speak well," General Li said, after composing himself. "But be patient, my son. Remember, if you wait by the river long enough, the bodies of your enemies will float by."

20

REAGAN WAS JOGGING along the National Mall in Washington, D.C., with the reflecting pool to her left and ancient American oaks overhead, when she got the encrypted text from the agent, Kathy Sullivan.

A man came under cover to Crow's room. They spoke, and Crow gave him a picture that he burned. All targets secure.

Reagan studied the reflecting pool's dark water. It was a mirror showing blue sky above. She had a million unanswered questions, but they all came back to this: could she still trust Jackson?

She typed back. *Were you seen?*

No.

Keep it that way.

21

JACKSON WALKED ACROSS the lobby of the Mandarin Oriental, stopped by the concierge, and asked loudly in English where to go for good sushi. The concierge handed a map to him, another to Lily, and circled a spot within walking distance. Jackson said thanks and walked with Lily out the front door. He walked two blocks toward the circled restaurant, then dropped his map in the trash.

"Didn't like his recommendation?" Lily asked.

"I know a better spot." Jackson also knew that whoever was trailing him would ask the concierge where he was going. He needed to lose any followers so he could eat his sushi in peace. "Up for an adventure?"

"Sure," Lily said. "It's my first time here."

The night air outside the hotel was not as fresh as Jackson had hoped. It was a sickly sweet fragrance of soy sauce and gasoline, with a hint of pavement. They were in the heart of Tokyo, not far from the Imperial Palace, but far enough that they could not catch a whiff of the Palace's beautiful gardens and blooming cherry blossoms.

Jackson headed away from the Palace and toward the Sumida River. It took him two turns to spot the American following him. There were other Caucasians in the crowded streets, but only one who loomed a head taller with a square jaw and a Marines haircut. Jackson recognized him as the same guy who had been watching them in Washington from a white news van, and from the back of the plane. Whoever he was, he must be a rookie.

After another turn, Jackson leaned over to Lily and whispered: "Is your phone off?"

"No, why?"

"Keep moving and turn it off," Jackson said. "We're being followed."

She didn't look around or ask any questions. That was good.

She took out her phone and powered it down. They continued along the sidewalk, bright neon signs giving their skin a pinkish glow.

"Stay close," Jackson instructed. Then he took a sudden turn down a set of stairs in the sidewalk. Lily followed at his side as they entered the vast Tokyo underground mall, with hundreds of shops and restaurants. No better place to shake a tail.

Jackson turned quickly into a large grocery store, a few stores before one of the city's most touristy sushi spots—one that the concierge had circled. Jackson grabbed a magazine and led Lily toward the back.

"Kneel down, look at the noodles."

Lily did as he asked, studying the dozens of brands that lined the aisle. Jackson could hear her heavy breathing. He opened the magazine in front of his face and peered over it toward the mall corridor outside. The agent passed a few moments later.

"Let's go," Jackson said.

They would have one minute, max, before the agent checked the sushi place and came out again, backtracking. He rushed Lily out of the store and up a different set of stairs.

A little luck waited for them outside. A couple was climbing out of a cab right beside them. Jackson pulled Lily toward it and got inside. Jackson told the driver the name of a sushi place twenty minutes away. The driver sped off.

Lily hurriedly buckled her seat belt, then turned to Jackson. "Want to tell me what's going on?"

"Yes, soon."

Lily nodded. She looked calmer than he expected under the circumstances.

Jackson leaned back, breathing easier as he watched the blur of city lights. By the time they arrived, after a dozen turns and a stretch on a highway, Jackson felt sure they'd lost whoever was following.

The sushi place was exactly as Jackson as remembered it, tucked into a quaint neighborhood where the same families had lived for decades. The sign outside had small black letters, and no neon. Inside, the wood-paneled walls had faded into a light gray. The sake bottles behind the bar gave the tiny room a greenish hue. The hostess greeted them. Jackson requested a table in the back. He sat facing the front door. A model sea turtle the size of a manhole hung above his head on the wall.

A waitress brought hot green tea. He and Lily ordered. As the first nigiri rolls arrived, they chatted casually about Tokyo and sushi. It almost felt like a date, except that she was obviously thinking about what had just happened. She seemed to be formulating her line of questions before she began.

"So, where did you work before the State Department?" she asked, holding a raw slice of fatty tuna delicately between her chopsticks.

"The CIA."

She looked surprised. "Aren't you supposed to keep that secret?"

He sipped his warm tea, holding the warm earthen cup between his hands. He noticed a man enter the restaurant, wearing a grey suit, white button-down shirt, and no tie. The man had a mop of pepper-gray-and-black hair and kept his head turned so Jackson could not fully see his face, but he had a slight limp that looked familiar. He sat at the small sushi bar, with his back to Jackson.

"You have a security clearance," Jackson said. "Besides, you already guessed it."

"So who was following us? And why? Because of the murder?"

"The CIA, among others. I'm not sure why. I need your help to figure that out."

"Why me?"

"You worked on the treaty."

"So did you." She sounded defensive.

"I reviewed it a week before it was signed," Jackson said. "Did anything change between then and the signature?"

Lily finished chewing, thinking. "A few things. Little things."

Jackson considered his words. He could still remember the first time he'd learned about someone targeting him, when he was younger than Lily. He'd been used to taking risks in the digital world, but the thought of a bullet whizzing at his skull had taken some getting used to.

"Hina might have known something she wasn't supposed to know. You might, too." He spoke slowly, quietly. "I want to understand this as much as you do. Tell me everything that happened with the treaty, the week before it was signed."

"Okay…" Lily took a deep breath. Her voice came out composed, analytical. "A few days before the signing, Hina and I had to make a small correction. It was to the English text, so the Japanese official had to sign it."

"What was the change?"

"Just one word."

"Which one?"

"We changed *administration* to *sovereignty*."

"A very important word." Jackson set his tea down, thinking. He was surprised this change had not been raised to his level. His eyes went to the man at the sushi bar, who was eating quietly. He recalled the exact phrase from the treaty, article five. The U.S. would protect Japan if there were an attack against *the territories under its administration*. With this change, it was *the territories under its sovereignty*. This meant the treaty would no longer apply to disputed territories, including many islands that Japan and China both claimed to own.

"Who ordered the change?" Jackson asked.

"Ambassador Blair," Lily answered, defensive again. "He said it came from the White House. He said there was no need to run it by you."

Jackson's throat tightened. "I asked you about the treaty yesterday, in my office. Why didn't you tell me then?"

"I—I guess I was thinking about Hina."

"Right, I'm sorry. But this is huge. This could explain everything."

"Why?"

Jackson saw no reason to hide the stakes. "Somebody could be trying to start a war. Now, if China moves against disputed territories that Japan administers, we would no longer be obligated to protect Japan."

"Wouldn't that *prevent* a war?"

"No, it's deterrence that keeps peace. China won't attack if it knows we'll defend. If that changes, well, China could push too far, Japan could strike first, our own military bases in the Pacific could be at risk. This is like pulling a card out from the bottom of a house of cards."

"I see your point…"

"Hina knew about this change in the treaty, and she was shot. You could be the next target."

Lily didn't flinch. "The killer could have just shot me at the same time. He didn't."

"It's harder to get off two shots." That was true, but Jackson knew Lily was right. If someone thought it was worth the risk to kill Hina over the treaty term, they would have taken out Lily already. And maybe him. They would not have sent a spy just to burn up a picture.

"Do you think whoever was following us is—" Lily's voice wavered—"trying to kill me?"

"I don't know. Back there it was the CIA. But others are following, too. The Chinese, probably the Japanese, too."

"Why do you think that?"

"Because I think one of them is sitting in this restaurant."

"Now?" she whispered.

Jackson took another sip of tea. At least Lily kept her surprise quiet. She was tougher than Jackson thought. She might be able to handle this. "I thought we shook them with the cab," he said. "But a man sat down in here a few minutes after we did. You turned off your phone, right?"

"Yes…well, I did, but I turned it on again once we got here. I needed to check—"

"No." Jackson glared at her. So that's how the man at the sushi bar had found them. "You know what your phone is?"

"The State Department issued it. Has to be clean."

"It's a tracking beacon."

"I turned off the location services."

"Doesn't matter. The Department bugs everyone's phone. And everyone who travels has to slide their phone through the airport metal detectors. Our diplomatic passports are like red flags that scream, *Official U.S. Government business. Please monitor me!* It's not hard for any country to add their own tracker."

She slipped her hand into her bag. "Sorry. It's off now. So the Japanese are following us?"

"Yes." Jackson started to rise. "Stay here, and be ready to leave fast. I'll go ask why."

He left a 5,000 Yen note on the table and moved toward the man at the sushi bar. The bar had only three seats, and the man was sitting alone.

"Is this seat free?" Jackson asked in Japanese.

The man's hand went to his pocket as he turned. Jackson had no doubt what was hidden there.

"It's saved for you, my friend," the man said in English.

Jackson immediately recognized him. It was Daisho, a man he had not seen in fifteen years. He had not aged well. His peppered grey streaks and, apparently, bouts of plastic surgery had hidden his identity until Jackson heard him speak and saw him up close. Daisho was a spy with Naichō, the Japanese equivalent of the CIA, and a specialist in tracking down money launderers who used cryptocurrencies. Jackson had worked with Daisho in one of his first government operations. They'd set up a sting together in Osaka, at a huge gaming arcade of the sort that existed only in Asia. They'd hit it off as the rare breed of spies who lived in virtual gaming worlds with major real world consequences. Jackson took his involvement here as a serious sign—important people in the Japanese government were concerned.

Jackson smiled as he sat beside Daisho. "It's been a while."

"Too long, Crow-san," Daisho said. "You were always easier to follow in person than online. Why haven't you visited?"

"I'm a lawyer now."

Daisho eyed Jackson doubtfully. "I've heard that one before."

"It's true. I left the old work. I advise the State Department on legal matters."

"I see." Daisho smiled, with an eyebrow raised as he looked past Jackson to where Lily was sitting. "Interesting that your legal advice involves guarding a beautiful young woman who the Chinese want dead."

Jackson did not respond. This was helpful information. The Chinese *did* want Lily dead, or at least the Japanese thought they did.

"Tell me, Crow-san, why do the Chinese want that?"

"I'm just a lawyer," Jackson said. "I was hoping you'd tell me." He glanced over his shoulder to Lily, who was looking down and cradling her cup of tea as if it was a wounded bird. Jackson turned back to Daisho. "She was in the Treaty Room when they shot Hina Himura. They could have brought an extra bullet."

"Maybe," Daisho said. "But perhaps they didn't think she knew what Hina knew."

"And what's that?"

"We don't know, and we could use your help finding out. Whatever it is, they must now think that your colleague knows, or that she has the clue planted with her. She's in serious danger."

That made sense to Jackson. Lily had worked closely with Hina, who could have left information with Lily, even if Lily didn't know it yet. "I'll keep her safe."

"Not without our help," Daisho said. "And maybe not even with it." He paused, his voice becoming soft. "They killed one of ours. Moto Tachibana."

"No…" Jackson could not hide his surprise. "I just talked to him, hours ago."

"He died in a terrible car crash, on the highway from the airport. It was no accident."

"I'm so sorry." Jackson's fist clenched. Moto's message had been clear: Hina had known about the changed treaty term, and she'd been killed. Moto had known, and now he'd been killed. That left Lily…

"Moto was like you," Daisho said. "An international

lawyer…with certain other skills. He will be greatly missed here."

Jackson nodded gravely. "What's behind all this, Daisho?"

"The Chinese are flexing their muscles, especially around neighbors like us. It's no secret your military has been pulling back from Japan, from Taiwan, from Korea. If they moved against one of their neighbors, and you don't defend, well…you can imagine what might happen."

"You think they're planning an attack?"

"You really haven't been gaming, have you? Lots of hackers are talking about a secret project in China. Something involving military and construction, moving lots of dirt. Maybe it's about the islands they're building in the South China Sea. They already claim an area as vast as the Caribbean. They've deployed another aircraft carrier, too. We don't know what they're planning. The Chinese can't keep everything from leaking, but they run a very tight ship."

"Any other details?"

"Nothing credible. The point is, if the Chinese attack our territory, we'll fight back even if you don't. Maybe we can't win an outright war, but we Japanese are a proud people. We will not let anyone take our territory. And we've never been conquered. We prefer to strike first."

Jackson shook his head. "That's how wars start…"

"Exactly. It's the assurance of American defense that has kept this region stable since the last world war. Now that's changing. Hina's murder must have something to do with it." Daisho glanced again toward Lily. "You need to find out what it is from your friend over there."

"I'll see what I can do," Jackson said.

"That's all I'm asking, Crow-san. You're one of the only Americans I trust." Daisho bowed politely, then his eyes flicked toward the window. "But you're rusty, my friend. You let yourself get tracked by the Chinese, and now a few of them are waiting outside for you."

Jackson blinked in surprise. How had that happened? He was tempted to blame Lily's phone, but maybe Daisho was right. He *was* rusty. "Got a plan?"

"It's your lucky day," Daisho said. "We have them surrounded. We'll start a little fight to cause a distraction. That should give you cover to get back to your hotel. Then you need to get your friend back to the United States. It's not safe for her here."

"Understood," Jackson said. "*Arigato*."

"Just doing my job. World peace and all that."

Jackson smiled and motioned for Lily to come. He introduced her to Daisho. They had been speaking only a few moments when Daisho's phone rang. He answered, listened, and then told Jackson it was time to go. He pointed to a cab that had stopped outside.

"Good luck, you two," Daisho said.

They said goodbye and Jackson moved out quickly with Lily. He heard a gunshot about a block away. Lily grabbed his hand, squeezing tight. They ducked into the cab and Jackson told the driver to take them to the Mandarin Oriental, fast.

22

KATHY HAD BEEN watching the screen for hours while Grant got some sleep. He'd blamed fatigue for losing track of Jackson and Lily outside the Mandarin Oriental, in the streets of Tokyo. Kathy knew better. Jackson must have detected him and shaken him. Grant had a lot to learn.

She sipped a lukewarm cup of coffee. Watching and waiting was the worst part of the job. Sensors could tell her when someone came, but they couldn't read body movements. They couldn't tell when a room-service guy moved like a soldier, or when a cleaning crew brought their own surveillance equipment to install. Only six people had passed through the penthouse hall of the Mandarin Oriental in the past six hours. Four cleaning maids and one stranger visiting his room with an escort hanging on his arm.

It was 9:03 pm when she saw the familiar stocky Chinese man with the bald head, the same one who had talked to Jackson.

"Hey," she said, nudging Grant awake. "The room service guy is back. At Lily's door."

Grant yawned and leaned forward, studying the screen. "Is she in there?"

"No."

The man opened the door and entered. They had one camera inside that showed most of the bedroom, but after a quick look around, the man went into the bathroom. They did not have a camera in there.

"Definitely not room service," Kathy said. "We have to warn them."

"Sure, let's disobey the Deputy National Security Adviser." Grant rubbed his hands over his short-cropped hair. "We'll just stop Lily in the hall and say, hey, we're the spies who have been watching you, heads up, there's a Chinese agent waiting in your bathroom…"

Kathy knew he was right, but she didn't like the orders. She didn't like Reagan. She was not going to have innocent blood on her hands, not this time. "I'm warning Jackson."

"How?"

"Stay here, watch."

She was already moving. She grabbed the Do-Not-Disturb sign from their own room's door and scribbled something on it before walking out. She stopped in front of Lily's door and hung the sign there. Then she moved to Jackson's door and hung an unmarked sign there.

When she came back, Grant asked her what she'd written.

"Something Jackson will understand," Kathy said.

"But you wrote only on Lily's sign. What if he doesn't come back with her?"

"I know him. He's not letting her out of his sight."

23

ON THE CAB RIDE to the Mandarin Oriental, Jackson told Lily the basics of what Daisho had said in the sushi restaurant. He told her Moto had been killed. Lily had fallen silent at that, with the same ashen expression that she'd had in the Treaty Room, after Hina had been shot.

When they reached the penthouse floor, their footsteps sinking deep into the plush carpet, Lily stopped at her door and waved goodnight to Jackson as he headed down the hall to his room. She slid her key card into the slot. The green light flashed. Her hand was on the handle when Jackson rushed back and stopped her.

"Wait," Jackson whispered by her ear. "Let me go in first."

It had only taken a moment for Jackson to realize something was wrong. He had not hung a room service sign on his door. And then he'd seen the sign on Lily's door, with the word "danger" scribbled in Dari. Only a few people in the world would use that language from Afghanistan here in Tokyo. And Jackson knew one of them was Kathy Sullivan. So maybe she was here, watching him, and wanting him to know that she was here. But if so, why hadn't she revealed herself? He didn't have time to figure that out. This warning plus Daisho's meant an attack was coming.

He readied his weapon in his sleeve. "Stay back," he ordered under his breath.

Lily stepped aside quietly. Now he was the one opening the door. He was the one who could have the red sniper dot on his forehead in seconds. The last thing he needed was for Lily to follow him into the attack, but he might be able to use a distraction.

"In thirty seconds, call the room," he said.

"I don't know the number."

"Call the front desk. They'll route it. Okay?"

She nodded, fear heavy in her eyes.

Jackson knew the best thing to do was to charge inside to catch anyone off guard. But if someone was inside, they would expect Lily to be coming. He needed to enter like she would to maintain the element of surprise.

So he slowly turned the handle. He stepped in at a normal pace, crouching low, drawing his dart gun.

It was dark and silent in the room. He didn't see anyone, or any red dots. The bathroom was ahead to the left. That was the most likely place of the attack, if it was coming. Assassins liked bathrooms. It's where people were most vulnerable, and the mess easiest to clean up.

He wanted to wait, to listen. But he still wanted to sound like Lily entering the room. So he flicked on the light. No motion.

He moved towards the bathroom steadily. He peeked inside, but saw nothing out of the ordinary. The ivory shower curtain was made of heavy material that obscured whatever was behind it.

He had eight more seconds before the phone should ring.

He couldn't stand still. Lily would be moving, going to the sink. So that's what he did, keeping his eyes on the shower curtain.

Staying low, he reached up with an outstretched arm to turn on the water in the sink. He counted *four, three* before the phone should ring, then turned the faucet on.

The curtain flung open.

A man leapt forward in a blur. Hitting thin air instead of Lily's body, he slammed into the glass mirror beside sink, shattering it into a million shards that clinked loudly on the tile. He recovered quickly and turned in surprise.

He was the same man who'd been in Jackson's room. He was drawing a gun.

The phone rang, and the man glanced into the bedroom.

Jackson blew a dart at the man's face. He didn't wait to see if it hit. He dove under the man's outstretched gun and tackled him hard into the wall. Tiles broke behind the man's head. They crashed down into the tub.

Jackson felt the heavy blow of the gun against his back. He slammed his knee into the man's groin. Then he did it again. Like clockwork the assassin crumpled into the fetal position.

By then the tranquilizer had taken effect. The man went motionless at the bottom of the tub, with the red-feathered tip of a dart protruding from his cheek. Jackson grabbed the dart and tucked it back into his sleeve. He eyed the body, thinking fast. If he'd sent a man on this mission, what precautions would he have taken?

He frisked the man and found no phone or ID. No surprise there. Using both hands, he carefully pried open the man's jaw and reached inside. He wiggled the teeth one by one. He found a loose molar in the back and gently pulled. It came out easily. An implant.

He studied the tooth's ivory contours in the bathroom light. It could contain potassium cyanide—lethal if swallowed, to keep a spy from talking. Jackson could handle that risk. He used the sharp point of his dart to prod at the top of the tooth. A small wedge of ivory popped off, revealing a hollow cavity. He shook it out.

A tiny data chip fell, like a tic-tac on his palm. He pocketed it to inspect later.

He would leave the rest to Kathy. If she really was here, and watching, she could clean up the mess and find a place to ask questions.

The phone was still ringing. Jackson went to the bedroom and answered it. "Hello."

"Are you okay?" Lily asked. "I heard…"

"I'm fine. Come on in."

Lily entered a moment later, cell phone in her hand. She sat on the edge of the hotel bed, staring wide-eyed into the bathroom, where the shattered mirror showed a broken reflection and an arm dangled over the side of the tub.

"What happened?" she asked.

"He thought I was you."

"Is he dead?"

"No, he'll just be out a couple hours."

She eyed Jackson, relieved but confused. "How'd you learn to do that? The CIA?"

"Some of it." Jackson sat beside her and put his arm around her shoulder. He reminded himself this was not his sister, Jules. He had learned from his mistake in Manila. He had protected Lily. She was safe now. "We'll get you back to DC. I have a friend there who can make sure you stay hidden for a while."

She sniffed and wiped her hand across her eyes. "I don't want to leave you. I mean, you could be in danger, too, here...alone."

"I'll be fine."

She studied him. "Who are you really, Jackson?"

He saw the distrust in her eyes, and it hurt him more than he'd expected. She needed to trust him, for her own safety. *Just for her safety*, he told himself. "I tried to leave my old work behind," he said. "But the person who got me this job did so on one condition—that I take on assignments when strictly necessary."

"So I'm an assignment?" She leaned away from him.

"No, it's not like that." He hesitated. *What is it like, then?* "I was told to monitor things and report. Maybe this is about the treaty, but I'm starting to think it's bigger."

"Like China starting a war? You know that's not going to happen."

"Then why do you think Hina was shot?"

"I—" Lily looked down at her hands on the white bed. "I'm not sure."

Jackson knew her well enough to know she wasn't saying something, and to know that it was fear and uncertainty—not distrust—behind it. He resisted the desire to take her into his arms, to comfort her. He put his hand over hers. "I'm going to make sure you're safe, Lily. If you have any ideas about Hina, please tell me."

"She told me not to tell anyone." Lily spoke evenly. Her body was motionless. "But...she had dinner with Ambassador Blair."

"What did she say about it?"

"That it was no big deal."

Jackson could hear the doubt in Lily's voice. "You didn't believe her."

"I've heard about Blair's reputation. I've worked with him..."

Jackson's jaw clenched. "Has he ever tried anything with you?"

"No." She paused. "You think he had something to do with this?"

He thought again of Kathy Sullivan and Afghanistan. Her assignment there had been to watch a government contractor bribed by a warlord. She usually got the jobs watching Americans, because she was the best. Maybe she was here because she was watching Blair, too. "I'm going to find out," Jackson said.

Lily's large dark eyes studied Jackson's hand before rising to meet his gaze. "And if he did, then what?"

"Then he'll wish I never set foot in the Treaty Room."

24

IT WAS DARK NOW. No land could be seen. But that didn't stop Donghai's pulse from quickening as he sailed closer than ever to Okinawa. He thought of his father's words, quoting the ancient master of war, Sun Tzu: *Let your plans be dark and impenetrable as night, and when you move, fall like a thunderbolt.*

His fleet had been venturing east from the Diaoyu Islands, testing the limits of the Japanese and, more importantly, the Americans on their Pacific base. Only 240 nautical miles separated Okinawa from Diaoyu. The space could be covered in minutes by jets. Pushing east, almost within sight of Okinawa, gave Donghai confidence that his brother Zhang was right. This time the Americans were not going to fight back.

Donghai studied the papers stretched out before him. One was an old map that mattered—an ancient map from the Ming Dynasty. It showed the Diaoyu Islands as Chinese territory, clear as day. Chinese fishermen had frequented the bountiful seas near the rocky outcrops. No one lived on the islands. They had no fresh water or flat land for building.

The past century changed nothing about China's ownership. The Japanese had sent out their Okinawa Prefecture to survey the islands in 1885, and they claimed them. It was baseless. It was ridiculous. Donghai had the 19th century Japanese report open before him: *Large numbers of albatross gather on the islands. Large amounts of wreckage lie along the shore, washed up here from boats from Ryukyu and China that have foundered nearby, but there was no sign of inhabitation.* So the Japanese understood, from the beginning, that the islands were owned by China.

Within ten years, just before the close of the 1800s, the Okinawa governors had pressed their cause and convinced the Japanese authorities to claim the Diaoyu Islands as their own. They called them the Senkakus. They established a small fishing expedition there. They overhunted the albatrosses on the island and decimated their population.

And they set up this conflict. They could only blame themselves. It was simple: Japan had taken what belonged to China. Donghai was going to take it back.

The lawyers and scholars and policy-makers had their arguments. They cited treaties and international law. Donghai found them absurd. He had the map. The Diaoyu Islands belonged to his people. If they could take them, then that would be the end of the matter. The original people of Okinawa, like the original people of all lands, should understand. The Ryukyu tribe had governed the Okinawa islands for centuries before the Japanese invaded and captured the Ryukyu king in the 1600s. Japan strengthened its hold on the islands, trying to eliminate all that the Ryukyun people had held dear. If the Ryukyu could have taken back their islands, surely they would have.

Then the other imperialists had come. During the Second World War, Japan had lost to the Americans. They had to give up territory to the American troops on Okinawa, in exchange for America's protection. But now the Americans would not be coming to their defense. The thousands of marines and fighter pilots and ships with the stars and stripes would stay on Okinawa, under its tropical sun, while Donghai took the Diaoyu Islands, likely without a fight.

The stakes were more than a few specks of land isolated in the East China Sea. Whoever controlled these islands—situated almost halfway between mainland China and Okinawa—controlled nearly 20,000 square nautical miles of ocean and the resources underneath. If Chinese scientists were accurate, and Donghai knew his people had greater scientific knowledge than any alive, the oil and gas resources in the vast area around the Diaoyu Islands could rival the Persian Gulf.

"Sir." Donghai's lieutenant had appeared in the door. His body was rigid as he saluted.

"What is it?" Donghai asked.

"Sir, our radar shows four approaching jets from the east."

From Okinawa. Donghai knew he could not trust his brother completely. The Americans would not roll over and play dead. But he also knew they would not fire, not on a first pass. This was the warning.

"Hold fire," Donghai said.

"Yes, sir." The lieutenant rushed out, issuing orders through his headset.

Donghai watched as the jets approached, streaks of light soaring straight towards him. They flew low over the aircraft carrier, their sound trailing behind with the familiar sonic boom of jet-engine propulsion.

The lieutenant appeared again, still rigid but breathing heavily. "They are coming again, sir."

"Hold fire again." Donghai sighed. His people had waited so long. They could wait a few days longer. "Begin to reverse course, back to the Diaoyu Islands."

25

JACKSON DREAMED HE was walking at dusk in the midst of a crowd crossing Memorial Bridge—the road resting on elegant arches over the Potomac River between Arlington Cemetery and the Lincoln Memorial. He reached the middle of the bridge when a man in the crowd stopped him. He was a tall man with severe eyes and a dark overcoat. He made some kind of sign over Jackson, then he let him go. Jackson looked out and saw smoke-filled sky and a Chinese warship floating in the Potomac River. Jackson tried to warn someone passing by about the warship, but his lips wouldn't part. And he knew, as he woke up, that it was the man who had sealed his mouth shut.

Whatever. Just a dream.

Jackson had plenty of wild ones. His old life had made sure of that. Dreams were just projections on projections, the necessary mechanics of a brain storing long-term memories. No use worrying about it, he told himself.

He climbed out of bed and started doing pushups to put some order into his mind. He'd been up too late. He'd blame jet lag, but it didn't help that he'd spent the night's early hours fighting off a Chinese assassin, getting Lily a safe military flight back to Washington via Okinawa, and worrying about the meeting that Ambassador Blair would lead with the Japanese in the morning.

He stopped the pushups at sixty, got the coffee brewing.

He thought of Vin. It had been years since they'd talked, but Vin had sworn he'd do anything for him, anytime, after he'd saved him from the government's sweep. If anyone could still track BitStones, it was Vin. He had more conspiracy theories than the JFK assassination theorists, but at least one in five of his leads was good. Vin also had the resources to crack any file. Jackson had found the minuscule data chip in the hollowed-out, but he couldn't risk accessing it on his own. Not here. Not on a laptop. Who knows what virus it could hold?

Jackson poured his coffee and sent an encrypted text to Vin: *I need to see you asap.*

The response came within a minute. *Finally! In person?*

Yes. I'm in Tokyo.

Come to the Hong Kong Jockey Club. Today, 8 pm.

See you soon.

The timing would be tight, but Jackson thought he could pull it off. He had to attend the meeting with Blair, then he could leave in the afternoon. He quickly booked the earliest flight possible to Hong Kong. If all went well, he should make it to Vin by 8 pm.

He showered, water steaming up around him, thoughts of the warship dream running through his mind again. He toweled off and stood before the mirror. There was a small gash and bruise on his shoulder, from tackling the assassin. *You're skin and bones*, his grandmother would say. She hadn't seen him in his bulky Agency days—she would've been proud. He'd shed that muscle, though it would have been useful last night. His body fit better in a suit now.

He went to the closet and eyed his two blue button-down shirts, then the safe peering out between them. He opened the safe and took out his passport and the data chip.

It was still early. He needed to start digging up what he could find before he met Vin.

Thirty minutes later he was walking into the U.S. Embassy in Tokyo. It could be confused for any boring gray office building if not for the American flag and the Marines posted outside. Inside, the building was a ghost town, except for the buzzing government-issued fluorescent lights along the halls. It seemed the lights were a leading export of the main State Department building in Washington.

Jackson walked to his guest office for the week, confirming that no one had arrived yet at any of the offices near this one. At least the foreign service officers could sleep normal hours wherever they lived, unlike those in Jackson's former line of work. He flicked on the lights and sat at the computer.

While the system started, he got the coffee going in the suite. He could go for another cup. It was also his good deed for the day, and it would tip him off if anyone arrived soon. Who wouldn't go straight for the coffee at this hour? He sat back down and typed in his passwords.

The classified system came online.

THIS IS A UNITED STATES GOVERNMENT COMPUTER SYSTEM.

Yeah, I got that.

Blah, blah, YOU WILL BE MONITORED.

I know...

UNAUTHORIZED USE MAY SUBJECT YOU TO CRIMINAL PROSECUTION.

Okay.

CLICK TO CONTINUE.

Jackson wiped a sheen of sweat off his forehead. No air conditioning this early. It was stuffy. Jackson leaned back, staring at the ceiling. It was so quiet. The coffee was finished.

He got up and poured himself a mug. The mug said WORLD'S GREATEST AMBASSADOR and had a picture of Blair's face. Jackson paused in front of the door to the Ambassador's office. *How was Blair involved?*

He sat again at his desk, took a deep breath, and clicked to continue.

A search page appeared on the screen. The State Department still communicated officially through cables—the electronic vestiges of telegrams—stored in this classified system. Cables had never been the same since thousands of them went public through Wikileaks, but they could still provide a wealth of information the public did not know.

Jackson typed "Blair" and scanned the few items that came up. None were highly classified or seemed relevant. Jackson was not surprised. It wasn't like Ambassador Blair would be broadcasting his connections with China or a murdered Japanese lawyer.

Next Jackson searched for "China" in the past 30 days. A list of cables filled out the screen. Jackson scanned the headlines. *Foreign Minister seeks compromise on environment... American citizen detained for illegal... Jets strafe warship near Okinawa...*

Warship. He remembered his dream.

Jackson guided the cursor over the link to the cable. This might be nothing. It was probably something. *Jets strafe warship...* Lily had been passing through Okinawa. If anyone could keep her protected, it was the military. Under that headline was the classified stamp: SECRET/NOFORN. That meant no foreign nationals were permitted to see it. The cable reported that one of the big, brand-spanking-new aircraft carriers from China had cruised closer to Okinawa than usual, and then had circled back to the Senkaku Islands after the Air Force gave its fly-by, middle-finger warning. No shots had been fired.

Jackson went back further in time, reading everything he could find on the Chinese military. It was no secret that China had the largest land army in the world, almost three million soldiers strong. But a series of cables reported on strange troop movements in southeast China. An agent in Pingtan—the closest point in mainland China to Taiwan—had seen soldiers arriving in droves, but the agent had not located any base there. The agent noted in the cable, "It's like they disappeared."

The reports on China's navy were more harrowing. They had been building aircraft carriers, battleships, and nuclear submarines at a rate the American government could never pull off. Technology had been stolen from U.S. defense contractors. The Russians had been advising. An American admiral warned that the Chinese fleet could, for the first time, win in a surprise confrontation in the Pacific. Everyone knew the Americans needed to keep the strongest navy to remain the world's policeman. Apparently the Chinese were ready to start policing themselves.

Two hours later Ambassador Blair arrived at the Embassy and passed by Jackson without a glance. After a few minutes Jackson went to Blair's office, where he found the Ambassador, with bloodshot eyes and still-wet silver hair, crouched over in front of his computer screen. Posture like that could kill a man.

"We had to send Lily back to Washington," Jackson said.

"I heard." Blair did not sound happy about it. "You should've requested my permission. I'm responsible here."

"We tried to contact you."

"I had other affairs to attend."

Affairs. Good word, Jackson thought. "Would you have disagreed with sending her back?"

"We could have protected her. We're only here another day."

This was going to be delicate. It was better not to arouse Blair's suspicions—to play the boring lawyer. But Jackson still needed information. He relaxed his shoulders and made his voice casual. "Why do you think Lily was attacked?"

"Beats me," Blair said, straightening his tie. "Probably the same reason they killed the Japanese girl, whatever that was."

"Did you know her?"

"Not really. As much as you know anyone after a couple meetings. It's awful what happened."

"Yeah…" Jackson leaned against the doorframe. "You think it has anything to do with the treaty?"

"No." The Ambassador waved his hand dismissively. "It's a scrap of paper. It doesn't change anything."

"Even the changed term? It went from *administration* to *sovereignty*."

"Legalese. So what?"

"This means we no longer have an obligation to defend disputed territories, like the Senkaku Islands."

Blair eyed him cautiously. "Lily told you about this? I doubt it matters, and definitely not enough to kill someone over." He shrugged. "Anyway, I'm just the messenger. That change came from the White House, and the Japanese agreed to it. They're tired of depending on us. They want to start rebuilding their own military. So we'll let 'em do it."

From the White House. Reagan must have known. And she hadn't told Jackson. "Why'd the White House want the change?"

TREATY OF WAR

"The last thing the President wants is a war. If the Chinese and Japanese want to fight over a few rocks in the middle of nowhere, let 'em." Blair leaned forward with his hands clasped on his desk. "We've got our own problems at home, and a couple thousand miles of Pacific to keep us out of the problems around here."

For once Jackson was glad to give his legal advice. He knew that ever since the United States had returned Okinawa to Japan in 1972, it had been clear under the Japan-U.S. Security Treaty that America would protect any attacks on territories controlled by Japan. China would not try to take the Senkaku Islands, because it knew that would bring America into the fight. "Just because we're not *obligated* to defend the islands doesn't mean we can't," Jackson said. "It's the threat of that defense that keeps the Chinese at bay. The Pacific's size doesn't matter as much as it used to."

"We're not turning our back on Japan," Blair said. "You know our generals are always hungry for action. They might see an attack where others don't. Heck, they think it's a threat when fishing boats sailing near the Senkaku Islands. Well, what if the Chinese sent an aircraft carrier instead? Our generals might attack. Then we've got World War III on our hands."

"The Chinese must believe that we *will* fight," Jackson said. "That's what prevents war."

"Not every war's worth fightin'. That's the President's decision, not yours."

Jackson couldn't argue with that, but he didn't have to like it. He started to leave, but noticed a large, open box full of books on the floor. The two books on top of the stack had the titles, *National Security Law* and *The Geneva Conventions*. Lily had told him about this. Blair had asked her to give him the titles of leading books on the laws of war, and his assistant arranged to send them in the diplomatic pouch. Apparently, Lily had said, he wanted them in the meeting to impress the Japanese.

Jackson asked him, "What are those?"

"Gifts for our friends at today's meeting. Lily picked the books. How'd she do?"

"These are about the laws of war. You think the Japanese are going to appreciate that?"

Blair leaned back in his chair and smiled. "I never go to a meeting empty-handed. We need every advantage we can get. We'll be saying sorry. Then we'll be listening. It's mainly for the soldiers to talk."

"So why the books?" Jackson asked.

The Ambassador rose from his desk and stepped past Jackson. "Come have a look."

He knelt down beside the box and pulled out one of the brand new thick books. Holding it out to Jackson, he said, "open it."

"Okay…" Jackson lifted the cover. Inside was a hidden container, which held an expensive bottle of bourbon. A bit different than a data chip in a tooth.

"See," the Ambassador smiled, "gifts!"

Jackson looked down at the open books. He figured each had a secret cavity that held a bottle. "It's creative," Jackson admitted, "but we could have picked different books…"

"You're always overthinking," Blair said. "The Japanese love bourbon, and little tricks like this."

Jackson waited until he was back in his office before he let himself sigh and roll his eyes. It was a shame an ambassador post as important as Blair's could be bought. Japan deserved better.

An hour later, Jackson joined the Ambassador in the back of a black, armored SUV with little American flags flying on its sides. He and Blair rode in quiet. Jackson wished Lily could have joined this meeting. He stared out at the Tokyo streets. The SUV stopped at a red light where an old man stood on a street corner under a black umbrella, selling bright red flowers. Dozens of pedestrians passed by him without a glance.

Their car arrived at a Japanese government building. It was modern and plain, glass and steel. The soldiers stationed outside gave away that it was a military headquarters of some sort.

"It's like the Pentagon," Blair said. "Only a lot taller."

They passed through a security point and met a group of

American officers who had already arrived. One of the men saluted Ambassador Blair, who raised his hand above his bloodshot eyes with the rigor of a dead fish.

The American group numbered ten. Jackson counted six decorated soldiers, including four Navy officers in crisp white uniforms, one staffer from Treasury, one from the NSC, and Blair and himself from the State Department. A young Japanese man in a black suit greeted them formally and began to lead them through the building.

The stiff procession made its way to a conference room on the building's top floor. The huge table in the center could seat twenty or more. The Japanese escort motioned to the side of the table facing the windows. As the group began to sit, Jackson took the seat to the right of Ambassador Blair, at the far right edge of the table. The sunlight streaming in was bright in his eyes and shadowed the Japanese man's face as he sat on the opposite side of the table.

Admiral Rodrick, from the Navy, sat at the center of the American delegation. He had short-cut white hair and leathery bronze skin, probably from a lifetime at sea. Jackson had never been good with military decorum, but he guessed the guy had enough little flags, pennants, and stars on his uniform to have risen to the absolute top of the Navy.

A few minutes ticked by in awkward silence. Then a door opened. The Americans rose to their feet to greet the Japanese.

They streamed in without any noticeable order. The groups met in a haphazard collision of handshakes, bows, and half-smiles. They began to take their seats on the other side of the table. At first, Jackson could hardly tell who was leading their group. The odds were on the oldest man, but he sat off-center, and his long, scraggly beard was not the mark of a diplomat. Maybe it was the younger man to his left. He was at least ten years junior to Admiral Rodrick, but he met the American's gaze with calm competency.

"We have come with a request," Ambassador Blair began smoothly. A Japanese interpreter translated the words as they were spoken.

"We bear great sorrow and grief over your colleague's death." Blair's gaze swiveled from person to person, as if trying to make them all feel important. As he explained the great importance of the meeting, and the reasons for the request, the Japanese group eyed him calmly. No signs of agreement, or of discord.

It was about ten minutes before the Ambassador finished his apology, during which he managed to give out the gifts of books containing bourbon and say something mildly offensive about common bonds of alcohol. "And so we have come simply to ask you to forgive us."

The older man, the one with the spindly beard, rested his elbows on the table and folded his arms. There was a boyish curiosity in his eyes, hiding as they were behind oversized glasses. "You may have our country's forgiveness," he said in English. "But we must know that you will defend us, as always."

The room fell quiet.

Admiral Rodrick was shaking his head almost imperceptibly. "I must be frank," he said. "We are not in a position to offer the protection we have in the past."

"But you still have forces, on our territory," the Japanese leader said. His voice rose with each word—the sign of his calm breaking. "We ask that you use them when necessary. We believe the Senkakus are at risk."

"Your military is stronger now," Admiral Rodrick said. "You can defend the islands if you would like. We have never taken a position on their sovereignty. We have no obligation to defend them."

"But you are obligated. It is in the treaty."

Admiral Rodrick looked to Jackson. "I understand this has changed."

"It has changed," Jackson said, keeping his voice composed. These were the facts, whether he liked them or not. "We have an obligation to protect your sovereign territory against any attacks. We no longer have an obligation to protect territory under your administration."

"I was not aware of this change." The man looked down the line of Japanese men beside him. Several of them bowed their heads as if in shame. "But it should not matter," the man continued. "Even if there were this change in the treaty, it is not relevant. The Senkakus *are* Japan's territory."

"That is disputed," Rodrick said, and Jackson reluctantly nodded agreement.

As the two leaders' eyes met, the bearded Japanese man showed no intimidation, no sign of budging. Their gazes stayed locked, oblivious to the others in the room.

"We will look into it, okay everyone?" Blair sounded nervous, as if unable to tolerate the silence or the tension. "In all events we would consider all appropriate defenses to any acts of Chinese aggression. There is no reason to think there will be any."

"Not yet," the Japanese leader said. "But there will be. Very soon, I fear."

"You will keep us informed if there is," Admiral Rodrick said. It was not a question. "We will evaluate the situation."

"As allies," Blair added. "Close allies."

26

THE SMOKE FROM General Li's cigar drifted up into the cloud that encompassed Beijing like a cocoon. He sat on a balcony overlooking the city from his office, with his black boots on the railing. His breathing was slow, his eyes closed. It helped him think fifty moves ahead.

His chief of staff came to the door and knocked. "Sir, it is the American Ambassador to Japan."

He bowed as he held out a secure cell phone on a silver tray.

General Li took the phone. The chief of staff left quickly. "Hello."

"General, it is great to talk with you again."

General Li could hear the worried tone underneath the American's thick accent. He would use that fear, but only as a last resort. He'd learned in his first tour of duty, in Vietnam, that the best starting point for the acquisition of information was gentleness. "Likewise, Ambassador," he said. "What news do you bring?"

"We had the meeting with the Japanese this morning."

"How did it go?"

"As well as we could hope. They are concerned about your ships, passing so close to the islands, but you expected this. They asked about the treaty. Their most senior leaders were surprised about the changed term, of course, and now they know its significance. We didn't agree with their sovereignty over the islands. We said it's disputed."

"How did they respond?"

"They didn't. I assured them that we remain their faithful allies. I used the exact words you suggested—that in all events we would consider all appropriate defenses to any acts of Chinese aggression. Admiral Rodrick agreed with what I said."

"You have done well." General Li took a puff of his cigar,

watching the smoke drift into the grey-brown sky as he mused about the ambassador's vulnerabilities. It was almost too easy. This man's company had been most useful in their secret project. And using his company had killed two birds with one stone—take the Americans' technology and compromise one of their leading political donors. Blair had never questioned the General's explanation that the project's purpose was trade and commerce, and that secrecy was critical for public relations to stage a surprise unveiling for the world, when the time was right. The project had paid Blair enough to silence any hard questions. His tryst with Hina had been icing on the cake. So many Americans lacked discipline. It would be their downfall. Now Blair could be blackmailed through his Chinese investments *or* through Hina's murder. He just needed to keep his mouth shut about the project for a few more days.

General Li smiled as he asked, "And what of the young woman?"

"She was not... I mean, which one?"

General Li, with some difficulty, managed not to laugh at the ambassador's fumbling response. He had no need to inquire about Hina, who could no longer speak of what she knew. He wanted information about the girl who lived, who apparently had been her friend. "Lily Sun."

There was a noticeable pause. General Li did not like that.

"Someone tried to kill her," the ambassador said. "The other lawyer, Jackson Crow, was with her. He stopped the attacker. Now she is on her way back to Washington."

"We will handle them," General Li said, fuming inside. He was already formulating the command to Zhang and wondering whether his impatient son could actually carry out an order for once. The boy had not only failed to kidnap the girl, but had let it look like an assassination attempt. Zhang had grown weak in America. "What do they know?"

"I'm worried that Lily knows about Hina...and me."

"I see." That concerned General Li. No one could know Hina's true role. She'd served him too well. She was one of the few agents who was worth ten times what they'd paid her. If only she hadn't learned about the project from Blair and starting asking too many questions… He'd have to eliminate this ambassador—and maybe even Zhang, his own son—if that secret was at risk. *All warfare is based on deception.*

"And Crow, what does he think?" the General asked.

"I'm not sure. He asked if the killing had anything to do with the treaty." Blair took a breath. "What happened with Hina…it's only between you, Zhang, and me, right?"

"Yes." *For now,* General Li thought. He enjoyed the ambassador's tone of innocence, because the further Blair had to fall, the more willing he would be to do whatever was asked. "We will make sure this stays quiet," General Li said warmly. "But in return, you must keep the Japanese assured. I would also like to speak with your President again. I trust you can arrange that?"

Yes, of course, the ambassador could arrange that. He was old friends with the President, after all.

27

LILY LANDED AT Andrews Air Force Base and adjusted her watch, making the twelve hours she'd just spent on a plane disappear. In fact, with the time change, she'd arrived at 9 am, half an hour earlier than she'd departed from Okinawa. Her body wouldn't believe it. She hadn't been able to eat. She had barely slept. No one had tried to kill her before.

She was exhausted as she stepped down the military plane's ladder and found her driver on the runway, wearing dark aviator glasses and one of those little earpieces with the transparent curly wire that secret service agents always wore. If this had been a normal airport, he probably would have held a sign that said "Sun." But this was witness protection. They knew who she was.

The driver led her to a black Chevy Suburban with tinted windows. In minutes they were speeding along the George Washington Parkway and across a bridge over the Potomac into the nation's capital. The white-stoned memorials and monuments were more comforting than ever. Lily was glad to be home again. She would be safe here.

Lily had guessed she'd be hidden somewhere out in the country. She knew the government had compounds scattered around Virginia and Maryland for secret missions and trainings. But the driver surprised her by going straight into the city and turning onto Pennsylvania Avenue, towards the White House. Instead of turning into the white Georgian mansion at 1600 Penn, the car turned into a brick townhouse on the opposite side of the street, beside Lafayette Square. Lily knew the place, and it made her all the more surprised.

This was the Blair House, named after a newspaper baron who built it in the early 1800s. Now it served as a historic residence for special guests of the President. Foreign dignitaries stayed here, not junior State Department lawyers under witness protection. Lily wondered if it was only a coincidence that the building shared a name with the ambassador. Blair *did* come from family money.

One of the secret service guys opened Lily's door and led her inside. The hallway had plush red carpet and curtains straight out of the 19th century. She glanced into the rooms as they passed and saw antique cherry tables and chairs. She half expected to see Thomas Jefferson inside, writing with a quill.

The guard led her up a flight of stairs to a bedroom upstairs. He held open the bedroom door and motioned for Lily to enter. "This is your room."

Lily nodded and stepped inside.

"Someone will be up with your bag and more instructions soon." He closed the door, and it locked on the outside.

She took a deep breath to calm herself. She would be protected here.

She studied the room with a measure of awe. The walls had broad yellow and white stripes. There was ornate molding everywhere, and deep blue curtains hung from golden rods beside the window. An antique desk with a crystal lamp was to her left, and to her right stood an immense four-poster bed covered in white lacy linens. One of the pillows bore embroidered American flags.

She walked to the window and glanced outside, where there was a small interior courtyard. The plants were perfectly manicured around a bubbling fountain in the center. She spotted black-suited agents at each entrance and exit. She tried to open the window to get some fresh spring air, but it was locked.

As she fell onto the bed, she couldn't help but wonder what on earth she was doing here. Her apartment was only a few blocks away. Maybe it wasn't safe, but wouldn't this place only draw more attention? At least no assassins would be sneaking in.

Her mind chewed over the possibilities as she began to drift to sleep. It had been a long night, and a long flight.

A knock on the door woke her up. She didn't know how much time had passed.

She rose from the bed, straightened the sheets, and checked in the mirror. Her eyes looked tired, her hair was in disarray, but what could she do about it? She quickly tidied herself up as best she could and went to the door.

Another knock came.

The view through peephole made her swallow. It was an attractive woman in a crisp navy suit, with freckles, bright green eyes, fiery red hair. Lily would have recognized her anywhere: Reagan Murphy, the President's Deputy National Security Adviser.

28

REAGAN HOPED THIS would be quick, but now the girl had her waiting outside the door. It had been, what, a minute, maybe two already? She knocked again, harder.

She needed to get this over with before the Treasury meeting. Mike wanted her to handle this in person, and to make the cover explanation compelling. So here she was, but only because he was the President. And because of Jackson.

The door finally opened. Lily was shorter and prettier than Reagan had expected. She had the kind of cheerful face that could sell magazines, even if she looked exhausted. Reagan could have some sympathy. The Chinese had tried to kill her yesterday and she'd just arrived from Tokyo.

Reagan held out her hand. "I'm Reagan Murphy."

"Lily Sun. Nice to meet you."

"I'm here on behalf of the President to make sure you are comfortable. He wanted to come himself, but an urgent matter required his attention."

"Oh." She seemed genuinely surprised. "Well, thanks for coming. I'm doing fine."

"I understand we have a mutual friend, Jackson Crow."

Lily nodded. "He saved my life. How do you know him?"

"We were college classmates." *And more.* "You can learn a lot from him."

"I already have."

"I would imagine so." Reagan heard the admiration in Lily's voice. She knew she no longer had any claim to Jackson, but she didn't have to be happy about it. "I know this must seem odd, having a room here at the Blair House, right?"

"I'm not exactly a head of state," Lily replied.

"They're not the only ones who stay here. The President reserves a few bedrooms for government employees with special situations."

"What makes my situation special?"

Reagan smiled patiently, but it was obvious that Lily knew something was off. "We usually invite people who have faced targeted attacks abroad. Everyone thinks they know how witness protection works, but it's different in this kind of situation. We don't know yet whether there will be more attempts against you. Think of this as the first stage. We just want to keep you here, under close protection, until we figure out how much more will be needed."

"Okay. How long do you think I'll be here?"

"Not sure. Probably a few nights."

"Can I leave?"

Maybe this girl wasn't as smart as Reagan had been told. It should have been obvious that she wasn't allowed to leave. "Soon, we hope," Reagan said. "Our security staff is assessing the situation. We'll make sure you're comfortable while you're here."

"A comfortable prison."

"No, of course not," Reagan said gently, though it was true. "Think of it more like a military base. Your life is in danger, and the President has decided to pull out the stops to keep you safe. It's a rare honor."

"Why does the President care so much?"

Because you know too much, Reagan thought. She had to be careful with this answer. "It was actually Jackson's idea. You serve our country well in the State Department, but you probably weren't prepared for that to put your life in danger. So I proposed this to the President, and he agreed. We protect our own."

"Okay..." Lily studied her clasped hands. "Thanks."

"Any other questions before I go?"

The young lawyer met Reagan's eyes coolly. "I think you've told me what you can. I'm good for now."

"Great. Get some rest. I'll check in again tomorrow."

29

KATHY FELT GOOD to be back at Langley. The events in Tokyo had been too close for comfort, but all the rules had been obeyed. She and Grant had watched Jackson and Lily, kept them safe, and not been discovered…technically. Jackson had to suspect that Kathy was involved now. He'd left the Chinese man unconscious in the bathtub when he'd taken Lily to his room to arrange her travel, as if inviting whoever was watching to take the man. Kathy had accepted the invitation. She and Grant had searched the man and found nothing unusual, other than a missing tooth. They tied him and up and asked a few questions when he came to, just enough to confirm that he was a professional. Two local agents had taken him to a facility outside Tokyo, but she didn't expect any quick answers out of him.

Now she'd followed Lily Sun back to DC, leaving Grant to follow Jackson. She'd been in her office only half an hour when Director David Strassitch summoned her. She went straight there, and his assistant let her straight in. This had to be big.

The Director rose from his desk and welcomed her warmly. As usual, he looked like the consummate politician—navy suit, red tie, coiffed grey hair. They sat in a sitting area in the corner of his large office.

"So, how was Tokyo?" he asked, like a friend just catching up.

"Exciting," Kathy said. "Read my report?"

"Yes, it seems you accomplished your mission. Well done."

"Thanks. Another imaginary gold medal of honor. I keep a closet full of them." Her banter hid the genuine satisfaction she felt at his approval.

He smiled. "I thought I was the only one."

"Why'd you want to see me?"

"The White House called. They've asked us to stand down from watching Lily."

"Now? That makes no sense. Clearly someone wants her dead."

"She's on U.S. soil. The FBI can handle things."

Kathy studied the Director's amused eyes. He never liked deferring to the FBI, and when she'd first gotten the task of watching Jackson and Lily, it hadn't mattered that they were on U.S. soil. "You agree with that?"

"We'll do our job, won't we?" he said. "Anyway, I need to you track down something else."

"Oh?"

"While you were flying back your asset in Beijing proposed a rendezvous with you. Apparently there were some odd military movements in southeast China. He claims to have information about how the government is financing the operation."

Her asset, known as Mr. Chan, had claimed lots of things over the years. "You think this is reliable?"

"I think it's important that you check it out. Five days enough time to prepare?"

"I'll make it work."

"You always do. Thanks, Kathy."

She returned to her office and spent a while gazing at the Langley trees, trying to discern a pattern. She could smell a liar from a continent away, and something told her there were more than a few right here in Washington. And she had the tools to get to the bottom of it.

She started with the stack of reports waiting at her desk. It could be tedious work, but she'd been at this long enough to embrace the process. The analysts had reviewed everything relevant on Ambassador Blair and the Japanese victim, Hina Himura. The first report on Blair was hardly better than a Wikipedia entry, but Wikipedia was never a bad starting point. The second report was by her best analyst. He'd been studying the Ambassador's habits, using his receipts and emails and social media. In the list of credit card payments by the Ambassador, the analyst had highlighted a string of receipts three nights before the shooting. First, he'd racked up a three-hundred-dollar meal at one of the nicest sushi places in D.C.

That wasn't unusual by itself. The Ambassador had expensive taste. But the next electronic receipt was an Uber ride from the restaurant to the Willard Hotel. Kathy knew the Japanese delegation had been staying there. The last receipt was a fancy bottle of champagne at the Willard bar.

The analyst was good. He had already secured the video from the Willard. Kathy hit play and watched as the Ambassador strolled up to the bar, with Hina Himura beside him. The Japanese woman looked beautiful, in a tight black dress, but she was staggering drunk, leaning heavily on his arm. The Ambassador ordered a bottle and carried it away. The string of videos that followed—from the lobby to the elevator to the ninth floor hallway—confirmed that he had escorted Hina to her room, entered with her, and left twenty minutes later.

The rest of the analyst's report showed there was no further information linking the Ambassador to the young Japanese lawyer. No phone calls. No texts. The FBI had shared their autopsy findings, which found no evidence of sexual activity. The autopsy also revealed that the woman had been menstruating at the time of the murder, and likely several days prior. Maybe that explained it.

Kathy felt sure the Ambassador had taken advantage of Hina somehow, and she'd died three days later in the most public way possible. Too much for coincidence. But how could he have orchestrated this? He seemed like a bumbling idiot to Kathy, but that could be great cover for a flawed, complex man.

Maybe Chinese intelligence had learned this before the Americans. Maybe they'd exploited it. They would've been smart enough to keep it off the record. A conversation on the sidewalk would have been enough. Or a private visit to the Ambassador's home. Kathy considered how the discussion would have gone. *We know what you did with Hina*, they'd say, and they'd show him a picture or something. *I don't know what you're talking about*, he'd reply. Guilty people always said that. Then they'd show more evidence and threaten to go public. *We can dispose of her*, they'd suggest.

Blair would be even more vulnerable now that Hina had died.

If anyone knew he'd been out with her, and gotten her drunk, three nights before she was killed, he would be a suspect. The FBI would need to be informed, but not yet. What did the Chinese want from him? He was the spokesperson for the United States to Japan. They could use that.

Kathy put on her headphones. Her analyst had been listening to every conversation in the Ambassador's office. There had been two more calls with the President and a dozen staff meetings, but nothing had been noteworthy. Kathy wanted to be sure. She clicked the last call from yesterday.

After quick hellos, the Ambassador asked the President, "So how's Ms. Sun?"

"She's fine," the President said. "I still don't get it. Our friends in China got the terms they wanted. Why did they kill the Japanese lawyer? And why would they be after Ms. Sun?"

"Maybe they think we'll act anyway," the Ambassador replied.

Kathy paused the recording. She didn't know exactly what that meant, but now she felt sure the Ambassador had not told the President everything. Otherwise, the President wouldn't be asking questions like this.

She resumed.

"It doesn't add up," the President said. "I gave their President my word. We even put it in writing and signed it."

"I don't know, Mike. The Chinese don't like to take chances. This whole murder could be just a distraction. You know what they really want. It's not that different from what we want."

"True." The President paused. "I can't have another crisis, Steve. We're too close to the election. Did you see the polls?"

"It's temporary. They'll bounce back when you keep us out of a war."

"They better. We have to manage it well. You keep everything else calm, okay?"

"You got it, Mike. Calm as the water at dawn, when the decoys are still. When we're sipping our coffee and loading our ammo."

The President laughed lightly, and as they talked about plans for another hunting trip, Kathy took off the headphones and went back to staring out at the trees rustling in the wind. She was starting to understand. The Ambassador was lying, to the President no less. It was time for her to start following the liar. He'd lead her to the others, she felt sure of it.

30

GRANT KNEW THE ORDERS: follow Jackson Crow and don't be noticed. But Kathy said Crow was one of the best, and her little note on the door in the Mandarin Oriental had basically shouted to Crow that the Agency was watching. Now Grant had to trail the guy from Tokyo to Hong Kong. He figured it was better to accept that Jackson would detect him, and let the only surprise be that Grant didn't know he'd been detected. Kathy's spycraft was too 20th century, Grant thought. The digital era called for different tactics—more psychology than pseudonym and disguise. Still, Grant had his alias for the region and so had donned his best banker's attire—charcoal suit, slim briefcase, and tortoise shell glasses—before heading to the airport.

Now he inched down the aisle of the plane, making his way to the back. He was halfway there when a woman stopped in front of him to stow a bag in the cabin above. The timing was perfect. Crow sat in the aisle seat beside the woman. He was reading a newspaper and looked like a vanilla lawyer; no hint that he'd fought off an assassin the night before. Grant knew better than to underestimate him. He bent down, as if to tie his shoe, and fixed a tiny tracker to Crow's bag at his feet. This time when Crow shut down his phone Grant could still follow.

When Grant rose, Crow's eyes were still glued to his newspaper. Grant tapped his glasses to snap a picture. Kathy would be pleased.

The flight was smooth and touched down in Hong Kong after four hours. Grant hurried off the plane several minutes after Crow. He followed the tracker to find Crow at the queue of cabs outside. The line was long, and Crow was next.

Grant decided against a cab. He rented an electric bike instead. Maybe it didn't quite fit his alias, but it was fast. He trailed Crow's tracker beacon through the dense, rush-hour streets. Crow switched cabs three times, as if trying to lose any tails. It amused Grant, who had no trouble staying with him.

After an hour, Crow finally ended his spree of cabs. He got out and started walking beneath the skyscrapers. Grant parked his bike down the block and followed him. Pedestrians packed the sidewalk like sardines. A large group was waiting at a corner for the light to change when Crow spun and looked straight at Grant. He didn't register surprise.

Grant stood his ground, ready for anything. To chase, to fight, to talk.

The light changed and the crowd started to move. Crow went the opposite way, like a salmon swimming upriver, and stopped in front of Grant.

"Thirsty?" Crow asked.

"Yeah," Grant said.

Crow turned quickly into a small bar on the block, with a glance back to confirm no one was following.

"It's just us," Grant said.

The bar was too cramped for Grant's taste. It looked like a place for serious drinkers who didn't want to talk. There was only a bar, no tables. The five other patrons barely spared a glance at the two foreigners before turning back to their drinks and the glowing TVs on the wall. Crow sat at the seat closest to the door, and Grant sat beside him.

Crow ordered from the bartender in Mandarin, then he turned to Grant with a smile. "I got us the good stuff."

Grant nodded, keeping his face blank and his body ready for action. He didn't speak Mandarin. Crow could have passed a secret message to the bartender for all Grant knew.

"Where's your partner?" Crow asked.

So he knew about Kathy, Grant thought. Better not to confirm anything. "I'm here alone," Grant said. "Protecting your skinny ass."

"Thanks for noticing."

Two drinks arrived. They looked like whiskey on the rocks. Crow could've asked the bartended to drug them. Grant grabbed the glass that had been served closest to Crow.

"It's Jim Beam, and nothing else," Crow said, grinning and raising the other glass. "To the Certified Insurance Agency."

"Cheers," Grant said, before taking down the drink in a single swig.

"So Sullivan's involved?" Crow asked.

"Maybe. I'm here alone. To keep you safe."

"Very kind of you. Two more," Crow said loudly, holding up his left hand high.

Grant eyed Crow's uplifted hand with confusion. Why had the guy spoken in English and attracted so much attention?

Then he felt something sharp prick his thigh. He glanced down and the last thing he saw was Crow's fist moving away, leaving a red feather on his charcoal suit pants.

31

JACKSON CAUGHT THE spy's heavy body as he fell from the bar chair. He laid him gently on the ground. The guy had neck muscles like a wrestler and biceps like cannonballs under his fine suit. Some cover. Jackson knew he had to be CIA, and probably working with Kathy Sullivan. The more he'd thought about it, the more convinced Jackson was that she'd been the one who warned him about the man who tried to kill Lily. He was thankful for that. He was less thankful when he'd spotted the familiar square-jawed agent boarding his plane. He'd tried to shake him in Hong Kong traffic. But the guy wasn't too bad. He'd somehow managed to trail Jackson for an hour, standing out like a sore thumb with his American buzzcut in the crowd of Asians.

"Hey, everything alright?" the bartender asked in Mandarin.

Jackson rose and glared at him. "What'd you put in that drink?"

The bartender looked shocked. All eyes were on Jackson and the American sprawled out on the floor.

"Any doctors?" Jackson asked the room. As expected, no one volunteered. "Okay, I'll go get help."

Jackson walked out the front door, grabbed a cab, and didn't look back. The spy was big. He'd probably be out an hour max, then he'd wake up and have to report to Kathy Sullivan. Jackson didn't envy him that.

The cab driver took Jackson straight toward the Hong Kong Jockey Club. As they fought through traffic, Jackson prepared himself for Vin. He was a rag-to-riches boy from India, born as Vivek Balakrishnan. And he'd probably be serving a life sentence in prison if not for Jackson. Not that it made Jackson proud. His memories of those days were best locked away, but going to see Vin—about BitStones no less—brought them all rushing back.

BitStones were the reason why the government had found Jackson. He'd turned to gaming after losing his sister, Jules. His mom had brought him back from Manila to America as a junior in high school, but then she'd left him with his grandmother. She couldn't give up her global crusade for justice but also wouldn't put Jackson's life at risk after what had happened to Jules. Jackson had never fit back in. Never wanted to. He'd grown used to the freedom of a motorcycle in Manila, and living with a Cherokee grandmother in a little Indian tribe town tucked into the mountains of North Carolina made him claustrophobic. Games had been his outlet. They gave him the freedom to do anything, to go anywhere.

Jackson had kept his gaming secret from the start, with origins in the shameful primordial soup of high school romance. He'd never forget the girl who'd made fun of him years ago. Amy Martin was cute, smart, brunette. She may have even liked him. He asked her out. They were in line to buy popcorn at the movies, going to see the last of the Hobbit movies. She asked him, *How'd they make a single book into three movies this long?* Jackson had figured his answer would be safe. She had agreed to see the Hobbit after all. So he said, *Most of the plot was developed for the MMORPG.* Then she asked what an MMORPG was. And, trying to sound cool, he told her that it was a massively multiplayer online role-playing game, but it was as impossible to sound cool while saying those words as it was to remain an ice cube in the Sahara. She'd laughed a bit and hung around for the movie. But she'd passed on the hand holding and the kiss, and she never ran out of excuses to avoid a second date. She wasn't the only one.

For years after that Jackson's grandmother had nagged him for choosing games over girls. She said a boy handsome as he was should be out finding a wife and starting a family. But he was hooked, and he became exceptionally good. He and Vin led a huge guild in the most popular game at the time. They became multimillionaires in BitStones.

The government showed up at Jackson's house when he was twenty-one. Agents could have met him in a game—undercover agents were the worst-kept secret of the gaming world—but they shook him up by tracking down his identity and location and showing up at his grandmother's home in black suits with shades.

The two agents sat down with Jackson on rocking chairs on the front porch, overlooking the mountains and sipping iced tea. They handed him a folder and told him to have a look. It was evidence that could put him in jail for twenty years. Jackson had never tried to break the law or hurt anybody, but the amount of Stone-trading he did meant he'd facilitated a lot of transactions. The Feds had connected him with known money-launderers and drug cartels. Whatever, he'd thought. Criminal laws were always too broad, catching innocent activity in their net, especially when they couldn't keep up with technological advances. He wasn't a bad guy. But none of that could diminish the threat of twenty years behind bars.

"What do you want?" Jackson had asked them.

"We want you to work with us," one the agents said. "Spying isn't what it used to be. We can't just travel to cities and watch buildings and people in person. We have to go wherever the bad guys go, even in games."

"And in return?" Jackson asked.

"You'll never be charged. You'll get access to the most powerful gaming servers and databases in the world."

That had sounded a whole lot better than jail. "So you want me to double-cross my friends?" he'd asked.

One of the agents had laughed at that. "Have you ever met any of them in person?"

"Well, no."

They'd talked a while longer, and Jackson agreed to their terms. He told his grandmother that he'd been offered a job in Washington, D.C., to do some computer consulting stuff. It was true enough. He'd packed his things and left within a week.

The following years had been a wild ride. Jackson had kept up his gaming identities and helped the government put a dozen gaming friends behind bars. The government had told Jackson about all the bad things his friends had done—but it wasn't like they were real-life murderers. Jackson figured their worst crimes were no different than that of greedy bankers, except they didn't serve

Fortune 100 companies or the rest of the establishment. He'd managed to keep a few friends out of trouble. But most had gone to prison. He hated himself for it.

That's why he'd ultimately left the job. He gave up the ability to know more about the world than the freaking CIA, and in return he'd kept his friend, Vin, out of jail. Vin knew it and was forever grateful. They'd last met, and said their goodbyes, at the Formula One track in Manama.

Jackson had never expected to come back to him, but now he needed help.

The cab arrived at the Hong Kong Jockey Club, which was as impressive as a dirt racetrack can be, with a huge grandstand wedged between steep green hills. Jackson paid the cabbie and walked through the club's bright blue entrance. Inside there were pictures of famed horses and jockeys, with lists of winners. The horse names were ridiculous, even in Mandarin. Jackson decided his favorite was American Dust, which had apparently won a big race in 1997.

The rendezvous time, 8 pm, passed with no sign of Vin. Jackson tried a few doors leading inside, but they were locked. The place was empty. So he waited and studied more horse names. His second favorite was the winner a couple years ago, Monster Balls, which he guessed was either a mistranslation or a horse owned by a particularly egotistical billionaire owner.

At 8:20 pm Jackson decided to find a way to get to the track. Maybe Vin expected him there. There was one security guard who had been sitting by the front doors. Jackson talked to him and got stonewalled, until he mentioned the name Vin. Then the guard smiled and opened the door to the track.

Jackson sat alone on the immense grandstand and watched a rider racing around on horseback. A thousand lights flooded into the place, for this single rider. After one lap he noticed Jackson sitting there and stopped below him. The rider came up the stairs wearing yellow jockey gear. When he pulled off his goggles, Jackson saw Vin's familiar dark eyes. The red dust covering Vin's light brown skin gave him an orange hue of fake-tan spray.

"Crow, my friend!" Vin said in his raspy smoker's voice. "How are you?" Vin didn't wait for an answer before wrapping his arms around Jackson. He looked small enough beside Crow to be his adolescent son.

"Doing fine," Jackson said.

"Well you look like shit." Vin laughed so hard that he started coughing. "At least your hair's still black. Mostly."

Vin's mop of disheveled hair had gone grey at thirty-five. He was always sensitive about appearances. "You looked good riding out there," Jackson said.

"Yeah, new hobby. I bought a few horses. We won two years ago."

Jackson smiled. Vin had a good heart, but he could be a vile and profane little man. "Monster Balls?"

"No other! You heard about him, that's good. Now he just eats and mates all day. Nice life. I was riding one of his colts down there just now. Might sell for a million. Nothing like having a million dollars between your loins."

"It's good to see you haven't changed."

"Not till the grave, my friend. Then I'll come back as a stallion, or an ant, or something in between."

"My money's on a lion...with monster balls."

Vin slapped Jackson on the back. "I like that! Come on, I'll get cleaned up and we'll eat and talk."

Jackson waited while Vin quickly showered and changed at the club. He came out in a khaki linen suit and big green-rimmed glasses, with his grey hair slicked back and his skin no longer caked in red dirt. He looked paler and yellower than Jackson had remembered. Jackson would have suspected jaundice, but Vin loved tropical fruit. It was probably due to his steady diet of cigarettes and scotch.

Vin led Jackson outside to an insanely expensive yellow sports car. He drove like a maniac up the lush hills of Victoria Mountain that loomed above Hong Kong. Jackson was not surprised when they rode into The Peak, a neighborhood renowned for the world's richest price tags. A penthouse here had sold last year for almost a billion dollars. Vin's had to be in the same ballpark. The building had gold-plated lions marking the entrance and a foyer made of black marble with gold veins. In the elevator a retina scanner registered Vin's arrival, and took them up forty floors. The elevator doors opened to a vast room overlooking the city. Vin might always be hiding from authorities, but he'd never eschew luxury.

Jackson had to admit some awe at the view from the window. The skyscrapers nestled within Hong Kong's hills looked like they were stacked on top of each other. Even more impressive was the new bridge snaking over the Pearl River Delta and connecting the city to Hong Kong. It was one of the latest marvels of Chinese construction—twenty times the length of the Golden Gate bridge, with stretches of tunnel that rivaled the Chunnel between England and France. Jackson wondered whether there was any limit to Chinese engineering. Next thing they'd do is dig a tunnel all the way to Taiwan.

Jackson turned away from the view and met Vin's eager eyes. "Nice place."

"Not bad, right? I prefer Fiji, but sometimes I have to be here for business. In person meetings are the worst. Unless it's you, of course."

They ate dinner at a table that could have seated twenty, with Vin's own personal staff preparing and serving food like this was a five-star restaurant.

Vin talked a lot. He was smart, but hard to follow with his thick Indian accent and frequent skipping of logical connections. He just assumed others would connect the dots. Jackson always had, which was one reason they'd gotten along. Tonight Vin started with cryptocurrencies and suddenly was talking about mobsters owning cows in Ethiopia. The connection was money laundering, but Vin never took the time to make such things explicit. Unless he was ordering drinks. He ordered the server to uncork a second bottle of wine when the first bottle was served. He noticed Jackson's raised eyebrow and said, "What? I hate waiting, man."

They'd finished the wine and were eating dessert, and sipping a fine Portuguese port, when Vin finally asked Jackson why he'd come.

"I need your help." Jackson handed over the data chip from the assassin's tooth and brought up the screen on his phone showing the ten thousand BitStones. "A guy from China found me in Tokyo and paid me the Stones for a favor. He also tried to kill me, and I found this chip on him. It's got the whole gamut of Chinese encryption. I'll transfer the Stones to you. I need you to track them and see what you can find on the chip."

"Man, that's about the hardest thing on earth to do. You know the resources it takes."

"That's why I came to you."

Vin smiled. "Let's do it together, like old times. Stay here a while," Vin said, motioning grandly around the room. "I've got plenty of space. Play some games, enjoy life a little, you've earned it."

"Sorry…"

"No, don't be sorry, just log in for once. How many years has it been? Five? Eight? Our guild—the one *you* started—is over four hundred thousand members now. We have a presence in all the top twenty games." Vin pointed to his scrawny chest. "I run everything, of course, but you're still the legend, the figurehead, the namesake. You've gotta check out the latest game, Camelot. It's totally old school—elves, dragons, and damsels in distress. We'll be kings there with our BitStones."

Jackson couldn't deny he was tempted. It would be fun. And Vin, despite his riches, was a lonely man who could use the company. *Raven March* was the guild Jackson had started. The most exciting time of Jackson's life was when it had been growing by hundreds and earning enough BitStones to buy private islands. That was when the government had come. Things had gotten complicated, and they would again. The fun had stopped years before he'd left the games and promised never to return.

He met Vin's eyes and spoke seriously. "I'm sorry. I have to get back."

"To Washington? That swamp is the worst. Why do you put up with the misery?"

"I got wrapped up in another conflict. There was a murder."

"The one at the State Department? Hey, I heard about that! It was front-page news even here. Here's the juiciest thing. You know the victim?"

Jackson nodded. "She was a Japanese lawyer."

"Yeah, and guess what? She converted 10,000 BitStones into dollars two days before she was shot. Exactly what you got paid!"

"Insane!" Jackson failed to hide his surprise. He blamed the port. "You sure about that?"

Vin stood and took a deep breath. "Two years ago I happened to tag one of those Stones with *our* code. Guess it reached the victim somehow. So when the news hit, I ran a search in our database and found it."

"Who paid her?"

"I don't know, but more information is probably there. Let's log in and find out."

"I can't…" Jackson looked away, gazing out at the lights of Hong Kong.

"Let me guess, you're trying to protect someone."

"A colleague of mine was in the room."

"*A colleague?*" Vin's brow lifted. "You sound so…diplomatic. Don't tell me Crow has turned into a suit. So who was this *colleague?*"

"Her name is Lily Sun."

"Ah, so this about a girl!"

"It's not like that."

"I know you too well, Crow. A girl…now that I can understand."

Jackson would let Vin think what he wanted. "She's in danger. That's why I need to know what's on this chip, where the Stones came from, and who's after my colleague."

"I see." Vin lifted his glass of port, studied the dark purple liquid, then downed it. "Okay, Crow, for you, I will deliver. Just give me a couple days."

32

IT DROVE REAGAN CRAZY to see her boss moping around like he'd been the past week. The latest polls had him down three points to the fiery New Hampshire Governor. Three points. Six months until the election. The news spinning around about the murder in the Treaty Room hadn't helped.

Now she was in the Oval Office, waiting for the President to finish a call. He'd been making calls all afternoon to Senators he needed to sign a landmark piece of military spending. He needed any victory he could get these days.

When he hung up, he leaned back in his throne, eyed Reagan, and sighed. "I think we got Miller. He's up for reelection, too. He'll vote yes."

"Good to hear," Reagan said. "We'll get this bill passed."

"But will it put me ahead in the polls?"

She shrugged. "It might get us a point or two."

"Looks like we'll need more than that if stocks keep tanking." He paused. "Any leads about the Japanese woman who was shot? The press says I'm not doing enough."

"There's a new wrinkle." Reagan had spent the past hour thinking through this conversation. If she played it right, she could get the President his reelection, and she could get Jackson back on the right side. "The Chinese tried to kill one of our people in Tokyo. A young lawyer who worked on the treaty with Japan."

"And?"

"My undercover guy from State happened to be there. He stopped it. The CIA has the assassin."

"That's good, right?"

"Maybe. He hasn't talked yet." Reagan leaned forward. She noticed the President's gaze drift down to her chest. Men will be men, she thought, no matter how powerful. She sat up straighter. "We're now protecting our lawyer who was targeted. She's across the street in the Blair House. She was the one who worked with the Japanese lawyer and made the change in the treaty. She could figure out what it all means when the Chinese start taking disputed territory from Japan…if she hasn't already."

"What do you propose?"

Reagan knew the President hated blathering about talking points and ideas. He had no time for that. He liked to get straight to the point, so she didn't sugarcoat it. "We let our friends from China take her, and then they offer her for ransom."

He studied Reagan quietly as seconds ticked by. "You're serious."

"When am I not?" she said. "Think about it. This gives them a little victory. You know what they'll ask for in exchange for her."

"The islands."

"Exactly. And we'll take the deal. The treaty no longer requires us to defend the Senkaku islands, and this gives us a reason to back away. I can already write your speech. You'll announce that you've saved an American citizen—a Chinese American—and prevented a war."

"And General Li will announce that he's retaken islands that belong to China."

"Which the American people couldn't care less about," Reagan said. "They want good jobs, healthcare, and education. This kicks the China conflict down the road for a few administrations. It's not like anyone could secure *future* peace. Avoiding war *now* is the best we can do."

"If anyone ever finds out about the girl…"

"They won't," Reagan assured him. "No one will know but you and me. Not even Ambassador Blair has to know about this."

"He's a liability."

"I've been saying that a long time." Reagan knew the President was old friends with Blair, but the guy was a loose cannon. He never should have been an ambassador, no matter how much money he donated to the President's war chest.

"But I trust him," the President said. "He tells me your friend,

Jackson Crow, has been asking questions about the treaty."

"I'll take care of Jackson."

"Good." The President stood and turned his back to Reagan, looking out over the Rose garden. He was a handsome man, with shoulders that showed his college wrestling days. It was leadership and cunning that helped him win, more than skill. When he turned back to Reagan, his face looked tired. "I don't want anyone to get hurt."

"No one gets hurt," she said. "I promise."

After the meeting, she went straight to a secure office in the Eisenhower Executive Office Building, which stood like an ornate grey fortress beside the White House. Reagan kept her promises. Other aspects of the truth could be bent as much as needed for the greater good. But not her promises. They were personal. That's why she wanted to call her Chinese contact directly this time. She'd memorized the number and dialed it on an encrypted line.

"Hello."

"It's me," Reagan said.

They went through their normal security protocol.

Then Zhang asked, "What can I do for you?"

"We have an asset you can take. She knows about the treaty. You can sell her back to us in exchange for what you've been wanting. It'll be good PR."

"We want no interference with the islands."

"None whatsoever," Reagan said, "except you must return the asset unharmed when we say so."

"Deal. I will handle it personally." The man sounded positively cheerful.

33

"I NEED TO TELL you something." Grant sat in one of Kathy's office chairs, elbows on his knees. He looked like a quarterback who'd just staggered to the bench after throwing an interception. "Jackson saw me tonight. In the airport, DCA."

Kathy was pacing. She hated football, but she had no problem playing the coach. "How'd he recognize you?"

Grant looked down. "He also saw me in Hong Kong."

Kathy stood still, fists on her waist. "Again?"

"I'm sorry, I know I should have told you earlier. I thought I could find him, and I did. He was only out of my sight for an evening. We picked up his plane-ticket purchase in Hong Kong, and I took the same flight back here."

"Tell me how it happened."

As Grant went through the details, describing how Jackson had spotted him on the street in Hong Kong and taken him to a bar and drugged him, Kathy felt more desperate than ever to start talking to her former colleague. She wanted to know what he'd done that evening in Hong Kong. Had he gone back to whatever secrets he'd used when he was working for her? The Director would want to know this. Jackson could not be left to his own devices. And if the Ambassador was part of this, Jackson was at more risk than he knew.

When Grant finished, Kathy asked him: "What did Jackson say to you?"

"Nothing much in Hong Kong, but in the airport he told me two things: that someone had tried to pay off the victim, Hina Himura, and that Lily Sun's life was at risk."

"He must want us to dig into this. What else did he say?"

"That's it. He whispered it beside me at a urinal. Then he was gone."

"Subtle," Kathy said, shaking her head. "But our orders are

clear." She'd already been pushing the limits.

"I know," Grant said. "Sorry again for blowing our cover."

She put a hand on Grant's shoulder. She needed him confident for what was ahead. "Look, it happens. I was the one who tipped him off with that room sign. We're not perfect ghosts, and Jackson is an old hand."

Grant stood slowly, towering over her. "Thanks. It won't happen again."

"Your next job should be easier," Kathy said.

"What's that?"

"We need constant eyes and ears on Lily Sun. Bug her apartment, the works."

He smiled. "Done. You going to help?"

"No, you can handle it," Kathy said. "I need to talk to the Director about our orders."

34

TWENTY-FOUR HOURS could pass quickly, like when you were on vacation at the beach or binging on Netflix. But time moved like molasses when you were locked up, hidden away, life at risk, without anything to distract you beside a few old books. Lily was ready to go home.

She had given up trying to sleep. It was the best way to pass the time, she knew, but after snoozing fourteen straight hours her jet lag had passed and she had no choice but to stay awake, staring at the ceiling or out at the little courtyard of the Blair House where the black-suited Secret Service agents roamed. She knew there was some danger involved in leaving this guarded place, but the attack had happened in Tokyo, not Washington. The government could set up surveillance or whatever they needed to keep her safe here.

That's why the knock on her door, at 7:23 pm, made her spring to her feet. This time she didn't even glance in the mirror to see how she looked. She just wanted out.

The peephole showed the same person as before, Reagan Murphy, looking like a professional woman in a Brooks Brothers ad.

Lily pulled the door open. "Hello, Ms. Murphy."

"Hello, Ms. Sun." The woman scanned Lily up and down. "Looks like you've been getting some rest."

"Not much else to do," Lily said. "When can I leave?"

The woman smiled, but it only made her face look more severe. "You may go now. You'll need to stay in your apartment for a while. You'll be under protection there."

Relief washed over Lily. Lockdown in her own apartment would be much better—away from this woman's domain. "Thank you," she said.

"Gather your things. I'll escort you out."

After she loaded her bag, Lily followed Reagan down the plush-carpeted hall. She made mental notes of the antiques. She doubted she would ever find herself in the Blair House again. This would make quite a story, not that she could talk about it.

As they approached the front door, Lily stopped when she was passing the dining room. The white and blue Chinese porcelain, no doubt a gift to some prior president, reminded her of a question that had been rumbling around in her mind. Reagan might be one of the few people who knew the real answer. She doubted she'd tell all the details, but Lily figured it was worth a try. "Hey," Lily said, making Reagan turn back. "You know this porcelain is from China?"

Reagan glanced into the ornate dining room, then back at Lily. "Okay…so?"

"There's a long history between China and the U.S., but a much longer one between China and Japan. Anything that unsettles the balance of power between them could be a huge problem, especially for the territories they both claim to own. So why did the White House request the last-minute change to our treaty with Japan?"

Reagan looked as willing to talk as a captured spy. "A lot of factors were involved."

Lily went with the friendly approach. She didn't want to sound like a liability. "Oh, I'm sure there were. But once I'm back at my desk, our counterparts in Japan are going to be asking more questions. What should I tell them?"

"The Japanese agreed to this," Reagan said, nonchalant. "They've been wanting us to decrease our military presence so they can build up their own. That's part of the deal now."

"But what if China tries to seize disputed islands, like the Senkakus?" Lily asked. "The Japanese won't just let that happen. There are old wounds between these countries." Lily knew them well, having heard her grandparents—the sweetest old people you could imagine—spouting vengeful belligerence against the Japanese for what they'd done in the nineteenth century. "Are you familiar with the Rape of Nanking?"

"Of course," Reagan said. "I have a PhD in military history.

From Yale."

And I have a law degree from Yale. Big freaking deal. Besides, Reagan hadn't answered her question. "So, you get my point?" Lily asked.

"It's been over 150 years, and back then Japan was stronger. They took over half of China, for God's sake. No way that happens today. China would crush them without our protection."

"Maybe…but don't forget Pearl Harbor."

"December 7, 1941." Reagan's hands had curled into fists on her narrow waist. "My great-grandfather was there. I will never forget."

"Japan was a lot weaker than America then. But that didn't stop them from surprise attack, guns blazing and kamikaze crashing. They still have that warrior spirit, no matter how much bowing and courtesy they show. They'll fight back against China. Or they'll strike first."

"You're wrong," Reagan said, like a teacher admonishing a student. "We still have our security treaty. Only a few barren islands are no longer covered."

"How would the American people react if Russia claimed Hawaii?" Lily knew the comparison wasn't quite right, but she couldn't stop herself. She didn't like this woman. "Think that would help the President's polling?"

Reagan inhaled sharply. "I came here to escort you out, not to debate foreign policy." She spun on her three-inch heels and headed for the front door.

Lily followed and said a tense goodbye outside, before climbing into a black Chevy Suburban waiting on the curb. The driver took her a few blocks to her apartment. It felt good to see the city streets on a beautiful spring day, if only briefly and through dark tinting. Most of the pedestrians were smiling, enjoying the freedom that Lily had temporarily lost. No one paid attention to a ubiquitous black Suburban driving past.

She was dropped off at her building's entrance, where two men without uniforms not-so-subtly guarded the door. She went straight up to her room and gazed out the window. The SUV was still there, parked on the street, which gave her some comfort. She showered, put on jeans and a t-shirt, and ordered take-out—Chicken Lo Mein.

As she thought over what Reagan had said, her mind went back to the Treaty Room. She still had a pit in her stomach when she thought of Hina. Even if Reagan was right, and the President was truly trying to stop a war by reaching this new balance with China and Japan, that didn't explain why anyone would want to kill Hina. The last time she'd spoken to her friend, Hina had sounded afraid. She'd told Lily that she'd gone out to dinner with Ambassador Blair, but that she couldn't talk about it. Lily hadn't pressed. Now she wondered if *that* was what had unsettled Hina.

A buzz rang by the door to her apartment. It must be the take-out she had ordered. She was starving. She asked who it was through the call box, and a man said it was Chinese delivery. She pressed the button to open the building's front door.

A minute later there was a knock on her apartment door. She opened it slightly and was surprised by the delivery guy. She'd expected the usual old Chinese man with the friendly smile. This guy looked like he belonged on a gym's promotional poster, with close-cut hair, a square jaw, and biceps bulging as he held out a white plastic bag.

"You were expecting Chang?" the guy asked, leaning against the door frame. "He's sick today. I'm filling in. Chicken Lo Mein, right?"

"Okay, thanks." She reached out and took the bag. "I hope Chang feels better."

The guy bowed slightly and left without another word.

Lily sat down on her couch to eat. She still felt weirded out by the delivery guy. She vowed to not open her own door to any other delivery guys for a few days. If her life was in danger, she could make the trek down to the lobby, where the guards would be watching. But the Chicken Lo Mein, in the comfort of home, was worth it.

35

JACKSON WENT STRAIGHT to the locked file cabinet in his State Department office. He began spinning the knob of the lock. These old contraptions were a running joke. The rusted combination locks might deter people with a fear of tetanus, but they weren't keeping out many burglars, much less determined foreign agents.

Jackson spun it right three times—32. Left two times—14. Right one time—27. Left to 0.

He pulled on it. *Stuck.*

He jerked harder, making the whole cabinet rattle like a bag of metal beams. He peeked outside his office. No one was paying attention. *Quit being paranoid,* he told himself. *Only the CIA is watching.* He knew there were no cameras in his office, but he scanned the ceiling anyway. The speckled particleboard and fluorescent lights showed no sign of intelligent life.

He spun the combination again, going slower this time.

He finished, landing on 0, and tugged. This time the lock opened, and he lifted the bar that kept the cabinets shut. He bent down to open the bottom one. The backup copy of the picture had to still be here.

Crouching, he flipped through the hanging files until he reached the one labeled Caracas, Venezuela. Every document in there was a decade old and about the struggling South American country. It was the last place anyone would look, unless they knew. Jackson found the cable about an economic deal with Venezuela in the 1990s. He pulled out the picture from the folder, with Ambassador Blair staring straight at him. He was thinking about showing Lily. He stuffed it into his briefcase and locked up the cabinet.

As he sat down at the desk, Jackson checked the clock. He still had a couple hours before he would join Blair for a mid-morning briefing with the Secretary of State. He started catching up on a backlog of emails and briefings. He cleared a few packages for the senior officials, attended a staff meeting, and approved the hire of two new lawyers. Having one of his people get killed would not help their hiring pool.

He had cleared most of his pressing emails when he came across an ethics package. It was for a new ambassador to Peru. The woman was filthy rich, like most ambassadors, and she had to sell a fortune in Coca-Cola stock before she could take the job, due to the company's lobbying about a plant in the country. Rich ambassadors loved this process because any assets sold due to ethical obligations meant avoiding capital gains taxes. It could save them millions. The rich get richer.

It made Jackson think of something. Ambassador Blair would have done a form like this. They made any senior official's assets publicly available, except for the assets that an ambassador sold. Had Blair sold anything?

Jackson pulled up the memo recording Blair's divestments. He had sold holdings in at least twenty companies, most of them Chinese. Three of them were major gaming conglomerates. One was a construction company specializing in tunnels. Jackson knew Blair had made a fortune investing in China, but it seemed odd that he would sell all this to take his position in Japan. Next Jackson pulled up the public form, which like most bureaucratic things had a trite name, Form 278, masking its significance. The Form 278 showed that Blair still had millions of dollars and Yuan in bank accounts in China. Exposure like that might be technically allowed for the Ambassador to Japan, but it had to make Blair vulnerable.

Twenty minutes before the meeting with the Secretary, Jackson put away the files. He hadn't found anything concrete, but a mountain of circumstantial evidence said Ambassador Blair had reasons to do the Chinese government's bidding.

He went to the Ambassador's office, where he found the silver-haired fox reading the paper and sipping an amber liquid.

"Starting early?" Jackson asked with a friendly smile.

"It's late in Tokyo." The Ambassador put down his paper and

downed the last of his drink. He paused before leaving the room to straighten his pink paisley tie in the mirror by his desk. "You missed the funeral."

Jackson had left for Hong Kong before it happened. "No one asked me to come, and I needed to attend to other work. How did it go?"

"It was fine," Blair said. "Lots of black, bowed heads, and a few tears. A Buddhist priest said some words. It was very formal."

"How are our Japanese friends handling it?"

"I was with Ambassador Tanaka. His eyes were moist. So were others'."

"Did Tanaka say anything more to you about Hina?"

Blair met Jackson's eyes evenly. "Just that he was sorry for what she had done."

"What do you mean?"

"Tanaka had suggested I get dinner with her a couple nights before the treaty signing." Blair's voice was steady. "He said that she wanted to get to know me better, but was too shy to ask herself. I did it as a favor. She drank too much sake, though. Not a good idea for a beautiful young woman like her. I had to escort her home. Tanaka was a bit ashamed about it."

Blair's words made Jackson's stomach churn. He couldn't think of any reason why the Ambassador would talk about this dinner with Hina, unless he suspected Jackson knew something. Jackson downplayed it. "That's too bad. But it was good that you could take care of her that night, and be there with Tanaka at the funeral."

"That's what diplomats do. Alright, time for our meeting."

Blair headed for the door, and Jackson followed. They went up one flight to the Department's seventh floor—the top floor, where real decisions were made. They walked past the open door to the Treaty Room. Jackson glanced inside and saw the spotlessly cleaned parquet floor. The world keeps spinning, he thought.

A group of suited diplomats was waiting outside the Secretary's office. The Ambassador said a few pleasantries. He told them the weather had been nice in Tokyo for a change. The head of political affairs—with her intimidating title of *undersecretary*—was a dignified older woman. What her title lacked, she made up for by staring down her long nose at idiocy. She gazed at the Ambassador coolly as he blabbered on. Maybe she smelled the bourbon on his breath.

The Secretary walked out of his office a few minutes later and everyone straightened. Even the Ambassador shut his mouth. The group entered a conference room to the side. While the senior diplomats sat at the center table, Jackson and other staff accompanying the principals took seats around the edge of the room.

The group briefed the Secretary on a wide range of issues in the Pacific. After a while, the Ambassador gave his update. "No developments since our meeting with the Japanese delegation," he said. "We continue to express our grief for the woman killed here. They're concerned about China, but I've given my personal assurances to the Japanese that the United States stands by their country."

The Secretary looked thoughtful, and a little concerned. "China has been claiming they might try to take over disputed islands. Maybe they're just rattling their sabers, but what if they do? You told the Japanese we'd defend them?"

"Well, not exactly," Blair answered. "I mean, I haven't told them that."

"You promise too much," said a man beside the Secretary. "The President wants no comments from the Embassy about military issues."

"I never said anything about military issues." Blair looked around the group. "You know me, I'm schooled in vagueness. I never say anything concrete."

"From now on, follow your talking points," said the Secretary. "Especially at the gala tonight."

The meeting moved to other topics. While he waited, Jackson looked up the gala on his phone and discovered that the Chinese embassy was hosting a major event—a "cultural celebration"—at the National Gallery. He studied the invite list and saw Ambassador

Blair and a host of other senior officials, including the Deputy National Security Adviser, Reagan Murphy. No one had invited him. He needed to be there.

He texted Reagan, *Free for lunch?*

It was thirty minutes later, back in another staff meeting in his office, back on the topic of a multilateral treaty to protect Galapagos turtles, when he got her response.

No, but we need to talk. Meet me in 15 at old spot?
K.

The "old spot" was a rundown coffee shop a few blocks up the street from the State Department. Jackson excused himself from the meeting, grabbed his briefcase, and hurried there.

He arrived first. The place had sterile white floors and served sugar-cream with a trace of coffee. It would be dark in Tokyo and Hong Kong now. He could feel the time difference. He ordered a large from the sleepy lady at the cash register.

"Interesting accent," she said. "Where ya from?"

The question Jackson saw in her eyes was one he'd seen a hundred times before, and it screamed, you're different, aren't you? Jackson was too tired to be polite. He gave his usual snide answer. "The mountains."

"Which mountains?"

"The mountains of Moria."

The lady stared at Jackson blankly. Test failed. Not that he opposed small talk, but if you hadn't even heard about the mountains of Moria, there couldn't be much of a connection.

She handed over the coffee, and Jackson waited. Reagan came a few minutes later, entering the cold place like a fireball of red hair and freckles.

"Hey, Jackson. You look rough."

"Thanks. You're the one who got me sent to Tokyo. Just got back this morning. Guess I can't buy you coffee?"

She held up her metallic mug. "Green tea. Shall we walk?"

They left together and strolled down 23rd street to the National Mall. The misty morning rain had stopped, leaving the city with the smell of wet pavement. A few spring petals still clung to trees, although the rain had knocked many to the ground. Office workers with tired eyes and suits milled around as if reluctant to reenter whatever building awaited them.

After a couple blocks, Reagan slipped her arm through Jackson's, staying uncomfortably close. She'd probably say it was a cover—a couple out for a stroll. Jackson suspected more.

"You met Lily?" Jackson asked.

"I did. You're right. She's smart. We have her protected now."

"She was pretty shaken up by what happened."

"Good thing you were there."

"Yeah…"

"You better be careful," Reagan said, almost playful. "You know how girls fall for the men who save them."

Jackson glanced at her gleaming green eyes and thought he saw a hint of jealousy. "What level of protection for Lily?"

"We kept her safe at the Blair House for a day, and now she's back at her apartment. We set up a security detail."

"That's not enough. The situation is still too dangerous."

"Why?" Reagan asked. "What have you learned?"

"I think someone tried to pay the victim to stay quiet about something."

"How do you know?" Reagan was speaking fast, the way she did when she was nervous.

Jackson shrugged. "It's a guess."

They reached Constitution Avenue and Reagan turned toward her office, the White House. "The President is very concerned," she said. "Things are more tense than ever between China and Japan."

"Not surprising."

"Maybe, but now we're stuck in the middle."

"Someone wanted this murder to be very public," Jackson said. "And they wanted us to think it had something to do with the treaty."

"Doesn't it? You must know about the changed term."

It wasn't a question. Jackson wondered how Reagan had

learned that he knew. Maybe Lily had told her. He saw no use denying it. "Did the White House really request the change? You could've told me."

Reagan's voice dropped to a whisper. "The President is trying to avoid a war."

"By inviting the Chinese to attack?"

"You know it's not that simple," Reagan said. "We changed one word, in one treaty. So now, arguably, we don't have an obligation to fight if they take over some islands we should care less about."

Arguably... It reminded Jackson of their old debates. "It is simple, and unsound," he said. "Before this treaty was signed, everyone knew the United States had to defend if China attacked, so China would not attack. Now we have no obligation. It's all up to the President. It's uncertain. And uncertainty in this kind of thing is what starts a war, not prevents it."

"You sound like a lawyer."

"I am."

"It makes a nice cover. But turn your old brain back on, the one that could see to the heart of complex things."

"Oh, I still see." Jackson hesitated. He could trust Reagan only to a point, and she sounded defensive enough already. "I see what the President and his most trusted staff want most. It starts with a *Re-* and ends with *election*."

"Always the cynic," Reagan said, but she didn't deny it. "Even someone like you should see why that means we want peace."

"I'm not so sure."

"Careful, Crow." Reagan stopped and met his eyes.

She only used his last name when she was mad. They were one block from the White House, standing on the quiet sidewalk beside the grand Daughters of the American Revolution Memorial Hall. Reagan was a member, like all the women in her family before her. This was her terrain, not Jackson's. Maybe he'd gone too far. Or maybe she was still hiding something.

"Look," he said. "I haven't been talking to the Chinese like you and the President have. But it makes me nervous. There's a reason we rarely change our treaties."

"Stability…I know." Reagan crossed her arms, but her expression softened. "We're just shifting course slightly to accommodate a new power."

"So why the murder? Hina Himura wasn't part of this."

Reagan took a deep breath and started walking again. "We're not sure. Maybe she was. I'd hoped you'd find something out. The dynamics in China and Japan are just as complicated as they are here."

"Whoever did it is also trying to kill Lily, and now probably me. I won't let her get hurt."

"She won't," Reagan said. "But keep your distance from her. If you visit her place, you'll just put her at more risk. Okay?"

Jackson couldn't agree to that. Lily was smart, she could help, and, he had to admit, he wanted to see her, especially now that Reagan told him not to. So he said only, "I understand."

"Good. I need your help with something else. You used to be able to be able to crack into impossible places and get information the government needed."

"That was a long time ago."

"But I know you can still do it. You never gave up your secrets."

That was true, and it made it easy for Jackson put on his best smile. If she needed him, he could get something from her: an invitation to the gala, for starters. "What do you want to know?"

"The FBI has been investigating the murder," Reagan said. "They haven't been able to find anything on the assassin. He was an old man with a clean record. He arrived here just a few months before the killing. The investigators think someone must have paid him to do it—maybe for family back in China—but you know how hard it can be to track money, especially if it's done through cryptocurrency in China."

"Have the CIA and NSA look into it."

"I am. But your name keeps coming up. They say you're the best."

"I don't do that work any more." *Except I am*, Jackson thought, but that was on his own terms, not Reagan's. "I guess it would look good for you if I delivered some information, wouldn't it?"

"This isn't about me, Jackson. You want to know what's behind this as much as I do. We have to find out to protect Lily, and you."

He wasn't so sure of that, but he would play along. She was in a powerful position. "Alright, I'll see what I can find, if you'll do something for me."

"What's that?"

"There's a gala tonight. Take me as your guest."

She was quiet a moment. She knew him too well. She'd probably read right through his eager request.

"I just want to be there," he added. "Maybe learn more about what's going on."

"Fine." She smiled. "It's a date."

"What time can I pick you up?"

"8 pm. Outside my office."

She strode off, towards the White House. Jackson watched her go, waiting for her to look back, but when she didn't, he turned for Lily's apartment.

36

THE APARTMENT BUZZER gave Lily a welcome excuse to stop reading the news. She'd caught up on everything she missed on her whirlwind tour of Tokyo, reviewing almost every reporter's take on the shooting. The mystery of Hina's death only added fuel to the speculative fire. Some theories made Lily sick to her stomach—that Hina was having an affair, that she was a spy, and that China was deliberately trying to start a war.

Lily went to the call box and smiled. It was Jackson outside.

She rang him in, then hurried to brush her teeth and change into jeans and a purple tank top. Not too dressy, but better than the under-lockdown-surveillance-might-get-killed pajamas. At least she'd showered last night.

It took Jackson longer than expected to knock on her door. When he finally did, and she opened it, he held a finger over his lips for silence. His angular face looked intense, though his dark eyes offered a smile. He was wearing a suit, like he'd come straight from his office. He motioned for her to follow him.

She didn't say a word. She trusted him after what he'd done in Tokyo, even if she knew that was a dangerous thing to do with a former spy.

He led her to the apartment building's rooftop, which had a small lap pool eight stories up and a decent view of the Capitol building. No one else was around. They sat in two lounge chairs by the pool's edge. The sun had come out. It was turning out to be a nice spring day, despite a misty start.

"Sorry for the quiet." Jackson faced her from the edge of his chair, elbows on his knees. "I scoped out the building. We should be able to talk here without others listening."

Lily didn't know quite how to respond to that. She leaned back in her chair and stretched her arms over her head. After being cooped up in her apartment, it felt nice to be outside. "Wish I'd known you were taking me here. I'd have brought my swimsuit."

Jackson laughed. "Right, sorry."

"I was hoping you'd come."

"I could be putting you at risk."

"Your friend, Reagan, said the Secret Service would protect me here."

"Yes. I'm sure it'll be fine. I just don't want to draw more attention to your location."

"If you don't think the Secret Service is up for the job, maybe you should hang around. You saved me last time."

He smiled but turned away, gazing at the electric-blue, hyper-chlorinated water. "I learned something," he said. "About Hina."

"What?"

"She received a huge payment days before she was killed."

Lily was surprised. Unlike the press reports, this was real news. "A payment for what?"

"I don't know. I hoped you might have some idea. Here…" Jackson reached down beside his chair, took something out of his briefcase, and handed it to Lily. "The killer took this."

Lily shuddered as she studied the picture. She saw herself standing and smiling just to the right of Ambassador Blair. She remembered how they had lined up before the photographers, and how victorious and relieved she had felt about the treaty signing going well. Until…

Hina was staring directly at the photographer—the killer—with a beautiful, serene smile. But Lily knew her friend well enough to see the strain and fatigue in her eyes. Had Hina known something? The only other person looking directly into the killer's camera was Ambassador Blair, two people down the line from Hina. He wore his normal, charming smile.

"What do you see?" Jackson asked.

"Hina and Blair are both looking at the killer. Her eyes…she seems nervous."

"So did they both know something about him? Maybe it has something to do with that dinner with the Ambassador?"

"It could be... She didn't tell me any details about it. I wish I'd asked."

"Did she give any hints?"

Lily thought back to the final days leading up to the killing. She had been busy arranging for the signing ceremony. Hina had been doing the same within the Japanese government. She remembered Hina telling her about the dinner with Blair, and that she'd found an escape from the stress by playing Camelot. She'd asked Lily to play, like they had before, but Lily had been too busy. There was nothing unusual about that. And the last thing she wanted to tell Jackson, her boss, was that she'd considered gaming during such a busy week of work.

"No, I can't remember anything unusual," she said. "I'll keep thinking though."

A cloud drifted in front of the sun as Jackson studied Lily. There was a light breeze and the cloud passed. She was glad that he'd come to her place and given her an excuse to get some sun. She also liked the way he looked at her.

"What about the C-175?" he asked. "Anything unusual there?"

The C-175 had been Lily's responsibility. It was the formal package of documents required for every U.S. treaty, involving signatures from all interested offices, from any government agency. The amount of time and effort it took to obtain those signatures had surprised her, but bureaucratic processes came with the job. She had finished the C-175 several weeks before the treaty signing. The White House, the Department of Defense, and many other offices had cleared it. "No, it seemed normal to me, but it was the first one I've worked on," she said. "I had all the signatures well in advance."

"Then who signed off on the changed term in the treaty?"

"I was told no more signatures would be needed, since it was a minor change." She glanced away, sensing from Jackson's tone that she'd made a mistake. It wasn't a minor change. She knew that now. "The instructions came through Blair, from the White House."

"Were they in writing?"

"Yes, there was an email from Blair." Lily could almost remember the exact words. "It was just a few lines. It said something like: *For national security reasons, the White House has agreed with the Japanese to a modification of Article V in the treaty. The term 'administration' should be changed to 'sovereignty.' No further signatures are needed. Coordinate with Hina to make sure the change is made in both official languages.*"

"So Hina made the change for them." Jackson fell quiet, as if lost in thought. "Is it possible that she was the only person in the Japanese government who knew about this?"

"Their bureaucracy is even more complicated than ours…but I guess it's possible." Lily paused. "What do you think happened?"

"When I was in Tokyo, Blair told me the Japanese agreed to the change because they wanted to build up their own military. But then, in our meeting with the Japanese, their leader was surprised about the change. Maybe Hina was the only one who knew about it. A change made that late could slip under the radar."

"Why would she hide that from her own team?"

"I'm not sure." Jackson sighed. "Sometimes people do unexplainable things under stress, or for huge amounts of money."

"So they are actually explainable."

Jackson smiled. The sunlight gave his hair the luster of black opal, his skin like copper. "You're right. There's an explanation, and we need to find it."

"How can I help?"

Jackson put his hand over hers, like he had in the hotel in Tokyo. "You keep thinking of any clues Hina might have left. But your main job right now is to stay safe. You're protected here, but your apartment is probably bugged. We'll have to come up here again to talk."

Lily grinned. "Next time bring your swimsuit."

He laughed, and Lily felt warmer and happier than she had in days, with the sun on her skin and his hand over hers.

37

JACKSON LEFT LILY secure in her apartment. He didn't want to leave her, but he didn't have a good reason for staying any longer. Liking the way she looked by the pool wasn't a good reason. He knew he shouldn't have put his hand over hers again. But she was scared, he told himself, and he wanted to comfort her. Her vulnerability was his kryptonite. He'd never let what happened to his sister Julia happen again, not under his watch.

And maybe Lily really had some clue buried in her memory. She'd worked closely with Hina. The Japanese lawyer had accepted a payment, which meant she had to know something was amiss. If Hina had been savvy, she would've told someone. That knowledge—even the potential for it—painted a target on Lily.

Jackson walked out the building's front door and had just stepped foot on the street when he spotted a large man wearing a black suit, black tie, and black sunglasses. He was approaching Jackson, fast.

"Hey Crow," the man said. His shoulders were twice as wide as Jackson's. "Good visit?"

Jackson fingered the dart gun in his sleeve.

This must be Secret Service, who'd been watching Lily's place. Someone was probably not pleased with his interference.

The agent pulled his suit coat back an inch, revealing a badge. "Don't make this hard," he said. "We're just giving you a ride."

Jackson followed the man's gaze to a black SUV idling across the street. An instinct urged him to run, but his mind knew that would not be wise. Even if he could get away from this huge guy with the body of a sumo wrestler, they were supposed to be on the same team. Maybe he'd be reprimanded for meeting with Lily. Maybe Reagan was playing games with him. Whatever it was, he resigned himself to play the dutiful civil servant.

Jackson walked across the street.

The door to the SUV swung open, and Jackson climbed inside. The large man climbed in after Jackson, so that he was wedged between two agents with guns.

The door slammed shut.

"What's this about?" Jackson asked.

The man looked out the window as they barreled down Pennsylvania Avenue. "You've been summoned."

"By whom?"

"*Whom.*" The agent let out a muffled laugh. "See, told you he was just a lawyer."

"I still don't buy it," the other agent said. "None of our business though."

"He's right. I'm a lawyer at State," Jackson said. "Where are we headed?"

"You'll see soon enough," the bulky agent replied.

A few moments later they drove through a gate by the side of the White House. After Jackson exited the SUV, one of the Secret Service agents patted him down. Jackson squirmed as the man left no spot on Jackson's body untouched.

The agent took the dart gun.

He held it up and laughed. "Well, look at this."

"I'll want it back," Jackson said.

"Fine, but you oughtta try a real gun."

The men checked inside Jackson's briefcase, full of papers and the photograph of the Treaty Room. They let him keep it.

They flanked him as they walked into the Georgian mansion. Jackson tried to slow down and process why he was being summoned to the White House.

Reagan had to be behind it.

Not even a prohibited visit to a protected witness could justify this. The agents guided him through the Rose Garden and into a door in the portico of the West Wing.

Sure enough, Reagan stood waiting with her arms crossed, her lips pressed tight as if forced into a smile. "Welcome, Jackson. The President is eager to meet you."

"The President?" Jackson said, feeling his stomach sink. This was a first. He eyed the agents beside him. "A little time to prepare would've been nice."

"Hope they didn't rough you up too much," Reagan said.

Jackson smoothed his shirt, straightened his tie. "Why does he want to see me?"

"Follow me. We'll talk about it in the Oval Office."

She turned and led Jackson down a hall with plush carpet and framed portraits along the walls. A few turns later they stood before the Oval Office doors.

Reagan knocked, paused a moment, then walked in.

There were two men in the room: the President, Michael Wallace, and the CIA Director, David Strassitch. This had to be big.

The President wore navy slacks and a white-buttoned down shirt open at the collar. He was bigger in person than Jackson expected. He approached Jackson and shook his hand. The man's firm grip and steady eyes demanded Jackson's complete focus.

"Jackson Crow," the President said. "Nice to meet you. I'm Mike Wallace."

"It's an honor, Mr. President."

"You want to know why I asked for you."

Something about the President's tone reminded Jackson of a memory of his father, soon before he'd died. Jackson had been ten years old, and he and his friend had been caught red-handed stealing a neighbor's blackberries. His father had given them the steady glare of justice, and Jackson had admitted guilt and taken the punishment—grounded for a week. But Jackson had stayed silent about what they were doing right before taking the blackberries, which was peeking into a girl's locker room at a nearby summer camp. Sure, they got in trouble for a few berries, but no one ever found out about the locker room. The secret was to keep your mouth shut and let others reveal how much they really knew.

"I'm here at your request," Jackson said.

The President motioned to the couches in the center of the room. "Have a seat."

Jackson and Reagan sat on one of the couches. The President and Director Strassitch sat across from them.

The President leaned forward, elbows on his knees, sleeves rolled up on his forearms, and stared at Jackson like his father once had—a judge about to hand down his sentence. "You went to the Treaty Room after the Japanese lawyer was shot. Reagan has been monitoring this. She told me you received a picture."

Jackson glanced at her. *How did she know about the picture?* He remembered the warning hung on the door at the Mandarin Oriental. The agents must have seen what happened, and told Reagan. *Kathy Sullivan…*

Jackson had a sense where this was going, and he didn't like it. He felt his cheeks growing hot.

"We know about the man who visited you in Tokyo," Reagan said. "We know everything. We know where you were just before this meeting. I warned you not to go there."

"I'm not sure what you mean," Jackson said innocently. "What do you want?"

"It's not what we want," Director Strassitch said. He sat ramrod straight, formal as he could be in a dark grey suit with a red tie. "It's about the national security interests of our country. You have put us in a difficult position."

"How?" Jackson asked.

"You know what we mean," the President said. "You saw the picture."

Jackson knew there was no use lying about seeing it. "The picture wasn't special. It showed what every other photographer in the room caught on their cameras."

"Then why did the Chinese pay you off for it?" Strassitch asked.

"You have live footage of the assassination," Jackson said. "You know there was nothing unusual to see. I think the Chinese just wanted to see what I had."

"So do we," the President said. "You have a copy of the picture?"

Jackson opened his mouth to object, but decided against it. If he couldn't trust the President, who could he trust? Besides, the original copy with the message about BitStones had already been burned. He nodded.

"Good. Let's have it."

Jackson opened his briefcase and retrieved the photograph. He handed it to the President.

The President gazed down at it for a long time. Then he handed it to Director Strassitch and leaned back, with one of his arms stretched over the back of the couch, his hand gripping tight.

"What I'm about to tell you is highly classified," the Director said. "It stays locked in your head, okay?"

Jackson leaned forward. "Understood."

"We had a relationship with Moto Tachibana, the Japanese agent who gave you this. We understand he was killed. Like you, his cover was as an international lawyer. He'd been put in that position to monitor Hina Himura."

"Why?"

Strassitch took a deep breath. "She was a mole for the Chinese."

The victim, a mole?

If this was true, it changed everything.

Jackson's mind was reeling. "Then why did the Chinese kill her?"

"We don't know. We need your help to find that out." The President turned to Strassitch. "David, tell him what we know."

"Our intelligence has learned that the victim received a large payment before she was killed. A payment from the Chinese."

That's my intelligence, Jackson thought. He'd told the agent in the airport—the one following him—to tell Kathy Sullivan. She must have reported this up the chain. She must have used Jackson's name. It moved fast.

"Any leads?" Jackson asked.

"We believe they have an undercover agent operating actively here in DC," Strassitch said. "Someone with connections. Hina must have learned something she wasn't supposed to know. We need to learn what it is."

Jackson knew how well governments kept sensitive information contained, especially the Chinese government. "How could she have learned something worth her life?"

"She was beautiful, like a modern geisha," Strassitch said. "She would seduce powerful men and use them to acquire information. She had a long relationship with the Japanese Ambassador, Tanaka. And she was targeting our own Ambassador, Steven Blair."

"Did she succeed with Blair?" Jackson asked.

The two powerful men exchanged a glance. The President answered, "It doesn't matter. He had nothing to do with her death, if that's what you're asking."

He sounded certain, but defensive. Jackson knew this wasn't the time to push. He was still learning. "What do you want me to do?"

"First, do what Reagan told you earlier today," Strassitch said. "Find out who paid the killer. Second, find out what Hina Himura found out. I'm not going to ask you how you do it. We just need answers."

"Any guesses?" Jackson asked.

This time the President answered. "You talked with Reagan." He nodded to her, smiling. "She's been helping me avoid a war with China. We've found an elegant solution, for now. But I'm starting to worry the Chinese have an ace up their sleeve."

"Our agents have seen suspicious military movements," Strassitch added. "They could be planning an invasion."

"Where?" Jackson asked.

"We'd like you to help us find out."

Jackson leaned back and considered the request. He was doing this already with Vin's help, to protect Lily and himself...and America. But he wasn't embedded in the CIA like before. He didn't have the same protection. "You want me to do this alone?"

"Would that be any different than before?" Strassitch asked. "You never wanted a partner."

It was true. Jackson had always had Vin and others like him, so he'd mostly operated without others from the CIA. He'd earned their trust. But that was years ago. "I'll need passports, cash, the usual."

Strassitch smiled and glanced to Reagan. "They're here."

Reagan handed Jackson a thick envelope.

"I also want complete immunity."

The President nodded. "As long as I'm in this office, you have it."

Jackson knew he couldn't expect much better than that. He even had two witnesses—as much as he could trust the CIA Director and his own ex-girlfriend. "Alright, I'll do it."

"Thank you, Jackson," the President said. "And don't worry, we'll keep Lily Sun safe. Just stay away from her to avoid drawing any more attention."

"Understood, sir," Jackson said.

The group said goodbyes and Reagan escorted Jackson out. He tried to ask her more questions, but she stopped him and said they could talk later. She had several urgent matters to attend before the gala this evening.

He could tell she was avoiding him, maybe feeling guilty for dragging him into this meeting without warning, because she never looked him in the eyes.

Jackson exited the same way he'd come. He retrieved his weapon, the agent smirking at him. Then the agent led Jackson past the parked SUVs and out the high, wrought-iron gate surrounding the White House. He left Jackson standing on the sidewalk, where he was surrounded by hordes of tourists wielding cameras.

Jackson took the normal, convoluted path back to his apartment in northern Virginia—walk a few blocks, take a few alleys, then metro under the Potomac and walk some more.

He felt sure no one was trailing him.

It was dusk by the time he reached the usual Friday farmer's market set up near his building. He stopped to buy a carton of overpriced, undersized strawberries.

That's when his homeless friend found him. "Hey, man," he

said, smelling like malt liquor and holding out an empty hand.

Jackson began to hand over his usual twenty-dollar bill.

"Nah," the homeless man said. "It's hundred dolla' bonus time for me."

Jackson immediately tensed. "Why?"

The man pointed toward Jackson's apartment building. "Cuz I seen somethin' funny about ya place and now I'm tellin' ya."

38

ZHANG AND TWO of his men, dressed entirely in black, left the black van at dusk. Two others stayed in the van. They were parked three blocks from Jackson Crow's place. It could have taken a long time to find this apartment. He hadn't visited during daylight hours, and he'd managed to lose his tail every time on the way here. Usually it was in the metro. Once he'd left an agent tranquilized on a bench. Zhang had to respect that Crow was good at hiding his location.

But the Japanese had given it away. The man who had delivered the package to Crow, Moto Tachibana, had led Zhang's men straight here. The Japanese were always bad spies, Zhang thought. Too much order and courtesy. It's why China always had an edge over them.

They'd been watching Crow's apartment ever since. Crow had arrived early this morning, stayed an hour, and then left for the State Department. Now the day had passed, and they were ready for him to return.

His father's orders had been simple: take out Jackson Crow before kidnapping Lily Sun. The message came after his father had spoken with the American ambassador, who was spooked by this guy. Zhang could understand. There weren't many who had the talents to capture his agent in Tokyo. Zhang would have to handle it himself now.

He'd been sitting by the same dumpster for an hour. It had grown dark. The alley behind Crow's apartment building was almost pitch black, aside from a single light over the back door. Zhang wore a thick wool cap, a heavy black rain jacket with the high collar up, and old brown running shoes that might have been white years ago. Amazing what a fraction of a BitStone spent at a thrift store could do for the appearance of the son of the most powerful general in China. Zhang figured he should be able to get this over with and put on his white tux in time for the gala.

He finally heard someone coming. The man had his head down, with a hat hiding his face. The man surveyed the area as he walked smoothly down the alley, straight toward Zhang. It was too casual and careful at the same time. It had to be Crow.

Zhang toyed with finishing him here, before he even entered the building. But it wouldn't be pretty, and it would put himself at risk. There was also a chance this wasn't the right guy. It wasn't worth risking exposure.

As the man passed, he glanced toward the dumpster but kept going as if he'd seen nothing unusual. And he hadn't. Zhang picked this dumpster for a reason. When monitoring the building they'd seen a homeless guy loitering around. The guy had gladly taken fifty bucks to abandon the spot for the night. Zhang was filling his shoes now.

Once the man entered the building, Zhang felt certain it was Crow. He sent a text to his two men waiting inside Crow's apartment, telling them the target would arrive any moment now. They knew the orders: eliminate him quickly.

Zhang kept his eye on the window. More than a minute passed. Two minutes.

Then a light blinked on.

There was a quick blur of shadows at the window. All went still.

Zhang's phone vibrated. He glanced down at the Chinese characters that said: *Target down.*

Zhang started to smile but hesitated. The message wasn't quite right. He typed back: *Dead?*

Unconscious.

What? Zhang's orders couldn't have been clearer. It was to be a clean kill and escape. He waited for a response.

Something definitely wasn't right. He stood and gazed up. The lights were still on in the apartment window.

He pulled his gun from the worn winter jacket.

He felt the blow before he heard anything, like a hammer dropping onto his shoulder. The buckle of his gun strap blocked some of the hit, probably saving his clavicle, but the force still knocked the gun loose from his hand. It clattered on the pavement.

The next blow came at his head, but Zhang recovered fast. He blocked it, and the next one. He swept his leg at the attacker's feet.

The other man stumbled but stayed standing. They faced each other, fists raised.

"Who are you?" the man asked in flawless Mandarin. It had to be Crow.

The faint light from the door was behind Zhang, so he knew Crow couldn't see his face. Zhang considered his options. Fight or run. His gun was out of reach, behind Crow.

He needed to eliminate this obstacle now.

He feigned a high punch, then dove at Crow. He tackled him hard. Crow's back slammed into the metal dumpster. Zhang heard him grunt heavily, the air knocked out of him as he fell. Zhang lunged forward to pin him down.

But Crow twisted quickly and knocked Zhang to the ground. As they grappled for position, Zhang took two hard hits in the side and one to the mouth before he managed to roll away.

Crow had gotten to his feet and landed a kick hard into Zhang's ribs. He started to pull something from his sleeve.

Zhang sprang to his feet and kicked at Crow's hand, knocking a thin piece of metal loose. Zhang swept at his legs again, and Crow staggered back before finding his balance and moving toward Zhang. The guy just kept going.

They stood facing each other, tense and ready, when sirens sounded in the distance.

"I called them," Crow said. "Go with me, or go to jail."

Zhang didn't need to think it over anymore. His father would kill him if the police got involved, because that would lead to the FBI and worse.

He turned and ran as fast as he could down the alley. He could hear Crow chasing after him, staying on his heels.

Zhang's heart pounded as he rounded corners. He had three blocks before his ride. He just needed enough distance.

But Crow was fast. Without turning or slowing, Zhang flung

off his jacket and threw it back, hoping to slow Crow down. But still he could hear the footsteps.

He rounded the last corner and saw the black van. Its door slid open as Zhang raced forward. He wasn't going to make it before Crow.

But then he saw the driver raise his gun. Two shots crashed into the night.

Zhang didn't need to turn. He heard Crow go down. He covered the last twenty strides and dove into the van. The door closed, and the van sped away.

After Zhang had recovered his breath, he asked, "You sure you hit him?"

"Two shots to the chest, boss."

Zhang thought about going back to confirm. But Crow had called the cops. Zhang couldn't risk it. He had to trust his men.

He glanced at a hanger with his white tux. It brought a smile to his bloody lips.

Crow was gone, and it was time for the gala. That's where Zhang would report to the ambassador, who could give him the final go-ahead to kidnap Lily Sun.

39

JACKSON SAT IN HIS downstairs apartment, floor 8, staring up at the ceiling. Just above was his upstairs apartment, floor 9. His kevlar vest was on the floor at his feet. It had blocked the first bullet, right at the heart. The second bullet had nicked him, carving out a half-inch-deep groove in his upper arm. He had cleaned the wound, bandaged it up, and taken a couple painkillers, but it still burned like hell. Jackson smiled and shook his head. Sometimes you needed luck more than skill.

All of his security measures had worked. His homeless pal outside had tipped him off, so he'd entered this safety apartment on the 8th floor and listened to the quiet footsteps above. He'd guessed right, there were two of them, waiting in the main room of his 9th floor apartment. No one expected simple little apartments like these to have trap doors between floors. He'd pulled the hatch and climbed up the stairs, like a man entering his attic, into the upper apartment's bathroom. From there surprise was on his side.

The two men were waiting beside the main door, with their eyes focused on it. They never heard him coming. Like deer in the woods, they'd stood motionless while he snuck up behind. He'd blown a dart into the back of the first man's neck. By the time the man registered his shock, the second dart had hit the second man. Both were down in moments, with enough tranquilizer to keep them down.

Jackson searched the bodies and found what he needed: a phone with a recent text thread. He'd pressed the unconscious man's thumb to the screen to unlock it, then messaged whoever their partner was. Jackson had a feeling it was the man the President and Director Strassitch were looking for. The message came back, and Jackson tracked the location—right outside his building.

One thing had gone wrong. He'd snuck up on the guy outside, easy enough, but this time the dart didn't work. It had been too dark to get a clean shot. The guy must have been wearing some kind of protection around his neck, because the dart had fallen harmlessly, only drawing the man's attention.

Jackson had been on him in a second, but the guy could fight. Kung Fu style. They'd exchanged blows. Jackson hadn't gotten a good look at his face.

At the sound of sirens, the man had run for it and reached a getaway van. Someone inside the van had shot at Jackson. The first gunshot, the one that hit his chest, made him crash hard to the ground. The second shot grazed him on the way down, and no more came. He was smart enough to play possum when needed. He'd waited until the van was out of sight, then rushed back to the apartment.

Glad as he was to be alive, Jackson knew the trouble had really started now.

He went upstairs through the hatch between his two apartments and surveyed the scene. The guys hadn't disturbed much. A stack of papers still sat in order on his desk. The computer was unharmed. Clearly they just wanted him dead.

He needed to move the bodies. He'd picked this old apartment building not just for its location. It had no cameras and plenty of shady activity. He put the bodies in a cloth bag and rolled them to the elevator on a laundry cart. He took them out to the alley and left them by the dumpster. When they woke up they wouldn't remember anything from the past hour.

He was on his way back to the elevator when he got a text from Vin.

You have to log in. You're in danger.

Jackson hadn't heard from Vin since Hong Kong, and now his message was coming a little late. He wouldn't contact Jackson unless this was critical. Vin knew the risks of a single text.

I know, Jackson replied. *Danger has passed.*

I have information you need. Log into Camelot. Here's account info.

An avatar name, Raven, and a password appeared. Raven had been Jackson's old gamer name. Vin must have created this account for him.

Jackson took a deep breath and gazed out at the Pentagon's lights. He'd managed to stay away from this for so long. He'd been living a normal life—putting on a suit, going to a government office, sitting in meetings, and buying overpriced strawberries at a farmer's market. Next he and Reagan might get back together, have a couple kids, and buy a minivan. Not after today. He should've felt more upset about it. He'd *wanted* normalcy, the boring life, the American dream. Now his blood was pumping, adrenalin coursing, feeling the pain of a bullet gash. The moment that gunshot fired in the Treaty Room, he knew deep down he was going to get dragged back into it. This time it was China instead of Afghanistan. Wherever there were people, there was conflict—it just changed in shape and form and consequence. The scale of this potential conflict was huge, and he and Lily were caught in the middle of it. Someone had tried to kill him, but that only made him feel more alive than anything since he'd stepped away from the CIA and the spies and the games.

So he typed back to Vin: *Okay, I'm coming.*

Come to the tavern. I named it for your sister, like old times. I'll be waiting.

Jackson went to his downstairs apartment, barren except for the encrypted computer and the headset. He'd never been able to bring himself to get rid of it. The hardware was probably dated now, with new gear coming out every year, but it had been the best at the time. This was the first edition that allowed retina scanning, so headsets tracked eye movements and presented them just as they appeared for every player. The games were inching ever closer to reality.

He booted up the computer and quickly downloaded Camelot. It was free to play, and you could spend however much you wanted in the game. That was how the Chinese hooked players young and built their BitStone empire. What teenager wouldn't grab an opportunity to turn gaming into a fortune?

A small icon showing a castle and the word "Camelot" appeared on the screen. Before placing the headset onto his head, Jackson glanced around to confirm he was alone, and that all was in order. It seemed secure. The apartment was bought with BitStones and owned by a series of LLCs that could not be traced to him. Even if the apartment above was compromised—as it had been ever since someone had found him and slid an envelope under the door—this unit below should be secure for at least another hour. The two unconscious guys in the alley would be out that long. Jackson could finish this and leave for the gala.

He put on the headset.

He was suddenly in a medieval town square with a fountain in the center. Stone buildings surrounded the square, with shops and taverns. At least fifty others were milling about outside. There were gnomes, elves, dwarves, and humans. Except they were all people wearing headsets, trying to escape from something, whether it was reality or law enforcement.

The character Vin had made for Jackson was a tall elf named Raven. He wore a long green cloak and a sword at his side. There was a red silken sash across his chest. He checked his inventory. He had 10,532 BitStones—over a million dollars if he ever wanted to convert…and get the authorities after him again.

Jackson drew his digital sword and turned down the familiar main road toward his guild's headquarters. He heard singing from a tavern up ahead. He checked the tavern's name.

Jules Inn.

For your sister, like old times.

Jackson had long made a habit of naming things in Julia's honor. Now he shuddered outside the game, thinking of how he'd lost Julia in Manila, and of the danger Lily was in. He would *not* let Lily get hurt. He'd never let that happen again.

He moved forward toward the tavern. Its name said a lot about Vin. Not even a player with his resources could have built this overnight. The man must have been angling to get Jackson back in the game for a long time. Through the window Jackson saw the tavern was as raucous as a digital place could be, with busty serving maids and frothing tankards of ale. Vin was sitting with two elves and three humans at a table in the far corner.

Jackson waited and watched. He trusted Vin, but it had been a long time. Vin seemed almost too prepared for this. He was holding court, laughing and talking, drinking ale and smoking a pipe. He was the smallest in the room, which made sense because he was a gnome. It was a good choice, Jackson thought. Vin was like a gnome in real life—always talking and doing something crafty.

Jackson, as Raven, walked into the tavern. The room fell silent as heads turned to him, like seeing a legendary cowboy return to his old saloon after years away.

Vin rushed to him, bouncing lightly on his slippered gnome feet. "Raven! How are you?"

"Good." Jackson looked past Vin to the others who had been sitting with him. He didn't say more, trying to figure out what Vin wanted to show him.

"I've been telling everyone you'd be back. Come on, let me show you how the guild's doing." Vin the gnome turned and walked to the back of the room, where stairs led up.

Jackson followed him to a room upstairs. Vin locked the door behind them and pointed to a huge mirror hanging on the wall. "This is the guild's vault."

The place brought a flood of memories back to Jackson. In every game they'd played, Vin had set up a vault like this. Games allowed these places to represent a true vault of BitStones—completely encrypted and safe. This was how he and Vin had made a fortune together and built an international guild worth billions. This was also what had led Jackson to decide, years ago, to leave the Agency rather than betray Vin. He hoped it was the right call.

Vin, in his little gnome body, sat at the small wooden table, and Raven sat opposite him.

"You created this character for me?" Jackson asked.

"I had to keep up appearances," Vin said. "In every game I've played Raven has been there. When you dropped off the map, we needed to keep things stable."

"Raven is dead, Vin."

"But you're here!" He paused. "Look, I'm sorry, but at least you're in friendly territory. This should quiet the talk of changing the guild name for a while." Vin tapped the desk eagerly. "And this was worth it, I promise. You're going to like this game. The company that created it set up a perfect way to transfer BitStones without detection. If you duel another character and win, you take the loser's Stones without question. Not even the Chinese agents can monitor the transfer. Go ahead, look in the vault. Check the Stones."

Jackson turned to the mirror. He paused before the reflection. It had been a long time since he'd seen his real eyes beside pointy ears. It would've felt like pure fantasy if not for the Stones behind this vault, the permanent and invariable link between this world and the real one. That, and the retina scanner on the vault door. It read his real-life retinas. A light blinked green, and the door slid open.

The inside looked like any highly protected bank vault. Vin had wanted it to look normal. The vault stored their code. It exploited a glitch in every game that ran on blockchain and BitStones. The blockchain was completely transparent, so anyone could see transactions. But gaming added a protective layer, because no one could see who controlled which avatar. Except the Chinese government…and Vin and Jackson. For every stone tagged, Jackson could see here exactly what the Chinese could see. Vin had stumbled upon the glitch when he and Jackson were trying to mask their identities, years ago. A bunch of gamers in their guild had teamed up and developed code to exploit the glitch. Jackson had betrayed all of them except for Vin.

"What am I looking for?" Jackson asked.

"Pull up Stone 80A036B."

"Okay." Jackson entered the term, and a unique page of information appeared about this particular Stone. It showed when it had been created and every person who had owned it or exchanged it for dollars. He saw a character named Himura. This must have been the Stone Vin had mentioned in Hong Kong—the one paid to the Japanese lawyer days before she was shot.

Jackson studied the other owners and transactions, but he

didn't recognize anything revealing. He saw no need to tell Vin that Hina had apparently been a double-agent for China. "What am I missing?" he asked.

Vin smiled, clearly enjoying this. "Go back two transactions."

Jackson studied the record. The prior transaction was from a Camelot character named Archer. Jackson figured this player must have started with the game's very beginnings, because common names were usually taken early. Archer had gotten the Stone as part of a large conversion of dollars, in cash. Then Archer had paid the Stone to Hina.

"So who is Archer, and how'd he get the dollars?" Jackson asked. That was the main weakness in their tracking system. Any time cash was involved, they could lose the trail. And the U.S. government could find it.

"No clue about Archer yet, but I traced the dollars. It took a lot of digging." Vin leaned forward, then tapped his small gnome chest. "Yours truly has his ways. First I used that data chip you gave me. You said it was from a guy who tried to kill you. Any idea who he was?"

The data chip from the tooth. "Not really. Probably a Chinese agent."

"That thing had some seriously wicked viruses on it. You were smart to give it to me."

"Anything useful?"

"Yeah, it identified a series of Chinese bank accounts. The guy must have had the chip as a sort of cross-reference. I ran these accounts and this cash transaction by some banking friends, so they could run the serial numbers of the converted bills through their databases. One of them happens to be a banker in Beijing. He owed me a favor for facilitating an unsavory payment for one of his clients. Anyway, this guy found a match. There was a large cash transfer, including one of the bills that this player, Archer, converted into dollars and paid to the victim."

The victim. Hina Himura was still a victim, Jackson thought, even if she was a double-agent. "Who made the transfer?" he asked.

"Look, this is why I sent the text to warn you," Vin said. "This same person recently made another transfer and cash payment to Archer. I think it was a bounty on your head."

"Why? And who?" Jackson needed the name.

"Archer converted the dollars into Stones today. Then he made payments to four other characters—all in the Red Silk guild. These were big payments. One of them talked here in the game. He bragged about all the stuff he was going to buy, and all he had to do was kill a...*crow*. One of my moles in their guild told me about it. I think they're talking about you."

"Yes. They tried."

"*What?* Someone tried to kill you?"

"I'm fine. But who's behind it, Vin? Who transferred the cash?"

"Don't know, but my friend in Beijing should. He said he'd tell you. But there's a catch. He'll only tell you in person."

Typical, Jackson thought. "You trust him?"

"Like a drug dealer trusts his delivery guy."

"Super." Jackson saw little choice. He hated to leave Washington again, especially with Lily still in danger. But she had Secret Service protecting her, and he had a feeling that if he found out who had tried to kill him, he would find who was after Lily. And he could stop them. He might even accomplish what the President asked—finding why the Chinese had killed their own agent, Hina Himura.

"Alright," Jackson said, "I can leave anytime after midnight." *After the gala*. He wanted to talk with Reagan first, and Ambassador Blair would be there. "There's just one thing, I can't fly commercial."

"I know, the Chinese have your data, right?"

"Yes, and it takes forever."

"No problem," Vin said. "You can take my jet."

40

THERE ARE PARTIES, and then there are galas. The Chinese Embassy spared no expense in decking out the National Gallery in red and gold. There was champagne and caviar, tuxes and gowns, lipsticked lips and tight-tucked tummies. The men tried to look like James Bond, and the women exposed selective bits of flesh through designer dresses worth enough to feed a third-world family for a year. Jackson hated the exorbitance, but he understood it. The elites had to gather and decide the fate of the world somewhere, somehow. Why not make it a gala?

He had Reagan beside him and a glass of bubbly in his left hand as he surveyed the hundreds waiting to enter the dining room. Some faces were familiar. Most not. Dozens had come up to Reagan and complimented her on the dress, and the man by her side. No one knew who he was, but something about the copper skin gave him an exotic look. He felt no qualms posing as arm candy. She'd invited him, after all.

Jackson had to admit she looked good. Never one to shy from attention, she'd gone with red silk. It hung from her shoulders loosely, with two strands spilling like waterfalls over her chest, merging into a thin silk river at her waist, and cascading violently to the floor. It almost outshone her blazing tower of curls held up by diamond-studded butterflies. Almost.

"Reagan Murphy!" A middle-aged Chinese woman approached, wearing a black gown and golden accouterments. "You look amazing!"

"Thank you, Min." Reagan flashed a wide smile. "You are elegance defined, as always. Where's your date?"

"He's by the caviar bar. He loves his Beluga."

"Don't we all?" Reagan said.

The Chinese woman laughed, then caught Jackson's eyes. "And who is this?"

Jackson slipped his arm out of Reagan's and held out his hand. "Jackson Crow."

She bowed. "Min Wang. A pleasure to meet you."

"Likewise." Jackson glanced to Reagan. "So how do you two know each other?"

"We're old friends," Reagan said. "Min did her graduate work at Yale while I was there. She taught me how to make the best rice noodles."

"Weren't those years the best? I always knew Reagan Murphy was destined for big things."

Reagan grinned. "I could say the same of you!"

Before Jackson could ask what Min did, a Chinese man joined her side, with a small plate that looked covered in dark little bird droppings. He was nearly Jackson's height, with a white tuxedo and a square face. He had faint scars, like a man who's spent a lot of time in a boxing ring, and a puffy spot on his lip like he'd taken a punch on his way to the gala.

Introductions were made, hands were shaken. The guy was Min's boyfriend, Patrick Li, who worked as a reporter for the DC branch of a Beijing news company. He seemed to know Reagan. They talked for a few minutes about some recent reporting on a trade deal with China. Jackson was ignored, which gave him the perfect opportunity to study the crowd. He spotted Ambassador Blair on the opposite end of the room. He also saw the same agent who had followed him in Hong Kong, with the square jaw and the buzz-cut hair. Jackson wondered if he'd been right to tell the agent about the payoff to Hina. That's what had gotten him summoned to the White House. Tonight the agent was with an older blond woman. She had her back to Jackson, but something about her stiff posture looked familiar.

"So Jackson, what do you do?" Patrick's question brought Jackson's attention back to the conversation. The guy was smiling, friendly, but his limbs moved with a fast, nervous energy.

"I—"

"He's a lawyer," Reagan answered dryly as she looked to

Jackson. "Sorry, did I make that sound boring? We just have so many of them in this city."

"I don't think it's boring," Min said. "Lawyers keep the world in order. What kind of law do you do?"

"International," Jackson said. "I work at the State Department."

"Oh, interesting!" Min leaned closer as if trying to get a better look at Jackson. "You're not a spy, are you? I hear they often use the State Department as cover."

Jackson laughed, genuinely. "No. I'm just a lawyer. How about you?"

"I'm a political officer at the Chinese Embassy here."

"So a spy!" Jackson smiled.

Min shook her head. "Nothing so glamorous. I've been in Washington for a decade, and I work with lots of your colleagues. Every day we have to fight against our own domestic hawks. I like to think your colleagues and mine are the ones that hold our countries' peace together."

"A noble task," Reagan said, turning to Patrick. "You really should report more on the positive aspects of Chinese-American relations, like Min's work."

"You're probably right." Patrick shrugged. "But you know as well as I do, it's bad news that sells. People don't want to hear about meetings and trade deals. They like to hear about warships."

Warships. Jackson started at the word. It made something click in his mind about this guy, like he'd talked to him before.

"You report on military affairs?" Jackson asked.

Patrick nodded. "Nothing like an arm's race to keep people riveted. It's like the old Cold War days. My latest article, about one of China's new aircraft carriers, has been my most-read so far this year. You Washingtonians can't get enough of it."

"Especially in an election year..." Reagan tapped her empty champagne flute with a red-lacquered fingernail. "Some people think my boss is weak because he allows China to build up its navy without pushing back."

"In China we know he is not weak." Patrick held up his hand, then bent it backwards. "My country is like a strong young tree, and your President is wise not to push it. A tree bends in the wind, then snaps back with force." He snapped his hand forward for effect. Jackson could see the control of his movement, and he recognized the phrase as a principle of Shaolin Kung Fu. Maybe this guy fought, which would explain the busted lip and the scars.

"I will tell him you said that!" Reagan put her arm in Jackson's. "Looks like they're opening the doors for dinner. Shall we?"

41

KATHY SULLIVAN AND Logan Grant paraded into the gala's grand dining room, where a hundred tables filled the space like lilies floating in a pond. On white tablecloths there were red napkins and immense red orchid displays rising from the center, as if grasping for more of the dim red-hued light from the ceiling high above. It would have been magical, except it was work.

Ambassador Blair had been moving through the crowd, shaking hands like a politician. Kathy had not noticed anything unusual, although she was surprised when she saw that Jackson was here, as Reagan Murphy's date no less. At least Kathy had properly disguised herself with stiletto heels, a blond wig, and enough makeup to look like she was in her 40s again. The makeup hid the pink that came to her cheeks when she'd met Grant and he'd said, "Wow."

Their table, as planned, was beside the Ambassador's. They made small talk with the other guests sitting near them. As they ate dim sum dumplings, the group chatted about how China's team would do in the upcoming World Cup.

As the servers were delivering the main course, Peking duck, the Ambassador rose. Kathy nudged Grant, who stood and followed him out of the room. It always pissed her off at events like this that she couldn't be the one to go, but not even she would attempt a disguise to get herself into the men's restroom. She couldn't exactly stand beside the Ambassador at a urinal. Grant could.

He returned a couple minutes later, drawing eyes as he crossed the ballroom. He gave Kathy a light kiss on the cheek and sat beside her.

"What happened?" Kathy asked, leaning close to him.

"Looked like a normal bathroom break," Grant said quietly.

"But wasn't?"

"No. There was a handoff. A Chinese guy in a white tux passed the Ambassador as he walked out the door. They made it appear casual, but I saw the Ambassador slip something to him."

"What was it?" Kathy asked.

"Couldn't tell. Something small, maybe a note or thumb drive."

"Did you get a good look at the guy?"

"Yeah. Didn't recognize him, but he's sitting…" Grant turned slightly, glancing to the far side of the room. Then his eyes opened wider. "Wait, he's gone."

Kathy hurried to her feet. The Ambassador could have given this guy an order, and now they might lose him. Only Grant knew what he looked like.

"Let's go after him," she said.

42

Zhang was beyond annoyed as he rushed out of the gala.

Jackson Crow had survived. Maybe the guy could dodge bullets. He didn't even look hurt in his black tux. Zhang had summoned every ounce of self-control to hide his surprise when he found himself talking to the man he'd just tried to kill. He played the perfect gentleman and detected no recognition by Jackson.

But it worried Zhang that Jackson was Reagan's guest. If Jackson learned about their deal, that would be a disaster.

After escaping the encounter with Reagan and Jackson, Zhang had focused on connecting with Ambassador Blair. When Blair headed toward the restroom, Zhang seized the opportunity. An accidental bump gave the Ambassador a chance to deliver the note. Zhang had read it, fuming, as he stood in front of a urinal.

POTUS has warned Crow. He knows about Hina. Take the target now.

Zhang wanted to ask, *what does Crow know about Hina?* But he couldn't risk a conversation with the Ambassador. The statesman was surely being watched. Zhang felt sure he'd keep his mouth closed about the project—Hina's death ensured that. But had *Hina* told anyone about the project?

Either way, Zhang had his mission now. He went straight from the restroom to his driver outside the gala, without finishing his dinner or saying goodbye to Min Wang. She was a casual sort of asset, not a spy, but she'd served as Zhang's date at enough events to expect he might vanish without a word. Their government had done enough to help her career that she was beyond asking questions.

As Zhang climbed into his car, he glimpsed two Americans rush out the doors from the gala. One of them—a bulky looking man—looked straight at Zhang, then quickly whispered something to the woman at his side.

Zhang ducked into the car and slammed the door. The driver

took off fast, going straight to the Chinese embassy. The spies must have been watching him or Blair, Zhang guessed. Whatever they suspected, he felt sure they had no clue what Blair's note had said. And there was no way they could follow him into the embassy—his fortress and sanctuary on foreign soil. There he would have all the resources he needed to prepare. He was going to get the leverage they needed to keep their plan secret a few more days. He was going to take Ms. Sun.

43

REAGAN ABANDONED SUBTLETY when she asked Jackson to join her on the ride home from the gala. Sitting beside him now, in the back of a black towncar crossing the Potomac River, she admitted to herself that she'd enjoyed the evening more than expected. Jackson had seemed distracted at first, but perhaps it was natural at such a splendid event with its fascinating guests and décor. The Chinese knew how to impress. After dessert and a couple glasses of champagne, Jackson had agreed to dance, and Reagan enjoyed the feel of his steady hands on her waist, his dark eyes meeting hers. His attention had returned to where she wanted it—herself.

The car stopped outside her house, a five bedroom Tudor mansion bordering the Washington Golf and Country Club in Arlington.

"Nice place," Jackson said, gazing out the window.

Reagan smiled. "Thanks. I've been here two years now. Come on, I'll give you a tour."

She began to climb out of the car, but Jackson hesitated and glanced at his watch.

"Just come see the view out back," she said. "I won't bite."

He agreed, more reluctantly than she'd hoped, and he asked to driver to wait.

She led him through the front door, telling him how she'd fallen in love with the home on first sight. The former owner was a Supreme Court justice, which had sealed the deal. It was amazing what a few years of high-end lobbying could buy.

They went to the great room in the back, with wood-paneled walls and floor-to-ceiling windows overlooking the lights of the Washington Monument. Reagan stood close to Jackson, her shoulder brushing against him. "I love this view," she said.

"I can see why."

She turned toward him and looked up into his eyes. "It's better with you here."

"Thanks for taking me to the gala," he said.

It sounded too much like a goodbye. She reached up and brushed a strand of black hair off his forehead. Their chests touched. "Almost like old times."

"Almost..."

Before he could finish, she leaned forward, her lips parting.

He stepped back.

"Sorry," he said. "Look, it's been a nice night. But I have a lot on my mind, and I have to leave town in an hour."

Reagan recovered fast, refusing to feel embarrassed and putting on her professional smile. "That's soon. Where are you going?"

"Out of the country."

"I see." Reagan didn't need to ask more. She had ways to find out where he was going. "Well, I hope we can get together again once you're back."

"Okay, sure. Thanks again for a great night."

She saw him out the front door and they waved goodbye as he got into the car. Her heart sank as he rode away. She felt sure there was still a chance for them, even if Jackson didn't want to admit it. Their time would come, though it might be a lonely wait.

An hour later Reagan sat in her home office, wearing a silk robe and slippers by a fire. She'd learned that Jackson had flown away in a private jet, destination unknown. She'd learn more soon enough. For now her comfort was a glass of red wine and a game called Camelot.

Her friend Min Wang had convinced her to try the game when it first came out. She wasn't the gaming type, but she had to admit it was fun with the headset. Min had shown her around the virtual world, and it felt like they were really together, exploring a land of castles and dragons. Reagan had created a broad-shouldered man as her character, with the name Archer. Come to think of it, he looked a bit like the President.

44

TWO HOURS AFTER the gala Kathy sat on her faded beige couch in her faded brick rancher in Arlington, Virginia, drinking a Budweiser and watching a recorded episode of Seinfeld. She might have felt sorry for herself, but there wasn't much else she could be doing now. Her mission following Jackson and Lily was basically finished. Neither she nor Grant could follow Jackson after he'd flown off in a private jet—at least not without raising too many red flags. They'd also lost the Chinese agent at the gala, and Ambassador Blair had done nothing but take home a woman ten years his junior for a consensual evening together. Kathy still had live microphones in Lily's apartment and the Ambassador's office, which would be triggered if there were any voices. For now she just had to wait.

And to be fair, Kathy told herself, this was only her second television show this evening—first Friends, and now Seinfeld. She was going to watch just one more. Who could skip the Puffy Shirt episode? It was a top-5 favorite. Even she lost her stoicism and laughed out loud when Jerry—

Her phone buzzed. It was the unique ringtone that was triggered by sound in the Ambassador's office. She knew keeping this tap was illegal, but lives were at stake. She paused the episode and fell quiet, listening to the live audio feed. There was no legitimate reason for Blair to be in his office this late on a Saturday.

"Wow, nice place!" whispered an unknown woman's voice, apparently right by the microphone wedged into the doorframe.

"Ever been in an ambassador's office?" It was Blair's voice.

Kathy rolled her eyes.

"First time," the woman said. "You even have a couch. And what a view! You can see the monuments, and the lights, and—"

"Yeah, not bad, right?" Blair slurred. "Just let me look…damn, it should be…it's not here."

"What're you looking for?" the woman asked.

"I usually keep an extra bottle behind this shelf, for such a time as this. It's truly the best Scotch you've ever tasted, like molten gold. But hey, look what I got instead."

"Oooh, looks old. I love older things…"

Liquid poured.

"To a lovely evening," the Ambassador said.

Glasses clinked.

They talked a while longer before it was obvious they were kissing. Kathy wanted to cut the feed, but she couldn't. Instead she listened to the two of them, her fury building like a geyser about to blow. This man had no dignity. No respect for the office. People like Kathy and Jackson and a thousand others were out risking their lives, trying to protect America, while this figurehead was acting like a college kid on spring break. Worse. He'd slept with a foreign diplomat who was shot in the State Department two days later. Kathy felt more sure than ever that this was no coincidence.

She was going to find evidence against him—lawfully obtained evidence, the kind she could use in court—to put him in jail, where he could live his pathetic days away from all statecraft and Scotch and sex, and under a mountain of shame.

45

JACKSON FELT LIKE a billion BitStones as he stepped out of the Gulfstream G650. Vin had arranged for the jet to be waiting at midnight, just hours after Jackson managed to survive the attack against him and, quite separately, the dancing with Reagan at the gala. He'd almost let her sparks consume him at her palatial home, but duty had clarified his mind. Whatever still simmered between them could wait. The whole night had fizzled into nothing—no hints about Ambassador Blair, and even the square-jawed agent he'd recognized had left before dinner was finished. After Reagan's house Jackson had made his way into the leather and wood-paneled paradise of a private jet. Fourteen hours of smooth flying later, Jackson was in Beijing, well-rested, well-fed, and wearing a brand new suit.

Vin had a car waiting for him at the Beijing airport. He'd refused to give the address, even in Camelot, so Jackson was completely in the hands of this driver. The man, black gloves and black glasses, clearly knew how to navigate through Beijing. He stayed at a steady speed, never above the speed limit, and changing lanes only when absolutely necessary.

Jackson could understand why. The Chinese government monitored everything. They'd track the tags of this car, and their cameras would recognize the driver's face—glasses or not. Not even a private escort like this could evade scrutiny for long. Jackson wondered what the driver's citizen score was. Probably pretty good, if Vin was using him.

They'd been driving almost an hour when the car slowed in a traffic standstill. It was early Sunday morning, but that didn't stop an infinite mass of tourists from shuttling across the highway between Tiananmen Square and the Mao memorial. A vast desert of grey paving stones stretched between the two monuments to communism and Chinese greatness. That, plus the dense smog, made Jackson want to gag.

Beyond Tiananmen and the red monumental entrance, Jackson knew there was beauty in the Forbidden City. But here it was locked away behind the more recent communist history—Mao's portrait separating the two eras of China's history.

Jackson felt relieved as the car started moving again. It was not much further until they reached the financial district of Beijing, which lately held more clout than Wall Street in the world's markets. Skyscrapers stretched to the sickly brown sky, including one building that looked like two awkwardly shaped legs joined at the top. Beijing had done even worse than D.C. in harmonizing its iconic past, its 1960s communist blocks, and its modern steel and glass structures. Not every city could be Paris.

The car stopped in front of one of the anonymous-looking towers.

"This is your stop," the driver said, accent heavy.

Jackson climbed out and went to the glass doors of the building. No one was around. It was Sunday, after all. He knew knocking would be foolish. He didn't trust using his phone, which he had kept shut down. So he sat on a bench and waited.

Ten minutes later a man came to one of the glass doors. He nudged it open and looked to Jackson. "Mr. Vin?"

"My friend, yes."

The man nodded and motioned for Jackson to follow. He entered the building and was escorted to a conference room on floor 41, which looked out to the east, over the Forbidden City and Tiananmen Square. There were islands of green between them—lush gardens secluded from Beijing's hordes.

"You made it!" came Vin's familiar voice.

Jackson turned and saw his friend—in a suit for a change—standing beside a middle-aged Chinese man with carefully groomed black hair flecked with grey. He wore an immaculate grey three-piece suit. His red tie was a swirl of golden dragons.

"Jackson, this is Mr. Chan." Vin stood between them, with the anxious pose of a girlfriend introducing a boy to her father. "Mr.

Chan, this is Jackson."

Mr. Chan bowed but did not extend his hand.

Jackson bowed back. "It's a pleasure, Mr. Chan."

"Likewise. I have long hoped to meet you." He spoke slowly, with a heavy accent, in the familiar way of someone fluent in a language but thinking in his native tongue. "May I call you Raven?"

Jackson tipped his head but didn't reply, as his eyes shot to Vin. It had been a long time since someone connected him with his avatar.

"Mr. Chan is a member of the Red Silk Guild," Vin explained quickly, as if sensing Jackson's discomfort. "I told him Raven had been back in gaming, and that I could arrange an introduction. Mr. Chan requested this, so that he might better assist us."

Jackson did not like this. Vin could have at least given him a warning. He focused his attention on Mr. Chan. The man must be the one Vin enlisted to figure out the identity of Archer—the character who paid Hina Himura before she was shot. "I understand you can tell us who transferred cash that was redeemed for a particular BitStone."

"Yes," Mr. Chan said. "Vin has given me the Stone's number."

"And?" Jackson asked.

"My clients do not provide names. I work only face-to-face. I can show you the client's picture. You will need to come with me to my hutong. It is not far."

Jackson looked to Vin again. He had mentioned none of this, and a hutong—a traditional neighborhood of walled homes in Beijing—could be a dangerous place for an outsider. The last time Jackson had been inside one, he'd barely gotten out.

"It's safe," Vin assured Jackson. "Mr. Chan maintains this banking office, but the real work is done from there, where he cannot be monitored."

This was stretching Jackson's faith in Vin. But he'd come too far to back out now, and Lily was still in danger. So he nodded. "Let's go."

46

THE LAST CHERRY BLOSSOMS of the tree in General Li's home courtyard had fallen, leaving a faint pink carpet on the small island of grass beneath it. The petals that fell to the pond encircling the island drifted lazily, while large golden koi swam below. The soft colors, pink and green and gold, were beautiful in the morning light, and the sweet fragrance bore no similarity to the smell of the streets outside the hutong.

General Li did not notice these things. He was an hour into his Sunday morning routine, reading a yellow-paged hardback copy of *The Art of War* by Sun Tzu. He had most of it memorized by now, but there was something in the rhythm of reading it, on the same pages that he had for years, that put his mind at ease. His son Zhang had disappointed him again, failing to control the American lawyers who knew too much, but Sun Tzu reminded him that wars were not won overnight.

In this restful frame of mind, he welcomed the officer who came into his courtyard like an honored guest, not as an interruption. No one would come to him here unless it was important. He placed his finger in the book as he looked up at the young man's eyes.

"Sir, one of our targets has just landed in Beijing."

"Which one?"

"Jackson Crow, sir."

General Li smiled and glanced down at his book again. His finger happened to be at one of his favorite lines—underlined decades ago, and highlighted multiple times since: *In the midst of chaos, there is also opportunity.*

47

JACKSON AND VIN followed Mr. Chan to his hutong. It was only a couple blocks from the financial district and surrounded by skyscrapers. But after stepping through a narrow gateway, the modern world felt a hundred miles away. The hutong's alleys and the walls were made of ancient grey stone, punctuated by red-painted doors with ornate bronze lions and dragons affixed to their centers. Strings of red and gold lanterns hung above them, bright against the brown smog sky.

Mr. Chan explained that this neighborhood was known as Gongmenkou Hutong. He said with obvious pride that these hutongs had been thriving places for families and shops for centuries, since the Yuan Dynasty 700 years before, when these residential areas had been built around the Forbidden City. The traditional architecture reminded people of China's ancient imperial history, before Mao, before the communists. "But now it is an endangered species," he said. "Our city grows, our government demands more density, and so they demolish the hutongs and build office towers."

They rounded a corner, where another alley of grey stones stretched ahead under lanterns. Jackson asked Mr. Chang why the hutongs were being destroyed. He sensed the man would welcome the question, and Vin's behavior—unusually quiet and polite—made Jackson think they needed to keep Mr. Chan happy.

Mr. Chan released a torrent of words, mostly speaking in Mandarin so fast that even Jackson, though nearly fluent in the language, could barely understand. Mr. Chan blasted the government for claiming they were trying to improve living conditions for residents. They claimed the hutongs were inefficient, overcrowded, and polluted. They had poor sanitation, water supply, and shared public toilets. The only reason the government allowed some hutongs to remain was for tourism and special memorials.

This hutong would be safe, Mr. Chan said, because it was a stone's throw from Lu Xun's home—a famous writer whom Mao Zedong had used to help fuel his own political rise. Whoever helped Mao would be safe. But what the government didn't understand, Chan said, was that people loved these places. They felt alive, in community, in the hutongs. The alleys connected siheyuans—or quadrangles—that held compounds of houses around a courtyard. "When they rip people away from this," Mr. Chan said, "and stack them like sardines in high-rise apartments, their souls wither. But enough about the government."

Mr. Chan sighed as they stopped before another red door. This one was larger and more ornate than the others they had passed, with two huge stone lions flanking the rounded frame. "Here," Mr. Chan said softly, "the noise of the city disappears. We can still be family here. Like my people once were, in the dynasties of imperial China."

Jackson and Vin followed him through the door and onto a serene courtyard with a gnarled tree that looked a thousand years old. The houses surrounding the courtyard had the sleek sloping tiles of traditional Chinese architecture, with sliding doors open onto the courtyard. Several people were around the space, talking quietly in the courtyard or within the homes.

"My father lives here." Mr. Chan pointed to a building to the far side of the courtyard. "My son lives here, my daughter too, with their spouses. And," he added proudly, "I have *four* grandchildren."

"That is wonderful," Jackson said, and he meant it. Four grandchildren might not have been much by American standards, but when most families here had been allowed only one child unless they were rich or otherwise curried great favor with the government, anyone who had four grandchildren would stand out.

"Come, we will talk in my home." Mr. Chan led them up the stairs of the main house, on the north side of the courtyard, and into a tranquil dining room.

Food and tea were served. Jackson ate and drank, but he barely noticed what he consumed. His mind was dominated by thoughts of getting information and getting out. He almost felt like this man was delaying on purpose. By the time they had been in the room over an hour, and even though Vin was playing along, asking friendly questions, Jackson had heard enough about the grandchildren's violin and math and martial arts classes.

"I understand you can help," Jackson said, more impatiently than he'd intended. "Who is Archer? And who paid him?"

"You Americans always hurry." Mr. Chan sighed. "I do not want a war between our people, but if it comes to that, I fear that is why we will prevail. Our leaders play the long game. Yours play in four-year increments."

Jackson would not argue with that, even though he believed impatience—and the quick action that came from it—could win battles too. "What can you tell me about Archer?"

"I will show you." Mr. Chan rose slowly and moved to the next room, where a stairway led down into the ground.

As Mr. Chan began to descend the stairs, Jackson looked to Vin. He did not like the idea of getting trapped underground. "You fully trust this guy?

Vin shrugged. "He's always been fair with me. He handles very sensitive clients. They trust him with their money…"

Some assurance, Jackson thought.

"Wait," Jackson called down the stairs. "What's down there?"

Mr. Chan's head appeared from around a corner at the bottom of the stairs. "My main operation. I like you, Raven. You are very lucky to get this access." He looked to Vin. "Only for my most important clients. Come along now."

He disappeared from view again, and Jackson and Vin followed. The light and sound of the room above disappeared as they rounded the corner after Mr. Chan, where they found yet another flight of stairs going down. Jackson counted his steps, and after several more turns and flights, he guessed they were forty feet underground. Mr. Chan was ahead in a long tunnel with ochre dirt walls braced by steel beams. It looked like a mining shaft—beneath the heart of Beijing.

Jackson took a deep breath and jogged forward, catching up with Mr. Chan just as he stopped before a plain metal door, one of several lining the tunnel into the distance.

They entered the door and found themselves in a sophisticated computer processing room. Servers lined the walls, and heavy-duty fans pumped air through the ductwork above. A handful of men sat at various computers, fully immersed with headsets. Jackson figured they were playing a game, mining BitStones.

Mr. Chan walked around a row of file cabinets to reach a large metal table near the center of the room. He activated a tablet that sat on the table and swiped it a few times, before handing it to Jackson. "This is who paid Archer."

Jackson looked down at the screen. His knees suddenly felt weak. It was Ambassador Steven Blair, staring at him just as clearly as he had into the killer's camera.

But it was more than that.

The tablet also showed the gamer whose character was Archer: an unmistakable picture of his ex-girlfriend, the woman who had just tried to kiss him.

No, impossible, Jackson thought. *Reagan?*

All the details lined up—they had tied her IP address to her real address in Arlington; they had her birthday, her driver's license, even her security clearance file.

Jackson couldn't believe it. Reagan could be ruthless, but this was too much. She wouldn't pay for a murder, would she? Besides, she was no gamer. Something had to be wrong.

He met Mr. Chan's eyes. "You're sure this is right?"

"You know BitStone ledgers do not lie," Mr. Chan said.

He glared at Mr. Chan. "I don't believe you."

"Look," Mr. Chan said, holding his hands up defensively. "I can show you the Ambassador's account. He has investments in many companies in China. Many are in debt. The government even began to prosecute, but they stopped. And he started directing me to make payments to Archer."

"Personally?"

"Yes. See the next page. You can review the cash payments there. But you didn't discover it here."

"You have my word." Jackson flipped through the transactions and saw the exact information he needed—cash transfers from the Ambassador's corporate account in Beijing to Mr. Chan, then to Archer, then to Hina. Jackson snapped a quick picture with his phone. He looked to Vin, who looked ashen. "I think we've got what we need. It's time to go."

Vin shook his head slowly. There was a noise at the door to the room.

Jackson turned and saw soldiers with guns raised, as he heard Vin say, "I'm sorry…"

The soldiers started shouting in Mandarin, *NOBODY MOVE, NOBODY MOVE*. Twelve of them had fanned into the room before Jackson realized what had hit him.

Vin had lied. Vin had set him up. He felt crushed, and furious.

Fully aware that it might be his last free act before a year of interrogation—sleepless nights, starvation, electric currents fired into testicles—followed by execution or a lifetime of imprisonment in a solitary concrete cube without feeling sunlight, hearing English, or seeing a woman's face ever again, Jackson set his feet, torqued his shoulder back, and slammed his fist into Vin's face. He felt the satisfying crack of a broken nose.

In the second that it took for Vin to collapse with a cry of pain, the first gunshots fired. Jackson had enough sense to drop to the ground, beside Vin and behind the row of file cabinets, even as he recognized that the shots were coming from the wrong place—the back of the room.

He pulled the only weapon he had on him—his dart gun—and risked a quick glance around the side of the cabinets. Many soldiers had fallen. The others had their guns firing at targets further away. Jackson missed his gun, but he did what he could. He blew a tranquilizer dart into the neck of a soldier. Then he blew a second, landing a direct hit in the eye. Both soldiers dropped, doomed for a couple hours of unconsciousness, but no one fired back at him, because the soundless dart gun was no threat compared to the munitions being fired from behind.

After fifteen seconds of chaos there was a moment of quiet—the eerie stillness that follows a gunfight, when the smoke hangs heavy and the damage has been done. Jackson rose slowly and saw that the soldiers were all down.

The noise came back in a hurry, with Mr. Chan shouting orders. *Shut down procedure! Now, now! Shut down! Evacuate!*

Mr. Chan rushed to Jackson's side and grabbed him by the arm. His grip was strong, even though he had a streak of blood running down his pale face. "We must go. It will blow in seconds!"

He raced off.

Jackson was confused. Had he been betrayed or not? He glanced down at Vin. He couldn't leave him, no matter what he'd done, so he picked up the smaller man's body and hoisted it onto his shoulder. He ran toward the door as fast he could, passing other men who were setting fire to computers, servers, and files.

Mr. Chan was there, waiting. He shouted. *OUT! NOW! CLOSING IN 5…4…3…*

A final man charged past them, and Mr. Chan typed in a code on the wall panel. The metal door slid shut.

Mr. Chan turned and ran the way they'd come, toward his home, without a glance back. Jackson managed to stay close, even carrying Vin's body. They were just beginning up the stairs when the whole tunnel shook with the force of explosion, followed by a sound like a nuclear bomb going off underground.

Jackson felt the burn in his legs, the fear at his back, as he leapt up the stairs two at a time. He was sweating and gasping for air by the time he reached the top of the stairs and was standing in Mr. Chan's home. Five other men were bent over, catching their breath.

"You must…leave," Mr. Chan panted out.

"Why did you—?" Jackson began to ask, but Mr. Chan's held up his hand, stopping him.

He pointed to Vin's motionless body. "Thank Vin. He saved your life."

"But—"

"He will explain. Tell him I knew what he was doing, and he will understand. Arrangements have been made for your escape...and mine."

Jackson listened beyond his own pounding pulse and heard a loud whirring sound, quickly drawing closer. A gust of wind whipped into the room as a helicopter descended overhead.

"This is your ride. It will take you to Vin's jet. You must leave the country now." Mr. Chan bowed formally to Jackson. "Goodbye, Raven. It has been an honor."

* * *

Mr. Chan expected the government to come within an hour. They would burn his home and kill everyone there. That's why they all had to leave. He had prepared for this, with passports, cash, and a residence ready in Taipei. He gave quick orders. Everyone began to pack up their essentials.

Just before leaving, as he looked over the quiet courtyard nestled within his quiet hutong, Mr. Chan sent a simple, encrypted text to his contact in Washington:

No need to visit. Crow is Raven. He flies with Vin.

48

AN ATTRACTIVE NURSE who doubled as a flight attendant had finishing cleaning up Vin's face when he woke up. His nose was still crooked—fixing that might require surgery—but the blood was gone and a sufficient dose of some painkiller had the diminutive guy smiling in his cushy leather Gulfstream seat.

Jackson figured they were over Japan right about now. It was far enough away from China for him to at least be willing to consider forgiving Vin, depending on his explanation. He'd come up with a few ideas. Maybe the Chinese government had something on Vin and so he'd agreed to lure Jackson into the country. Maybe Mr. Chan was the target. Either way, Vin had signaled to the People's Liberation Army, and they'd come with enough firepower to put a dozen holes in Jackson before he could move. That was not a danger to invite lightly.

He waited for Vin to speak, feeling his former friend's eyes on him. He clinked the ice around his crystal glass, watching the amber liquid swirl. He reached into his bag of organic, fancy chips, crunching away at the final fragments.

"Come on, man," Vin said. "You can't just ignore me."

Jackson held up the bag, studying the ingredients. "Plenty of saturated fat and oil and spices, but not a fleck of monosodium glutamate." He tipped up the bag and poured the last of its powdery contents down the crease and into his mouth. He talked as he munched, "There's nothing like the bottom of a bag of chips to explode into your life with all the titillating, addictive flavors man could contrive. Tastes like ambrosia, but probably closer to fertilizer." He washed it down with a swig of whiskey.

Vin was laughing. "Seriously, Crow?"

Jackson gazed out the window at snowy peaks of northern Japan, probably Hokkaido. "If you can't explain yourself in ten words, I'm breaking your nose again."

"That's against Gulfstream rules. Don't punch a man in his own jet."

"You already exceeded ten words."

"Come on, man, I'm sure you already figured it out," Vin said. "The Chinese have been onto me for a while, and onto you, too…Raven. I owed Mr. Chan a lot of money. And then this opportunity presented itself. I told Mr. Chan I could bring you to him. He's had his own troubles with the government, as you might imagine for someone in his line of work, and with his opinions against the Communist Party. The location of his operations had already been compromised. So he agreed to signal the authorities when you arrived, but then to fight back when they came, no survivors. Now the government might think all three of us are dead, and I'm even with Mr. Chan."

Jackson turned to Vin for the first time. He did not smile. "That's a terrible plan."

"Hey man, it worked didn't it?"

"Mr. Chan's men killed at least a dozen soldiers. Their location is compromised. Even if it was destroyed, skeletons will remain. The government can do the math."

"But *we* survived! Why are you so worried about Mr. Chan, anyway?"

"He knows who I am, Vin. He can talk. He *will* talk when the right questioner enters the room."

"Hey, we made it out, didn't we? And you learned what you wanted."

Jackson sighed and shook his head. "I still can't believe Reagan is Archer."

"Could he have faked what you saw?"

Jackson thought back to what he'd seen on the panel. It would have been difficult, but possible, to frame Ambassador Blair. And yet, after everything he'd learned, Jackson felt sure that Blair really was behind this. He had to talk to Reagan. If she wasn't Archer, he needed to find who was. That was the only way to find out what the Chinese were plotting.

"I want to find Archer," Jackson said. "Can we login here?"

"Of course." Vin stood slowly. "I had this baby custom-built. It's my home away from home." He stopped beside Jackson. He wore regret on his face. "Look, I'm sorry. I know it was a risk. I couldn't think of any other way."

"We got lucky, Vin."

"You always do, my friend. I was counting on that. But next time, could you please take it easy on my nose?"

As Jackson stood, looming a head taller and looking down at the man's twisted naval bone and large brown eyes, he could not help but smile. Vin had done what he'd said. That's as much as he could ask for right now. "Okay, sorry about your nose," Jackson said. "But don't ever lie to me again. And I'm never going back to China."

"Fair enough." Vin clapped him on the shoulder. "Let's go hunting."

49

LILY EARNED HER FIRST BitStone as a teenager. After months of begging, her parents had finally given her a BitStones game as a birthday gift. They'd told her the game was very popular in China, and that it could be a good way to spend time with family there. Maybe even earn a little money on the side. Her father—a classic, hardworking immigrant to America—was always in favor of that.

Starting out, Lily had made and abandoned many different characters. She'd had online romances. She'd fought battles. And she'd mined enough BitStones to pay for college. Then, when she was a senior in high school, her parents had cut her off. They said she was spending too much time on games, and not enough on her cello practice or her track team. Not even the Stones were worth it, they said, because a life lived in front of a screen was no life at all. So she'd given it up…mostly. A little playing here and there, earning a bit to cover rent and a meal, didn't hurt anyone. Besides, it was becoming acceptable in professional circles. She'd even played the hottest new game, Camelot, with Hina Himura. It felt like forever ago.

Now, locked in her apartment as some sort of permanent curfew against the risk of someone kidnapping or assassinating her, and with no sign of another visit from Jackson, she decided to visit Camelot again. She'd take any escape she could get.

When she logged in she ignored a queue of messages—mostly spam, she figured—and started trying to track down any real-world clues about what was going on in China. It was no secret that international criminals, whether government-sponsored or not, favored BitStones to finance their work. The criminals took just as much care in Camelot as they did in the real world to avoid getting caught, but Lily had an advantage. Her old character had risen to the level of baroness in the Red Silk Guild. The position was the equivalent of a mid-level manager, so it afforded access to interesting information.

After six straight hours of digging and asking innocent questions, she learned that a large band of Red Silk Guild members had been working together in a single, highly-classified mine for many weeks now. The orders for this project came from the highest level of the guild, which Lily knew was the highest level of the Chinese government. The band of workers expected their work to be finished very soon, maybe even in a day or two. Last but not least, she saw a notice on the guild's public board, posted by a guild member named Archer: *Bounty of 50,000 BitStones for any information relating to an American named Jackson Crow.*

Lily sat back in shock. She pulled off her headset, her mind racing.

Was this about the treaty? Or Hina? Or her? It was a huge sum of money. Jackson was in serious danger.

She stood and stretched as she thought it over, then she went to the kitchen for a snack. She might be trapped in her apartment, but she had to do something.

Her hands shook as she pulled the headset back on. She posted a response on the guild's public board: HAVE INFORMATION ON CROW. SEEKING ARCHER.

She guided her character to a dense forest that the guild controlled in Camelot—a place where a conversation could be private. She figured the worst that could happen was Archer or someone else would track her down and kill her avatar and take her BitStones, which after paying for law school and this apartment amounted to a few nice meals.

She didn't have to wait long.

Archer rode up on a black horse and dismounted with a flourish. He looked like what she'd expected from the name—black cloak with the hood up, black boots, and a long bow strapped across his back. It was almost haunting in the shadowy woods.

"What can you tell me?" he asked.

"How do I know you'll pay?" she asked Archer. Lily didn't take particular pride in this, but she'd made her elven character quite beautiful. Like a Disney princess, she wore a long blue gown and had flaxen blonde hair and blue eyes. She'd named the character Sunbolt.

Archer pulled an arrow, notched it, and drew, pointing right at Sunbolt's face. So much for appearances disarming him. "Tell me now."

She picked an innocuous, public fact. "He's a lawyer at the State Department."

Archer didn't flinch. "What else?"

"Why do you want to know?"

"Do you want the bounty, or do you want to die?"

She did something you could only do in a game like this. She stepped forward, around the notched arrow, and kissed the man. For a split second he started to kiss back, but then shuffled away.

She batted her eyes, playing to his ego. Every gamer had one. "Sorry, I have a crush on you, or your character, well maybe both."

"Who are you?" he asked.

"I'll tell you my name if you tell me yours."

"Patrick."

"Nice to meet you, Patrick. I'm—"

Before she could answer, Archer snapped around, grabbing at his side.

"Hey!" he shouted, as a small figure ran off. A thief, probably a gnome. They were rampant in forests like this.

As Archer drew his bow, another figure darted past Lily and leapt towards Archer, sword raised high. Lily saw the name Raven hovering above the character. Archer drew two daggers and started to fight back. Lily hunkered behind a tree to watch.

Archer and Raven were an even match—probably with the best gear BitStones could buy. Neither managed to make a dent in the other, but when the little gnome rejoined the fight, Archer had no choice but to run. At his level he could probably kill fifty average characters, but these two were not average.

Raven and the gnome did not pursue Archer. They came straight toward her. She stepped out from behind the tree with

Sunbolt's hands held up innocently. It was no use trying to hide.

The tall one, an elf, with long black hair pulled back into a ponytail, stopped in front of her, but kept his eyes on the surrounding trees. "What do you know about Jackson Crow?" he asked.

"He's a lawyer at the State Department," she said. "I was about to get my bounty until you showed up."

"We've gotta go," the gnome said. "He'll be back, with forces."

"She knows something," the elf said intensely. It was only a game, but she could have sworn she recognized the intonation of his voice.

"I got what we needed," the gnome said quickly. "Let's go. Now!"

"Fine. Thanks, Sunbolt." Raven ran off after the elf. As the two of them disappeared, a BitStone transferred to Lily's character, the equivalent of pressing a hundred dollar bill in her hand. Then she was alone in the digital forest.

50

It was Sunday afternoon when General Li received the report about the explosion in the tunnel underneath Beijing. He had called his entire staff into the office. They were on the cusp of action. He needed every resource available.

He'd sent a crew to dig out the bodies, but he had a feeling neither Wong Chan nor Jackson Crow would be there. It didn't matter. Zhang would be capturing the American girl any moment now. Even Zhang could handle that. General Li's reports assured him this kidnapping would lure Jackson Crow so that both American lawyers could both be brought to Beijing for questioning. General Li doubted they knew about his true plans, but it was better to be certain.

Either way, Donghai had his fleet in position. The final pieces would be in place tomorrow. They would take the Diaoyu Islands. The Americans would put up a show of force, sending a few ships and jets, but as they had agreed President Wallace would stand down from a fight. No one would be hurt.

Then General Li would make his real move. With the Americans backpedalling and their eyes on the Diaoyu, half a million Chinese soldiers would march. It would be too late for the Americans to try to stop them, if the U.S. military even could without the threat of nuclear attack. This American President would not resort to that, not with an election coming.

And so Taiwan's softened people would come back into China's hands. General Li, overnight and without a fight, would add 25 million people and $500 billion in GDP to their country. It would be the first domino to fall.

51

IT WASN'T EVERY DAY you almost got killed in Beijing and made it back to Washington in time for dinner. On the flight back Jackson and Vin had stolen another piece of the puzzle from Archer. Now if only Jackson could find Archer in the real world, he could stop him before Lily got hurt. He was going to start with Reagan. Jackson suspected she knew more than she'd told him after someone had hacked her Camelot account. Maybe she had the missing piece that would make the puzzle come together. He had to identify the enemy before he could fight back.

The jet landed at a small airport an hour west of Washington. Jackson texted Reagan as soon as they touched down, and she agreed to meet him anywhere private. He told her to show up at the waterfront in Georgetown at 7 pm.

"Good luck," Vin said as Jackson left.

"Sure you don't want to come?" Jackson asked.

"Nah, DC's never my speed." Vin patted his leather seat fondly. "Besides, much better to do some digging from the comfort of home. Just let me know if there's trouble."

Jackson arrived in Georgetown ten minutes early. He found Reagan already there, waiting on a bench overlooking a gorgeous spring sunset. They exchanged hellos and strolled along the boardwalk lining the Potomac River.

When they reached the boathouse, Reagan protested. "You are *not* taking me out on the Potomac."

He smiled. "Surprise."

"I can't. I mean, it's lovely, but if you want to talk, we can do that on land."

"Come on, it's a perfect evening. This requires privacy." Jackson pointed to a kayak bobbing up and down, tied to the boardwalk. "I'll help you climb in."

"Where'd you get this?" she asked.

"Doesn't matter. Please?"

"Fifteen minutes, max."

"Okay," Jackson agreed. He held Reagan's hand as she stepped down into the kayak. Then he stepped in behind her. "Your purse and phone?"

"What about them?"

"Give them to me."

"Why?" She eyed him, and Jackson tried to answer with his expression—eyes tense, finger to his lips. Reagan took a deep breath and then handed them over.

Jackson put his own phone in her slim purse, then he took off his shoes. He dropped them all in a bag that was sitting in the kayak and tied the bag to the underside of the dock, out of sight to anyone passing by. He shoved off into the water.

"Let's enjoy the river in quiet until we get out a ways," he said, picking up the paddle.

Reagan nodded, clearly nervous now. Her back was straight as a rod as Jackson dipped the paddle into the glistening black water and pulled. Left side, pull. Right side, pull.

They were in the middle of the river, far from everything and everyone, when Jackson finally spoke. "Okay," he said, "We need to talk."

She had a trace of fear in her eyes. "Is this some kind of game?"

"No, but I do want to ask you about a game. Have you ever played Camelot?"

Her face registered surprise, but she nodded. "A little. Why?"

"What's your character's name?"

"Archer."

"When did you last log in?"

"Last night." She must have seen the concern in Jackson's face, because she quickly added, "I hadn't touched the game in a long time. I just wanted a little escape, but the game had a weird glitch or something."

"What kind of glitch?"

"When I logged in, my character had over fifty thousand

BitStones. That's more than *five million dollars*. But I'd never had more than a few BitStones. They're for hardcore players, you know. Anyway, I reported it to the game's authorities and to the digital specialists in my office. Then I logged out and read a book instead."

Jackson breathed easier. His instincts were right. She wasn't the current Archer. "Someone hacked your account," he said. "It can't be a coincidence. Any idea why the Chinese might be targeting you?"

"Obvious, right? I'm the Deputy National Security Adviser. I guess they tracked my home IP address."

She sounded too innocent. She still wasn't telling him something. He didn't want to reveal what they'd learned from Archer…yet. He wanted to give her a chance to tell the truth. He might learn more that way.

"Reagan, I need you to be completely honest with me. Two days ago your boss hauled me into the Oval Office to take a photograph from me. That same night I was ambushed and shot before I went to the gala."

"You were *shot*? But you seemed fine…"

"I was lucky, it only graze me. Then I flew to Beijing and almost got killed again. While there I learned that Ambassador Blair paid to have the Japanese lawyer killed, and it turns out she was a double agent who'd slept with the Japanese ambassador and maybe Blair, too. You're the one who ordered Blair to change the term in the treaty. You're the one who knows what the President knows. You're the one who's supposed to be preventing a war. Help me connect the dots…please."

Reagan's mouth formed a tight line, lit dimly by the moon beginning to reflect off the water. After a few moments, she asked quietly, "I saw the photo. It could be a coincidence that Blair was looking towards the killer."

"I doubt it. The victim was looking at the killer, too. Lily told me Hina had gone out to dinner with Blair. There was something between them."

"So what?" Reagan asked. "Everyone knows about Blair. His

philandering is the worst kept secret in Washington."

"The President claims Blair had nothing to do with it. But if that's true, why did the President want the picture so badly? You saw it. There was fear in Blair's and Hina's eyes. He wouldn't have been afraid if he was in control...if he *alone* had paid the killer. Just imagine what your mom would say if she saw an expression like that." Jackson did his best impersonation of an Irish accent. "*Get thee to a confessional booth, or face ye the wrath of God.*"

Reagan smiled, but not for long. "So what about Hina? Why would she be afraid?"

"She and Lily wrote most of the treaty. You heard Director Strassitch. The Chinese were paying Hina to sleep with ambassadors and report any sensitive information she found."

"So why would the Chinese want her dead?"

Jackson did not answer. He leaned closer to Reagan. He knew her. She couldn't lie straight to his face. He had stolen the information from Archer, in Camelot. Her reaction to this would tell him everything.

"You should know," he said softly. "Code? Whale. Code? And then...silence..."

Reagan sat back and crossed her hands in her lap. She stared out of the boat at the water.

Jackson guessed at her thoughts. She must feel guilt. She had been talking to the enemy, and she'd hidden that from Jackson.

"I didn't lie to you about this, Jackson," she said, turning to him. "You knew about the changed treaty term and the reason for it. I knew the Chinese wanted a distraction. But I swear, I had no idea they were going to kill anyone."

Jackson studied her green eyes. They were magical, emerald eyes, capable of hiding universes. "What are you keeping from me?" he asked.

She looked away again, studying the water, where light from monuments glistened over the slight ripples. "I have a contact."

"With the Chinese?"

She nodded. "He knew about the shooting. After it happened,

I asked him why, and he said it was to sow chaos. I also learned…"

"What, Reagan? Tell me."

"He's going to take Lily."

Jackson forced himself to stay calm. It would not help to blow up in anger. "Take her where?"

Reagan met his glare. "It's not what you think. I've been assured that she will be kept safe. We are going to bring her back very soon."

"Did you order a *kidnapping*?" Jackson shook his head in disbelief. "This is treason."

"No, this is politics," Reagan snapped. "I'm just doing my job. The President needs a way to stop a war and save face. The Chinese are going to return Lily as soon as we agree not to interfere with their exercises in the East China Sea."

"*What!*" Jackson failed to keep his voice down. "This really is treason."

"No, Jackson. You know we cannot hold the Chinese back forever. They are too strong now. We have to give them discretion in their hemisphere, and we can keep our own hemisphere without a world war breaking out."

Jackson's mind was racing. He started rowing toward the shore. He had to help Lily. "When is this going to happen?"

"I don't know. Truly. Soon, I think."

"You put an innocent woman's life at risk."

"She'll be safe. They promised."

"*Who* promised?"

"I can't say."

Jackson swung his oar out of the water, furious, and held it to Reagan's throat. "Tell me now."

She did not flinch. "You won't hurt me."

"No, but you have to tell me, if you ever want a chance of my trust again."

"I never lied to you, Jackson."

"Lied…withheld facts…at some point there's no difference. Who's your contact?"

She bit her lip, then breathed out heavily, as if giving up. "You met him. At the gala. Patrick Li. He's the son of one of their most powerful generals, a successor to the presidency if our intelligence is correct."

"Thank you," Jackson said through gritted teeth.

The puzzle snapped together in his mind. On the flight back to Washington, he and Vin had stolen a BitStone from Archer. They'd tracked it back to a bar in DC where a man had paid with a fraction of the same Stone and signed the electronic receipt with the name *Patrick Li*. It wasn't hard from there to find that "Patrick" was actually Zhang Li. And so this Chinese agent who had been communicating with Reagan was the same guy who had taken the cash from Ambassador Blair, via Mr. Chan, and paid the old assassin who shot Hina Himura and himself in the Treaty Room. Then he'd tried to kill Jackson and showed up at the gala, right under Jackson's nose, with a white tux and a busted lip. And now he was going to kidnap Lily.

Jackson needed to tell Reagan, but not all of it. He didn't trust her enough for that. "He's been lying to you, Reagan."

"What do you mean?"

"Patrick has been using your hacked account in Camelot. He is Archer. He paid for the assassination in the Treaty Room. He tried to kill me."

"You have evidence?"

"Yes." Jackson couldn't say the rest without giving away Vin. "By the way," he said, "I think there's more to all this. I think Blair still knows something he hasn't told us. He is deeply compromised by his situation in China, whether or not he slept with Hina. The President knows it, but Blair is not even telling him everything. Why else would the President summon me just to take my copy of the picture that the assassin took?"

"I'm not sure," Reagan said. "I'll look into Blair's role, if any."

"Good." Jackson rowed harder toward shore. He couldn't waste more time before going to Lily. "Tell your friends at the CIA if you find something. I might run away for a while."

"What are you talking about?"

"I know they've been following me. They even helped save my hide in Tokyo, but I need to go off the map until this passes." Jackson grunted as he pulled the oar again. "The Chinese could be plotting something huge. We're completely blind to it."

"We have the Senkaku Islands under control," Reagan said. "This is not another debate. The Chinese will take them—in 24 hours if all goes according to plan—but that's the end of it. You can trust the President. You can trust me."

Jackson shook his head. *24 hours. A lot can change in 24 hours.* "The islands are a distraction. I'm sure of it."

"A distraction for what?"

"I'm not sure…" Jackson thought of the cables that he'd reviewed back at the Embassy in Tokyo, and of Blair's investments in Chinese construction companies. "There are reports of Chinese soldiers traveling in huge numbers to southeast China and then going off the map. I think Blair knows something. The Chinese have him under their thumb."

"How? Blair is loyal to the President."

"Loyalty only goes so far." The boat bumped against the dock. Jackson grabbed the wood tightly, before fixing a final stare on Reagan. "Tell your boss that if he doesn't shake down his old hunting pal, he's going to find a disaster on his hands. Tell him in language he can understand: either he trusts Blair, or he wins the reelection. He can't have both."

52

ON A SUNDAY EVENING like this, Zhang Li found the streets of Washington eerily quiet. The trees on 21st street rustled gently in the wind as a few people walked their dogs under pale yellow lights. Near his home in Beijing there would be hundreds shopping and talking under flashing neon. This made a difference when kidnapping someone. You could get away with it easier in Beijing. In Washington you had to silence the person quickly.

Zhang knew the easiest way to silence was a bullet to the head, but that was no good if the person needed to be alive. Chemicals were the second best option—either gas or an injection of the right stuff could knock a person out before they even knew what hit them. But Zhang's favorite method was old school. With enough secrecy and speed, nothing beat duct tape over the mouth.

No one suspected a delivery guy with a roll of tape at his waist, even on a Sunday, with companies now bending over backwards to make their same-day and next-day shipments to the ends of the globe. Not that Zhang expected much resistance, but he had been warned that there would be at least one Secret Service agent who would, to maintain authenticity, have no clue that Zhang planned to kidnap Lily. The agent might even try to fight, if Zhang let it come to that, but his instructions were to let the guy live, so he'd have to stop the fight before it started.

He spotted the agent the moment he drove up to the boring brick apartment building in his properly labeled delivery van. He parked in the reserved loading zone and put on the blinkers. He walked across the street and halfway up the block to the agent, who was sitting behind the wheel of a black SUV. The tinting on the driver's window was impenetrably dark, but Zhang had seen him through the windshield driving past.

Zhang tapped the driver's window. Nothing happened.

Zhang kept tapping, and harder.

Finally the guy lowered the window an inch, shook his head, and tried to wave him off.

"Hey!" Zhang insisted, tapping harder. "Hey, I need help. Help."

"Get lost," the agent grunted.

"Yes, yes, I lost," Zhang said, unleashing a thick Chinese accent. "I have package to deliver. You know 2000 F Street?"

The guy shook his head. He was smart. He didn't lower the window any further.

"But I lost!" Zhang said. "2000 F Street?"

"That way." The guy pointed ahead, down the street.

Zhang leaned closer to the window as if trying to follow where the guard was pointing. "How far?"

"You'll see it."

"But my map—" Zhang reached to his waist, pulled the tranquilizer gun, and shot a dart through the one-inch opening of the window. It was a direct hit to the agent's neck. The agent's eyes went wide before his head fell to the side, unconscious. He'd be out for an hour and would wake up in fine shape, except for the career setback. The person he was guarding would be gone.

Zhang hurried to his van and grabbed a standard, book-sized mailing box with the words "URGENT DELIVERY" written in large letters on the top. He carried the box to the apartment entrance and rang for Lily Sun, unit 401.

He knew she'd see him through the camera, with his delivery uniform, hat, and box. He also figured she wasn't expecting anything to arrive at 7:30 pm.

Her voice came through the intercom. "Can I help you?"

"I have urgent delivery," he said, accent intact. "Sender says it is from a Mr. Blair."

"Blair?" she said. "Okay, you can leave it at the door."

"Sorry, I need signature. It says urgent."

She didn't answer for a moment. "Wait there," she said loudly, probably because she suspected that her apartment was tapped and monitored by the agent on the street, who at the moment would not be listening. "I will come down and sign for it."

"Good," Zhang said. "I wait here."

He kept his head down while he thought. He had expected her to ring the buzzer and let him come inside, where it would have been much cleaner and easier to tape her mouth, tie her up, and put her in a large box to haul back down to the van. Now the building's entrance camera would be watching. Someone could be entering or leaving at the same time. Lots of unpredictables.

Zhang would just have to be fast. He waited a couple moments to be sure that Lily had left her apartment and would no longer be looking at the video. Then he rushed back to the van and grabbed a big box full of styrofoam peanuts, the kind that spill all over the place but that cushion a body quite well. Sometimes spies had to deal with messes like styrofoam peanuts.

He acted like the box weighed a ton as he lowered it onto a pull cart. The words "FRAGILE," "BREAKABLE," and "WASHING MACHINE" were printed all over the cardboard. He rolled the box to the apartment entrance and left it sitting—with no tape sealing it at the top—to the side of the glass doors. He yanked off a half foot of duct tape, which he cupped in his hand, hidden underneath the smaller, urgent-delivery box by his side. He stood in the exact same place he'd been when Lily had seen him. She might notice the washing-machine box, but she wouldn't necessarily assume it was his or, more accurately, hers.

She walked into the lobby a minute later, moving gracefully to the door. This was the first time Zhang had seen her in person. She wore skinny jeans, a black t-shirt, and no makeup. She was even prettier than the pictures.

It was a shame, Zhang thought. Another fine Chinese woman ruined by the Americans. Even as his country surpassed the United States by every important metric—population, GDP, math, science, culture—the Americans kept stealing his own people's best. He would steal her away from her cozy Washington apartment because that was his part in making the world—and certainly his own people—realize that China, not America, was the future. The next generation would have girls like this in Beijing, where they belonged, and not in this languid swamp.

When Lily reached the door, Zhang waved and smiled at her, mostly because that's what a good delivery guy would do. She glanced past him toward where the black SUV and the knocked-out agent, hidden behind a tinted window, sat on the street.

Then she pushed open the door.

Zhang held up the urgent-delivery box. The instant she took it in her hands, he jabbed a tranquilizing dart into her thigh.

She crunched forward in shock. He slapped the tape over her lips before grabbing her in his arms. In one smooth motion, he tied her wrists and ankles together behind her back, stepped to the washing-machine box, and lifted her gently up and over and down into the feathery bed of peanuts. He drew his tape and sealed the box closed for good measure before rolling it to the back of the van. The fragile contents were secure.

53

KATHY HAD JUST put a huge spoonful of macaroni and cheese in her mouth when her agency phone rang. She glanced at the clock on her microwave. The blue lights showed 8:12 pm. For a Sunday night, that meant it was either an emergency in Washington or a standard Monday morning report from Asia. Both were important enough to her that she opted for spitting out the mac-n-cheese. It was a benefit of living alone. No one would ever know.

She picked up the phone. "Hello?"

"You're not going to believe this." Grant sounded excited. "Our asset was just kidnapped."

So it was an emergency in Washington. "Status?"

"She's alive, I think. In transport."

"Are you at the office?"

"Yes."

"Good," Kathy said. "I'm coming now. Give me a second, but stay on the line."

Kathy left her bowl and stood from the kitchen table. Her bare feet clapped against the linoleum floor as she rushed to the door, stepped into her shoes, and grabbed her bag and coat. There was a reason she never took off her suit until she laid down to sleep. In twenty seconds flat she was driving her Honda Accord away from her little brick rancher.

As she pressed the phone to her ear again, she reminded herself that Grant had been shaken up after botching things in Hong Kong. Kathy couldn't blame him. Jackson was not a normal target. Still, she wanted to be gentle with her young partner until he got his swagger back. "You there?"

"Yeah."

"I'll be there in nine minutes. Talk me through what happened."

"I kept our tap on Lily's apartment like you said."

"Good."

"And seven minutes ago some delivery guy rang her unit. She sounded surprised, but said she was going down to sign for whatever he was delivering."

Kathy shook her head. People needed to learn to never trust the delivery guy, especially at night. "Did Secret Service pick it up?"

"They didn't make a peep. An agent was supposed to be watching, but they were MIA. I just tapped into the building's security cam. It showed everything. She never had a chance. The delivery guy was good. He had tape and a box ready. She was inside it before she could make a sound."

"You get a look at the guy?"

"Not much. He had a hat pulled down. But from the audio, he's Chinese. I'm running the comps now to see if we have his voice anywhere else."

"And the transport?"

"Standard delivery van. Couldn't see the plates, but we don't have to worry about that."

"Why not?"

"Remember what I said about drones?"

Kathy could hear the smile, and the swagger, in his voice. She wasn't going to backtrack on what she'd said. Agents still beat drones, but this could help…a lot. "I remember. A spy's best friend, you said."

"Exactly. It's cruising two hundred feet above them while they ride up I-95. I set the autopilot to track them. We have full visual."

"Bring it all with you and meet me outside. We're going after them." Kathy hung up, her stomach rumbling like a washing machine. She dialed the Director to give him the report. She looked forward to another imaginary medal of honor. Some compensation for leaving behind her mac-n-cheese.

54

JACKSON LEAPT OUT the kayak at the shore of the Potomac River. He retrieved his phone and called Lily, but got no answer. Reagan caught up and assured him that Lily should be at her place, under watch.

"Maybe she's just asleep," Reagan said.

It was just after 8 o'clock. She wasn't asleep.

Jackson didn't hesitate. Her apartment was only a mile or so away in Foggy Bottom. He sprinted off and was breathing heavily when he arrived at the door to the building. He used the call box. Still no answer.

He studied the area around the entrance and saw no sign of a struggle. Everything was tranquil. There were only a couple styrofoam peanuts on the ground.

He called her cell phone. No answer.

He sent a text and called again.

He felt his stomach sink. She would have answered, especially for him. He was too late.

He sat on the stoop and stared down at his phone, thinking. Maybe Vin could help. He texted him, *My colleague is gone. Can you help?*

Vin answered. *I found some things. Log in.*

He texted back, *I'll be on in 15.*

Same place.

K.

Jackson hailed an Uber and rode the short distance to his last secure apartment in northwest DC. He would need to find a new backup. But this one had what he needed for now: a computer and a headset.

In moments, headset lowered, he found himself in Camelot, at the Jules Inn.

Vin was waiting, again sitting with a group of others. His gnome avatar came to Jackson. "Great to see you again. We have important work to do." His little arms motioned to the table where he'd been sitting. "Some of these fine people are thinking about joining the guild. A few of them saw you last time you were here. I told them they could duel you if you came back."

"Are they good enough?" Jackson played along. He guessed where Vin was going with this. He must have wanted Jackson to take one of these players' stones. Vin had said dueling was the only way to avoid inspection by the Chinese agents.

"Now's your chance," Vin announced to the group. "Who wants to duel the one and only Raven?"

A red-headed woman stood. "Me. Let's do it."

She was a human knight named Sion. She had thick shoulders, full plate armor, and the hilt of a huge sword behind her head. If not for Vin's plotting, Jackson would have guessed she was controlled by a fifty-year-old man living in a Midwest trailer park, maybe on his sixth beer. Just enough to be bold in Camelot.

"Come outside," Vin said, turning away from the door. Jackson followed him to the town square without looking back. He drew his sword as the red-headed knight and a crowd of others approached. Over half of them bore the black sash of the Raven's March guild.

"Game time!" Vin announced, hopping up onto the edge of the fountain. A gnome needed height, but Vin didn't need any help with his voice, which came through with the same loud and raspy sound as in real life. "You know the rules. It's an official one-minute duel to death. Winner takes all stones. But if you survive, you get to join Raven's March. All members collect equal share of our loot, and pay a modest fee of 10 stones per month into the bank. Turst me, it's worth it. Last month we paid out 24 stones per member."

"I'm ready," the red-headed knight said, drawing her huge sword and holding it with two hands.

"Fight's on!" Vin shouted.

The knight charged. Raven spun away from the first attack, but it was closer than he'd expected. Vin had made Raven's character very strong, but Jackson was rusty.

The knight turned and came again. Their swords clanged and sent sparks flying. They stayed locked together, eyes meeting, as the seconds ticked away. The crowd was chanting. *Raven! Raven! Raven!*

But he was unnerved. The knight was staring hard at him. He recognized the eyes.

It was not a woman. It was Mr. Chan.

The knight shoved him back and swung again. Apparently they needed to keep up appearances. Jackson ducked and landed a hit to the knight's side.

"10!" Vin shouted.

"9!" The crowd joined in. "8!"

On "4!" Jackson decided to go on attack. If Vin wanted him to take Mr. Chan's stones, and make it look real, he would. He brought Raven's sword down hard at the knight, who staggered back. He leapt up in the air and swung, with every ounce of digital power, at the knight's neck.

"1!"

The sword cut clean through the metal and the flesh and bone, like a samurai's blade through bamboo, and the knight fell to her knees, head rolling.

"Victory!" Vin announced, then shrugged. "By 3 milliseconds. The system doesn't lie."

Jackson looked around at the group watching. He had to keep up appearances, so he made Raven raise arms, holding the sword victoriously overhead for the crowd.

As the crowd dispersed, Vin and Jackson went back to Jules Inn and the vault room on the second floor. Vin sat in the same chair at the table.

"That was Mr. Chan," Jackson said.

"Yes." Vin's gnome was smiling. "He's in Taiwan, safe for now. He found something he wanted you to see. As you can imagine, he's under the closest surveillance right now. You wouldn't believe the complex chain of games and characters he used to get you this information."

"Just so I could get the BitStones?"

"Untraceably, yes. The Chinese government has no clue what we know," Vin said. "Have a look."

Jackson studied the trail from Mr. Chan's BitStones, which had appeared in Raven's inventory immediately after the duel. The Stones had been mined originally by the Red Silk Guild, controlled by the Chinese military. Next they went to a series of rogue gamers, with multiple transfers into U.S. dollars and back, before reaching the red-headed knight named Sion. As Jackson reviewed the details for each Stone, he learned that they were the same 1,000 stones paid to him at the Mandarin Oriental in Tokyo in exchange for destroying the picture. He had then transferred these Stones to Vin.

"These were my stones," Jackson said.

"Yep. I gave them to Mr. Chan, who transferred them to one of his hackers on the inside. They work in the tunnels under Beijing. But keep going. You're almost to the interesting part."

Jackson followed the trail from Mr. Chan to the hacker, who had sent them to the familiar account of Archer. Reagan had identified him as Zhang. Just two hours ago, Archer had converted the stones to dollars at an address in New York City. But again, Mr. Chan had been the one to manage the conversion, receive the Stones, and now get them back to Jackson. Amazing how much bankers could know, regardless of the currency.

The pieces were not hard to put together. The Chinese military had mined these BitStones specifically for surveillance. They had paid the Stones to Jackson not just because they cared about the picture, but because they wanted to track him. Now Vin and Mr. Chan were using that same tracking against them, without them knowing it.

"What's the address in New York?" Jackson asked.

"It's the Waldorf Astoria on Park Avenue," Vin said. "Guess who owns it?"

Jackson didn't have to guess. "The Chinese government."

"Precisely. We don't have any access to video footage inside, but look what I found."

Vin showed Jackson a server full of files, accessible through the game, and he opened a video. The streaming footage seemed to be from a security camera. Jackson recognized it instantly—Lily's apartment, where he'd been just minutes earlier.

"This is 2000 F St., Washington, DC," Vin said, as the video played.

A delivery guy came to the door of the building and set down a huge box. Lily came to the entrance. It took only an instant for Jackson to see what was coming. Lily opened the door and the guy took her out with a tranquilizer. He loaded her in the box and carted her away.

"Tell me you tracked the van," Jackson said, looking to Vin's character.

He nodded.

"And now, with Mr. Chan's help, you know he took Lily to the Waldorf. You should have been a spy."

Vin's eyes lit up like gold in the gnome's face. "For you, Crow. Only for you."

"Thanks, Vin. This is excellent work. One more thing…" Jackson knew it was asking a lot, but… "Could I use the jet?"

"Sure, though it could take a couple hours to get a fresh pilot."

Jackson didn't have a couple hours. "I'll find another way. But I might need help getting back. Maybe arrange for a pickup in New York?"

"You got it. I'll have a helicopter ready."

55

WHEN HER PHONE RANG late at night, Reagan usually expected it to be the President. This time it was the individual who knew more about the world's dirty laundry than anyone on the planet: the Director of the CIA. The President had other things to keep him busy, like politics and elections. The Secretary of Defense had a massive bureaucracy of soldiers and contractors to manage. But the CIA Director spent his days with a finger on the pulse of the information that mattered most to national security.

That's why Reagan, phone to her ear and pacing at midnight in her White House office, was worried even before she heard the words from the Director. She'd been worried sick ever since getting out of the boat with Jackson.

The Director didn't even say hello before reporting, "Lily Sun has been kidnapped."

"What? How?" This was not good. Jackson would be even more furious. Reagan needed to feign complete surprise. "We had an agent guarding her."

"The agent was injected with something. The kidnapper posed as a delivery man. I have credible information that he has taken her to the Waldorf in New York."

The Waldorf? Damn. Her Chinese contact had assured her he could keep the location secret. Going to the Waldorf—which everyone knew the Chinese government owned—was like setting up a homing beacon. "I will inform the President."

"Two of my agents will be arriving at the Waldorf soon."

Reagan did not want them getting in the way of this, but the Director was a highly insightful man. She chose her words carefully. "Good. I will talk with the President about next steps. As you can imagine, this would be very sensitive if it were to get out."

"*When* it gets out."

"We'll see," Reagan said. "We have a contact in their

government. We may be able to work this out without a conflict, and without anyone getting hurt."

When the Director didn't respond, she worried that she might not have sounded concerned enough. She added, "Why do you think they kidnapped her, instead of…worse?"

"I'm not sure. We've received no message from our counterparts. We'll dig further."

"Not yet," Reagan said. "The President will want to clear anything. It's all very sensitive with China right now."

"Understood." But the Director didn't sound happy about it.

"Talk soon."

She had bought some time, but not much. It was time to wake up the President.

56

ZHANG COULD THINK of no place he'd rather unbox Lily Sun than the Waldorf Astoria on Park Avenue. He loved its tall grey lines and imposing shape, the art deco entrance with gilded gold, and the sparkling, luxurious interior. Above all, he loved that his people owned it.

The acquisition had not been difficult. A major Chinese company had purchased the historic property several years ago, and when that company ran into some financial difficulty (which can be readily produced when needed), a state-owned entity had taken control. They ran the hotel with the highest standards, of course. Most guests noticed only improvements when they had the pleasure of staying at the Waldorf. Several upper floors had been converted to condos, mostly owned by Chinese elite. And on floor 42.5, the more-or-less permanent guests had all the privacy and security that was required for running intelligence in America's beating financial heart.

This time, unfortunately, Zhang could not stroll into the Waldorf's main entrance. He drove his van into the delivery entrance at the back of the hotel and unloaded the washing-machine box onto a rolling cart. The box's contents began to struggle and shake. The low murmur confirmed that the duct tape was still doing its job.

He took the box to a service elevator that could reach the secure floor. He passed the retina scan to operate the elevator and rode up. Stepping out on floor 42.5, he rolled the box to room F. He nodded to the guard who stood before the door. They would keep an eye on things from the room across the hall.

Room F was a corner suite with a fine view of the city's evening lights down Park Avenue. He sat on the bed and watched the box rocking. He had enjoyed seeing the box's contents. He could understand why she would appeal to Jackson Crow. Zhang still couldn't believe the man had saved her back in Tokyo and survived his own attack before the gala in Washington. His father had been extremely disappointed. *You have failed me again,* he'd said. *Do not do so again.*

This time Zhang would not fail. He had taken the girl and left breadcrumbs for Crow to follow. Now he was finally on safe territory. If anything went wrong at the Waldorf, the Chinese management could shut down the exits and secure the building's premises. But things would not go wrong. Crow would come, and Zhang would handle him personally. He wasn't petty. It wasn't just revenge he wanted. Anything or anyone that got in the way of his father's will had to be eliminated.

Zhang didn't have to ask the girl any questions or try to get information from her. But if he did, that would certainly make his father pleased. It might even make up for failing the first time. The challenge would be conducting the interrogation without hurting her. His orders were to keep her without a scratch. To have any chance, he needed to avoid her recognizing him as the one who had kidnapped her. She'd only gotten a brief glimpse of him, without much light, so a mild disguise should work. He needed to change clothes.

He opened the hotel room door and closed it, loudly, as a delivery man would do after dropping off a package. Then he moved silently to the bathroom with the large walk-in closet. He picked out a nice, navy suit. Nothing too flashy, but properly tailored and stylish, with a red silk tie.

After he changed into the suit and combed his hair in front of the bathroom mirror, he put on a pair of black-rimmed glasses—rounded to give him an intelligent look—and then went back into the main room, where the box was sitting still.

He opened the room's front door as if entering for the first time. He motioned across the hall to the guards he knew were stationed in the opposite room. One of them hurried out. "Lock it," Zhang whispered. Then he closed the door and locked the deadbolt and the chain. Moments later he heard another deadbolt lock from the outside.

"Hello?" he called into the room. "Is anyone here?"

The box suddenly shook, then rocked back and forth.

"Oh dear, let me help you."

The box rocked again, this time so far that it tipped over on its side, followed by a grunting sound.

"I'm very sorry," Zhang said. "If you will be still, I will help you out immediately."

The tipped-over box went still. Zhang knelt beside it and slid a small knife along the tape holding it closed. Hundreds of styrofoam peanuts, and Lily, spilled out. Her wrists and ankles had dried blood and fresh bleeding from her attempts to get loose.

"Oh my. This is terrible." Zhang pocketed the knife and met the girl's eyes. She was stunning. Her black t-shirt fit tight and was wet with sweat. The ferocity of her stare only made her more attractive. He forced himself to focus on the task at hand. He spoke clearly and crisply, like a kind professor. "You were *not* supposed to be hurt in any way. I will cut you loose now and remove the tape. Then we can see about those wounds and getting you some food. But please, when I remove the tape, will you promise not to scream?"

She glared at him, but after a few heavy breaths through her nose, she nodded.

"Good, very good." He pinched a corner of the tape covering her mouth. "It will sting, but not so bad if it's fast."

Then he yanked.

She sucked in a big gulp of air through her mouth, then screamed bloody murder, the sound making Zhang stagger back and the room vibrate. She screamed again, and again. It even started to take on words like "HELP" and "I'M TRAPPED" and "GET ME OUT OF HERE!"

Zhang waited quietly for her to stop. None of it mattered. All the rooms on floor 42.5 were completely soundproofed, for occasions such as this. There were no cameras or microphones, either. Some tasks required discretion.

She eventually ran out of steam. Her eyes fell on Zhang, and her expression told him that she realized the screaming was pointless. He was slightly disappointed that it had taken her so long to figure it out. Even the smartest people could become unreasonable under pressure.

"Would you like me to cut your bindings now?" he asked, gently.

"Yes," she growled.

He did not ask her not to fight. He knew that she would. The best he could do was try not to get aroused while he knelt over her with the exhilarating expectation of a wrestling match. He would not resort to base acts. No, he represented his people to her, and his people were better than that. They were not like the Japanese or Yankee soldiers who raped and pillaged their conquests. They were not like their ambassadors who gave up secrets to bed Hina Himura.

He sliced the three cords in quick order—ankles, ankles to wrists, and wrists. To the girl's credit, she did not come at him immediately. Instead she bent forward, then side to side, stretching her body's tight muscles after hours of being bound up.

Then she slowly stood and gazed out the window. Tall, lit-up buildings stretched across the brilliant Manhattan skyline. Even at this late hour, near midnight, dozens of yellow cabs and pedestrians moved up and down Park Avenue. The pace of life here was far better than Washington. But none of it compared to the lines of this girl's lean back, standing in front of Zhang, silhouetted against man's finest constructions.

She turned to face him. She seemed calmer. "Who are you?"

"My name is Patrick Li. You?"

She did not answer his question. "Why am I here?"

"I would like to learn that as well." Zhang adjusted his glasses. "I was told that something special would be delivered to my room, and that I should not allow it to leave. That is all I know."

"Who told you this?"

"A friend who works in the Government."

She studied him quietly, her nicely shaped chest rising and

falling heavily with each breath, her nicely formed mind puzzling over her predicament. "When can I leave?"

"I'm not sure, but I will find out." Zhang took a step toward the room's phone, his hands up innocently. "Are you hungry or thirsty? I would be glad to order you anything you'd like."

She eyed him doubtfully. "How about a filet and a bottle of Bordeaux?"

He smiled. "How would you like your filet?"

"Rare."

"Just my type. I'll order two." He picked up the room's phone and flipped open the menu that sat beside it, pretending to read the words as he carefully studied the shadows and felt the air. He knew she would attack. He invited it.

"Room service," the voice on the other line said.

"Hello. I would like to order two Filet Mignons, cooked rare, and a bottle of Bord—"

A shadow passed over the menu. He dropped the phone and spun.

She came at him like lightning, charging and swinging a lamp at his head. He ducked the lamp and landed a swift punch to her solar plexus. As she doubled over in pain he brought an elbow down on her back. She fell flat on the floor. He was on her in a second, flipping her over and pinning her down and staring into her beautiful face.

"I don't know who you are," he said. "But I can protect you if you let me. Do not do that again."

Through a wince of pain, she nodded, then breathed out, "Why?"

"Because whoever you are…" He leaned closer to her face, smiling. "I think I like you."

He stood and picked up the phone again, turning away quickly so that she would not see his erection. He finished placing the order, with an extra bottle of Bordeaux, just in case.

57

THERE WERE MANY reasons why Kathy preferred Washington to New York. Manhattan was like a freshly delivered street-side hotdog—steaming and full of potential, but far less tolerable as it is digested. The thought of the hot dog made Kathy want to vomit, only her stomach was still empty after the speeding drive to the Waldorf and the command to stand watch at the exits. She'd drawn the short straw and was stuck monitoring the main entrance, while Grant was posted at the delivery entrance where the drone had recorded the kidnapper driving inside. Their drone might have been illegal in Manhattan, but no one shot it down. It gave them all the information they needed. Maybe she could come around to like drones, even if she'd never admit it to Grant.

Anyway, a drone couldn't do what she was doing now. It might show the live video and the heat sensors of bodies going in and out of the Waldorf, but it couldn't pick up on subtler clues. Kathy had seen a few normal rich tourists strolling out to start their days. But mostly she'd seen Chinese operatives. She wasn't one to stereotype, but it was no surprise that Chinese travelers overwhelmingly preferred the Waldorf these days. They felt safe here. And that made it all the easier for agents to hide among them.

The first one she'd spotted had stopped outside the entrance to tie his shoe. A small thing, tying a shoe. But these were nice wingtips. How often did those heavily waxed laces happen to come untied the moment one stepped outside? Not often. The agent's eyes had passed over the line of cars parked on the opposite side of the street, and had surely registered Kathy sitting there, in the same spot she'd been for three hours.

So they knew she was here. It hardly mattered. The Director had told her to stand watch. *Watch.* She was a field agent in her bones, trained to infiltrate places far less hospitable than the Waldorf and accomplish missions inside. Director Strassitch knew her track record. She'd rescued four kidnapping victims before, and she could do it again. He hadn't explicitly prohibited her from going inside. She'd earned more discretion than that.

She watched and watched as a half dozen other suspicious actions tipped her off to agents milling about, ensuring that all was right and proper at the gilded Waldorf on this fine Friday morning.

"Anything interesting?" she asked Grant, through her undetectable earpiece. He was still on the side street watching the delivery entrance.

"Yeah, the milk man," he said.

She couldn't resist a little laugh. "Just make sure our target doesn't get taken out with the empty bottles."

"Roger that. Any guesses how much longer we'll have to wait?"

"No clue," she said. "I'll keep you posted."

Another hour passed. The Friday sidewalk commuters were out in full force, walking with heads down and elbows out. Kathy couldn't understand why anyone would live in such a mess of people. For the money, she guessed, but she'd given that up a long time ago.

It was 8:42 am when she saw Jackson Crow.

He passed right by her car, wearing a trim grey suit, a plaid green tie, and a fedora hat. His eyes, sharp as an eagle's above his high cheekbones, were focused on the Waldorf's entrance and never glanced at her. He walked to the end of the block, crossed the crosswalk, then turned back toward the Waldorf and strode right through main entrance.

"Jackson Crow is going inside." Kathy watched him disappear from view in the lobby.

"What should we do?" Grant asked.

Kathy was tired of watching. She was tired of leaving Jackson to work on his own. "We're going in to back him up."

58

JACKSON KNEW THE ODDS weren't good. He'd been up all night, and now he was walking alone into enemy territory packed full of agents and cameras to monitor his every movement. But he had three advantages that he figured took his chances from 0% to about 2%: the element of surprise; a pretty good idea of which room Lily was in; and he'd pulled off something like this before.

The surprise part was simple.

Patrick Li had no reason to expect that anyone had discovered the kidnapping so soon. He would know it was only a matter of time before various pieces of video footage and identification came together to show where Lily was, but not this soon, not without Vin and his discovery in Camelot. Even if the Americans had tracked this down, the kidnapper would not expect a solitary lawyer to attempt a rescue mission in the bright morning light. So at least Jackson had surprise going for him.

The cost of surprise was a sleepless night. He'd ridden his motorcycle at speeds twice the legal limit up I-95, slowing only for the automated cameras, and arrived in Manhattan two hours later.

He figured it had to be some kind of record.

On the ride he'd come up with a rudimentary plan for finding out where Lily was—watching windows. Everyone says New York is the city that never sleeps, but watch a hotel for an entire night, and anyone will see that's just not true. This was particularly so for the Waldorf, because the upper half of the building had been converted into condos soon after the Chinese government became the building's owner.

Jackson had started observing—from a safe distance—on the north side, where only a few sporadic rooms still had their lights on after midnight. Then he'd checked the east, south, and west sides. After noting the lights he'd found an odd but simple pattern. One floor, near the top of the Waldorf, had far more lights on than the others. By his calculation, it was the 43rd floor. A little searching online revealed that this floor housed two exorbitantly expensive penthouse units.

At 4 am he'd called Daisho, his friend in Tokyo who had warned Jackson and helped him get out of a sushi bar without the Chinese taking Lily. Jackson told Daisho that he needed another favor, and that he might be close to learning something important.

"I knew you'd find something," Daisho said. "How can I help?"

"Can you get me into the Consulate General of Japan in New York?" The Consulate General's offices happened to be in a large building, mostly full of banking professionals, right across 49th street from the Waldorf.

Daisho did not hesitate in saying yes.

Twenty minutes later a sleepy looking Japanese woman arrived at the building's entrance with a key card and swiped Jackson in. She gave him a key card and left without asking any questions.

He owed Daisho a bottle of something nice.

Jackson found a nice perch on the 40th floor of the Consulate to study the Waldorf's lights. The floor he'd identified definitely had more lights on than the rest of the building, but he couldn't see anything through the tinting. By 5 am all but two of the rooms on the Waldorf's 43rd floor had flicked off or on at least once. By 6 am there was only one room left that had kept its lights on the entire time he'd watched—at the corner of Park and 49th.

It wasn't much, but it was a start.

He'd gotten changed, downed a coffee, and headed after Lily.

Now, inside the Waldorf, came the hard part. First step: get into the hotel's kitchen. It was every hotel's beating heart, sending out steaming trays of overpriced food on demand and at any hour. All he needed to do was find out which room had ordered enough food for two last night and then steal a server's uniform and make his way to the penthouse condos for a special delivery.

He approached the front desk in the lobby and flashed his best smile for a young Chinese woman at the counter, with the nametag Xun.

"Welcome to the Waldorf," she said. "How can I help you?"

"Good morning, Xun." Jackson bowed slightly. "I'm Jason Wright, the lead food reporter from the New York Times." He lowered his voice, smiling widely. "I normally don't even mention who I am, but I've heard amazing things about your new chef." Jackson had scanned recent news about the Waldorf and seen the chef's name all over the press.

"Oh yes," the woman said. "Mr. Wong is amazing."

"I believe it. The thing is, I'm supposed to do an undercover tasting for breakfast, of all things. This is a bit unusual, because I usually do dinner as you would imagine, but we are running a special article on the best breakfasts in the city. Do you know whether he happens to be here this morning?"

She blinked and nodded eagerly. "Wait just one moment. I will check right away." She picked up the phone and dialed, no doubt to the kitchen. After a few words in Mandarin—including a whispered "New York Times"—she hung up and looked to Jackson. "Yes, he should be arriving very soon."

"Excellent. Would you be so kind as to confirm whether the food prepared in the kitchen for the restaurant is the same as that prepared for the Waldorf's residents?"

"Absolutely," she said. "We offer the finest for our guests and our residents."

"I know this is asking a lot, especially without notice, but would it be possible to have a quick peek inside the kitchen before Mr. Wong arrives? I'd love to see where the magic happens."

"I might be able to arrange that." She winked at him. "Let me talk to our kitchen manager."

She exited the front desk through a door in the back and came out two minutes later. It seemed like just enough time for her to tell the manager, and everyone else in the hotel, that a New York Times food critic had arrived for breakfast. Hotels would do anything for a good review from a food critic.

She bowed her head toward Jackson. "The manager has offered to take you for a quick look himself."

"Thank you very much," Jackson said, just as a middle-aged man approached. He had thinning hair, a serious expression, and wore an outfit that looked a lot like room-service delivery. Best of all, he was about Jackson's size.

The man extended his hand. "I am Liang Xi. Xun tells me you would like to see our kitchen."

Jackson tried to read the man as they shook hands. This manager was serious, either because he really believed Jackson was a food reporter, or because he knew Jackson worked for the U.S. government. Regardless, the simple smile-tactic was not going to help, so Jackson answered professionally. "It would be an honor to see where Mr. Wong works."

The man nodded. "Please, come with me."

As Jackson followed the manager, he began wondering how long a hotel like this could go without noticing a missing manager. Maybe an hour, he figured, and he had some cover since the girl at the front desk thought he was playing tour guide for an important food critic. An hour had to be enough time. If Jackson couldn't get Lily out before then, he'd be in serious trouble. The lobby cameras might have caught his face and fed it into facial recognition software. It took only a few clicks from there for any watching Chinese intelligence to discover that an American agent had officially entered the building.

They rounded a corner and entered a hallway with kitchen doors at the end. A men's restroom was ahead on the right.

"Sorry," Jackson said. "Mind if I make a quick stop?"

The manager paused, then shrugged. "No problem."

Jackson entered the restroom and went to a urinal, confirming on the way that no one else was in the room. As he relieved himself, the sound of footsteps on the gleaming white tiles made him glance over his shoulder.

The manager stepped into the only stall. It was the perfect opportunity.

As the stall's door began to swing closed, Jackson stepped quickly and silently toward it. He drew the dart gun from his coat pocket and raised it to his lips.

A swift push opened the door. The manager's pants were down to his knees, and the dart hit squarely in his upper thigh.

Jackson caught him as he collapsed.

In one minute, Jackson had the manager propped up on the toilet seat, feet in the normal position, grey suit pants at his ankles and a coat and green plaid tie laid on his lap. Jackson put on the manager's suit; it was a decent enough fit. He locked the stall door and slid through the gap underneath.

He went through the kitchen's swinging doors and approached a stack of papers sitting on a desk near the doors, beside a phone. They were slips of paper with scribbled notes for recent orders. He flipped through them quickly and found one for two filet mignons, cooked rare, two bottles of Bordeaux, and a box of chocolates. The number written at the top was "43 station."

Jackson wasn't sure what that meant, but he intended to find out. He took quick inventory of the kitchen's activities. There were three rows where chefs prepared plates, with the last row hosting a set of trays. He watched two waitresses in red dresses retrieve orders and exit through the door he had entered. He saw one man in a room-service uniform like his enter a different door near the back, and he glimpsed an elevator just beyond. Acting on instinct, he walked past the row of ready trays, picked one up, and exited through the same doors as the other room-service guy. There were two elevators, but only one for the upper condo floors. Jackson pushed the button and waited.

When the doors opened, a room-service guy was inside, holding an empty tray.

"Hey!" Jackson said cheerfully, holding up the full tray in his hands. "This is for 43 station. Want me to take care of yours, and you take mine?"

"Who are you?" The guy looked confused. "43 station is my job."

Jackson needed to act fast. He glanced back to confirm they were alone in the elevator area. "Sorry! Here!" He quickly put his tray on top of the one in the guy's hands.

The guy was shaking his head. "What are you—?"

Jackson fired before the guy could finish the question. The trays clattered onto the floor as the guy grabbed at the dart protruding from his neck and fell unconscious.

Hurrying inside, Jackson let the elevator doors close and surveyed the buttons in the elevator. He saw the answer to what had been puzzling him: there was a floor 42.5. He pressed the button but nothing happened. Above the buttons was a panel that he recognized. A retina scanner. He hauled up the man's unconscious body and held open his eye in front of the panel, then tried button 42.5 again. This time the elevator started to move.

As they rose, Jackson knew he was in trouble. Security on this floor—for whatever secrets it held—was bound to be high. The doors could open onto anything and anyone, and now he had another motionless body to deal with. Plus, he realized, and not for the first time, even if he found Lily, getting out would be a challenge. He couldn't just climb out a window…

The elevator stopped, with Jackson hiding behind the edge as the doors opened. He peeked out onto a normal-looking hotel hallway lined with doors. Normal…except for the man holding an automatic rifle in his hands. To his credit, the man didn't shout as he charged towards the elevator and the body on the floor. He also didn't see Jackson until it was too late. Jackson spun and fired a dart, aiming for the thigh. No one wore body armor there.

Jackson dragged the body and trays out of the elevator and left them in a pile in the corner, except for one tray with a silver plate cover sitting in the middle, which he took with him.

Momentum and adrenalin fueled him down the hall until he reached the last door on the left—the one that had the light on all night. It was labeled Room F. He quietly slid away the deadbolt on the outside. Then he knocked and turned his back to the peephole.

He heard Lily's familiar voice. "I didn't order anything."

She sounded unharmed, but someone could easily be beside her with a gun to her head. Keeping his back to the peephole, he said, "But I have an order for Chicken Lo Mein."

"Jackson?"

He could barely hear her whisper, but then a deadbolt slid and the door flung open and Lily wrapped her arms around him as he slipped into the room.

59

THE ROOM HAD everything one would expect from a penthouse corner unit at the Waldorf, except for the body with the small puddle of blood by its head in the middle of the floor. There was no need to ask how it happened. A thousand broken pieces of a porcelain lamp surrounded the man like a halo of bright blue and glittering gold.

Jackson confirmed the room was secure and that Lily was okay, other than a few cuts at the wrist and ankles. Then he knelt down by the man's body. He'd been right. It was Zhang, Archer, Patrick Li—the same man he'd met at the gala.

"What happened?" Jackson asked.

"It was half an hour ago." Lily's words came out tense and rapid-fire. "It's been terrible. I pretended to give up last night. I cooperated while we had dinner and even slept a couple hours. Early this morning I told him I wanted to shower while we waited for breakfast to be delivered. I kept the water running and waited by the bathroom door. When I heard a knock, I slipped out and grabbed this lamp. I waited around the corner, and as he walked up with the tray of food in his hand, I swung. It shattered against his head. It was so loud. I can't believe no one heard it. The room must be soundproof. I've been watching him, standing close with the other lamp ready to swing, but he hasn't stirred."

Jackson confirmed the man's breathing was regular, like a deep sleep. He was initially surprised no one had come after the attack to help Zhang and secure Lily. But it made sense. No cameras and soundproof. This must be an interrogation room. For the Chinese, in the heart of New York City.

Jackson could make use of that. Zhang might not be unconscious for long. Jackson needed to make sure he couldn't fight if he woke up. "You still have whatever he tied you up with?"

"It's in the box." Lily moved to a large cardboard box in the corner. She reached inside and retrieved a few strands of rope. "He cut them with this."

She held out a small knife in one hand, and the cords in the other. They were short, but Jackson would have to make do.

Just as Lily handed the knife to him, Jackson saw her eyes flick past him. He jerked around and instantly realized his mistake. Zhang had been listening, pretending to sleep. As soon as he'd seen an opening, he'd risen and charged. Now he was swinging a roundhouse at Jackson's head.

Jackson didn't have time to dodge the blow. Stars erupted in his vision as he staggered back against the wall.

Zhang slammed a fist into Jackson's gut, then shoved Lily hard into the wall. Head spinning, Jackson forgot about the knife in his left hand and tried to pull his dart gun with his right hand, but the man knocked it to the ground. Then he reached for a real gun on the bedside table. Jackson got there first and hurled it across the room, but that left him exposed. Zhang landed another blow to the side of Jackson's head, knocking him back against the wall.

Jackson couldn't see straight, and Zhang was too strong.

He remembered what his grandfather had told him once about fighting a bear. If the larger, stronger creature gets you pinned against a tree, you are doomed if it knocks you down. The only hope is to dive under its legs and run zig-zags through the forest. Jackson didn't have a forest, but this guy was closing on him like a bear.

He ducked the next swing and dove between the man's legs. He used the knife to slice into the man's calf as he slid through. He expected the man to double over in pain, but instead the guy spun and landed a dropkick on Jackson's back.

Jackson fell hard to the floor, shards of porcelain lamp jabbing into him as he rolled to over to look up.

The guy glared down at him and growled, "It's over."

It was a faint hope, but Jackson started talking, trying to buy time. "We know about Hina."

"You know nothing." Zhang jumped forward, knee raised, and

foot dropping like a hammer toward Jackson's face.

Jackson managed to get his knife up just as the foot came down. The force of the blow slammed the blade's hilt into Jackson's forehead, but there was an unmistakable feel of stabbed flesh, like a foot stepping onto a nail.

Stars flashing in his vision, Jackson staggered to his feet as the man screamed and grabbed at his foot. The knife had stabbed all the way through.

Jackson dove for his blowgun, then fired a dart into the man's neck. He went out cold.

"Nice shot," Lily said, coming to his side. "Tranquilizer?"

"Yeah, he'll be out a while." This time Jackson didn't take his eyes off the motionless body.

"You okay?" she asked.

"Could be worse." Jackson took her hand and backed towards the door. "We have to go—"

Three swift knocks at the door interrupted him.

60

WHY AREN'T THEY stopping us?

Kathy stood at the hotel room door, glancing over her shoulder and expecting men with guns to be coming after her. But the hallway was empty. Not a soul in sight, other than Grant standing by the stairs, gun drawn.

She'd been at this business long enough to know something didn't add up. Maybe the Chinese really believed this floor was still a secret. Or maybe not even they knew yet about Zhang and Lily. Whatever it was, Kathy didn't like it.

The door swung open, revealing Jackson, and Lily Sun guarded behind him. There was another man's body sprawled out in the middle of the room.

Jackson failed to hide his shock. "Kathy?"

"Jackson." She looked past him. "And Lily. Good to see you're all right. Ready to get out?"

"What are you doing here?" Jackson asked.

Kathy couldn't blame him for not trusting her. It looked bad. She'd been following him and hadn't tipped him off. "I came in after you."

"Whose orders?"

"The Director's."

"So the White House knows..."

"I'm sure they do." Kathy caught Lily's eyes. "It's not every day one of our diplomats is kidnapped right out of DC." She motioned for them to come. "We have to go. Now."

Jackson leaned close to Lily and whispered something in her ear. She shook her head. He glanced down at his phone, quickly typed something, then looked back at Kathy with all the emotion of a granite wall.

"Tell me why you've been following me," Jackson said.

"I will...once we're out." Kathy held her gun ready and glanced out to the hallway, where Grant motioned for her to hurry. "The stairway is clear now, but it might not be for long. We have a ride outside the delivery door. We can talk on the way."

"I want to know what's going on before we walk straight into another trap. And this room is secure." Jackson looked over his shoulder, out the floor-to-ceiling window of the room. "Lily knocked out this agent an hour ago. Then he woke up and fought me. No one has come for him, which means no cameras, no mics. Tell Grant to come inside and close the door before he's seen."

"Grant," Kathy said. "You heard him."

Her partner obeyed and came to her side, but he didn't look happy about it.

Jackson glanced at Grant, and a look of recognition passed over his face. "You…"

Kathy was losing patience. "Yes, we've been working together the whole time. I got the mission from the White House right after the shooting in the Treaty Room."

A grimace passed over Jackson's face. "Who, exactly?"

"Reagan Murphy."

He ran his hands over his hair. "You warned me in Tokyo. I appreciate that."

"Our job was only to watch and protect you both."

"And you reported on everything you saw, which I do not appreciate. Some matters require discretion. Your partner can tell you about that." Jackson looked to Grant. "How was the rest of your time in Hong Kong?"

"Delightful," Grant said.

"I'm sure. Take it easy on the drinks next time, okay?"

"Enough," Kathy said, looking to Lily. The young woman's dark eyes revealed rapid processing, like a spinning cursor on an overloaded computer. "Somebody wants you gone," Kathy said. "And it can't be just because of the treaty."

"It is the treaty," Lily said. "Has to be."

"If so, they'd be after Jackson, too."

"They have been," Jackson said. "They tried to kill me in my apartment."

"So why'd they kidnap Lily but leave you alone?" Kathy asked.

"Not sure." Jackson turned to Lily. "You're more vulnerable," he said to her. "But I think there must be something else you know."

"About what?" Lily asked.

Jackson glanced to Kathy, as if deciding whether to speak his thought, then back to Lily. "How about Ambassador Blair?"

Lily didn't answer, but her eyes showed that Jackson had hit somewhere near the mark.

"What about the Ambassador?" Kathy asked, focusing on Lily.

"How do we know we can trust you?" Jackson demanded before Lily could say another word.

Kathy hadn't wanted to give up this information, but she needed Jackson on her side if she was going to get them out of here safely. She formulated her answer with the fewest words possible.

"My asset, Mr. Chan, told me," she said. "About Vin, and you...Raven."

Jackson didn't flinch. He held her gaze, poker stare, for a solid ten seconds. Then he gave a quick nod.

He must have seen the implications. If she knew he was Raven, but the news hadn't gotten out, then she was keeping his secret. It would mean he could trust her up to a point. But he would also understand the risks of her knowing what she knew.

He turned to Lily. "The Ambassador knew the murder was about to happen. And he's been helping the Chinese ever since. The question is: why would they kill her? You told me about Blair's dinner about Hina. What *exactly* did Hina tell you? She might have known her life was at risk. She could have given you a clue."

"I'm...not sure." Lily's eyes were locked on Jackson. "*You* are Raven?"

Kathy still stood in the open door, with Grant beside her, when she heard a door open. She snapped around as a group emerged from the room across the hall.

"Raven, Crow, blackbird—doesn't matter any more." It was Ambassador Blair, accompanied by five Chinese soldiers with semi-automatics.

They moved forward, trapping Kathy, Grant, and the rest of them in the room.

61

JACKSON QUICKLY DID the math. Seven guns were raised, with five semi-automatics for the Chinese and two Glocks for his side. An eighth gun was on the floor, still in the corner where he'd thrown it during his fight with Zhang, who lay motionless on the floor. By the time Jackson's side fired two bullets, or tried to make a move, enough bullets would spray the room to leave no one standing. But he doubted the Chinese were eager to test it. Two Glocks, if fired first, could still do some serious damage, especially aimed at Ambassador Blair's head.

For now, Jackson slowly side-stepped to the left, with both hands raised, so that his body was between the five men in the doorway and Lily. He looked down the barrel of the rifle trained on his forehead. The gunman wore a formal green uniform with red shoulder-patch insignia, like an infantryman dressed up for a ball. His hard, dark eyes must have weathered a thousand verbal assaults from a drill sergeant—enough to make him the perfect half-human soldier, eager to kill.

The uniformed men inched further into the room, fanning out as they came, allowing Ambassador Blair space to enter. He walked through the group with the grace of a consummate diplomat, just stepped out of the barber shop, with his fastidious suit, combed silver hair, and American flag pin on his jacket lapel.

"Lovely to see you all," Blair said calmly, glancing around the group and pausing on Kathy and Grant, who still had their guns raised. "Let's drop the weapons now."

"No." Kathy didn't budge. Her gun pointed right at the Ambassador's head, point-blank range. "Anyone shoots, you die."

Jackson lowered his arms, eyes still locked on the gunman targeting him. He reached back and took Lily's hand in his, as he shuffled slightly back towards the window. He didn't notice the body near his feet start to rouse.

Blair clasped his hands in front of him. "It would be a shame for you to die, Sullivan, especially in direct disobedience to your Commander in Chief."

"What are you talking about?" She sounded uneasy.

"We have come to bring Lily back home." Blair smiled as he peered around Jackson. "You're safe now, Lily. The Chinese government is not behind this. Apparently this man—" Blair glanced to the body on the floor—"he went rogue not long ago. He was an intelligence asset, but we all know they can get their own ideas of justice if they don't obey orders. Right, Sullivan?"

"If he went rogue," Kathy said, "then so did you. Why else would you, of all people, be here right now?"

"That is quite simple." Blair held out his hands innocently. "The President has learned that this man, by the name of Zhang Li, and not coincidentally, the son of a leading Chinese general, is responsible for the death of the Japanese lawyer who was shot in the Treaty Room. He was the one who paid the killer. Now he kidnapped one of our own. We made a deal. Our Chinese friends would take him into custody here, maybe ask a few questions. Then we'd toss him in a high-security U.S. prison. But looks like you killed Mr. Li…and saved us the trouble. Lily, we'll bring you home now. Everything will be fine."

Kathy tilted her gun accusingly at Blair. "You're disgusting. Zhang killed Hina Himura because you slept with her, and you paid him to do it."

"Ah, so you *have* been poking around, beyond your orders," Blair said. "I assumed you had my office tapped…"

"You've been lying to the President."

Blair didn't flinch. "Now that's a serious accusation. Hina and I had a fun night, no big deal."

"You bastard," Kathy growled. "That's a lie!"

"Steady, Kathy," Jackson said, as calmly as he could, trying to buy time. "Ambassador, we have questions, that's all."

"Well, it sure is a surprise to see you here, Mr. Crow," Blair said. "Just doing your lawyer work, eh?"

"Like I said, I look out for my associates."

"From what I hear, you've been doing a lot more than *lookin' out*."

Jackson saw a chance to learn more. "You've been doing a lot more yourself. You *and* your companies in China. It'd be a shame if that got out, don't you think?"

"Well…yes." Blair's lips pressed into a tight line as he tapped one of the soldiers and nodded to him.

Jackson stepped back, fearing he'd hit too close to the mark.

"Hold it," Kathy demanded, still pointing her gun right at the Ambassador's face. "If anyone shoots, I shoot."

62

ZHANG HEARD EVERY WORD. Face pressed against the thick carpet of Room F on floor 42.5 of the Waldorf, Zhang opened his eyes slowly and found himself staring away from the door, toward the corner of the room where his gun lay three feet away. His head throbbed and his foot was in excruciating pain. Each pulse felt like it gushed blood from the knife wound. He forced himself to take steady, silent breaths as he lay still and considered his options.

He'd learned several important things from the conversation that he'd overheard. First, Ambassador Blair, Jackson Crow, an American agent named Sullivan, Lily Sun, and at least a few Chinese soldiers were in the room, with guns locked and loaded. Second, his government—and probably his own father—had betrayed him, giving him up as a sacrifice to maintain the secrecy of their plans. Third, people were about to start shooting.

Zhang knew that if he stayed silent and still, he might survive. Most shootouts ignore motionless bodies on the floor. But he also had the element of surprise, and he wanted revenge. He wanted to spill American blood. If he could just slide a couple feet... he could put a bullet in the Ambassador's head, then Crow's...

* * *

The first gunshot was like a cork firing out of a shaken Champagne bottle. All the pressure inside bubbled up, the only thing holding that pressure back began to slide out, and then—*pop*.

Jackson reacted to the sound of the gunshot, from the floor beside him, before he even saw the dot appear on Blair's forehead and his smiling face freeze like a man who swallowed a bug. Only this time, Blair's brain had swallowed a bullet, and he went down as the other guns began to fire.

Spinning, Jackson grabbed Lily and dove to the other side of the bed. He felt a stabbing pain in his shoulder, but he managed to keep his body over Lily's, wedged against the wall of glass where it met the floor.

There were too many shots to count. It took seven seconds before the room went quiet.

Jackson took five breaths, hand pressed to his throbbing shoulder. He looked at his hand—covered in blood—then crawled to the end of the bed and peeked.

No one was standing. No one was moving.

He counted eight bodies. Zhang, Blair, Sullivan, Grant, and four Chinese soldiers. One of the soldier's bodies was in the doorway, propping it open. That meant one soldier had fled the room. Jackson had to get out, now. If Vin came through, they'd have a chopper ready.

He glanced back at Lily. "You okay?"

She nodded. Her face was unimaginably serene.

"Follow me." Jackson moved in a crouch around the bed and stopped by Kathy Sullivan. Her face seemed unharmed, but her white shirt was covered in blood in two places—the gut and the shoulder. He put his hand to her neck. He felt a pulse.

He had to take her with him. She had saved him…again.

He checked Grant and Blair, but both had flat-lined. He returned to Kathy's body and lifted it onto his left shoulder, the one that hadn't taken a bullet. He took her gun in his right hand, wincing from the pain.

He eyed Grant's gun. "Lily, can you take that?"

"Okay." She knelt beside the fallen man and picked up his gun with both hands.

"It'll be live. Point and shoot if it comes to that."

"Got it…how are we going to get out?"

"Our ride should be on the roof. Follow close."

Jackson rose to his feet, Kathy's limp body draped over his shoulder like a sack of potatoes. He stepped carefully over the fallen bodies and opened the door. The hallway was still clear.

Lily was moving faster, without a body on her shoulders, and passed Jackson as they hurried toward the stairwell. She entered first, and he follower her. There was shouting below. The sound of boots on stairs.

"Run!" Jackson grunted.

She charged up the stairs, gun raised. He took the steps as fast as possible, his legs and his shoulder throbbing. They were near the top of the Waldorf, so it was only a few stories to climb. At the top of the stairs, Lily stopped in front of a door with bold red letters: *Emergency Exit*.

"This way?" she asked, as Jackson caught up.

Jackson nodded, and she pressed her weight into the door. It opened, setting off an emergency siren. A rush of wind and a loud whirring greeted them. Two soldier's bodies were motionless on the roof, and just beyond them, a helicopter sat, propellers spinning.

Vin was leaning out the helicopter's open door, waving for them to come. Jackson ran with Lily to the chopper and climbed inside after her. He laid Kathy's body gently on the floor and put pressure on her wounds.

Vin shouted at the pilot, *go, go, go!* The helicopter lifted off just as soldiers burst out of the emergency door on the roof. They raised their guns and fired a couple hopeless shots as the chopper soared out of range and flew south over Manhattan, untouched.

Vin turned back to Jackson and Lily. He wore headphones so big they made his head look miniature, almost like a gnome. He eyed Kathy's body, then Jackson's shoulder, then Lily.

He smiled widely. "So you're the girl?"

63

AS THEY FLEW away from New York, Lily felt the same numbness she'd had after the Treaty Room. But this time was different because she knew who the man beside her really was. Jackson Crow was Raven, the character she'd seen in the game. It was no coincidence. He had fought Archer, the same man who was hunting for Jackson and who Lily had been trying to find. Adding that knowledge about Jackson to everything else that she'd learned about him—that he'd worked at the CIA, stopped the Chinese man who had tried to kill her in Tokyo, and now rescued her from the Waldorf—she was shocked that her quiet boss had been this man all along.

And yet, he still made her feel...safe.

"Hey, you okay in there?" Jackson looked up at her from the floor of the helicopter, where he was leaning over Kathy Sullivan, keeping pressure on her wounds. There was a large wet spot on the shoulder of his dark coat, like blood.

"I think so," she said. "Are you hurt?"

"A bullet grazed me. It'll be fine."

"Wow. I'll help bind the wound. But can anything stop you?"

"Many things. We got lucky."

"I know. There were so many shots. I can't believe we survived."

"What happened?" asked the small man in the cockpit, turning back from the passenger seat. Lily thought he almost looked familiar with his quick movements and over-eager eyes.

Jackson gave him a quick overview of what happened. Everyone dead except Kathy. "Oh, and Vin, this is Lily," Jackson said. "Lily, Vin. He's an old friend."

Vin's beady brown eyes studied Lily with an elevator gaze, up and down. "I can see why Jackson wanted to get back."

Jackson shot a harsh look at Vin. "My friend is dying here, Vin. Focus, please. I asked you to arrange a landing, ideally at a hospital in DC."

"Sorry, right. I'm on it. Should be just a little over an hour." The man turned around and started dialing on his phone.

"Ignore him," Jackson said softly. "He's crude, but he has a good heart."

"How do you know him?" Lily asked.

"We go way back."

Lily thought again of Raven from Camelot, and the gnome that had been with him. The way the two of them talked to each other made it suddenly obvious. "Vin's the one who was with you when you fought Archer, isn't he?"

Now it Jackson's turn to look shocked, mouth hanging open as he met her eyes. "How could you know…?"

"Remember the beautiful elf?" Lily held out her arms, posing. "Sunbolt?"

"Incredible…. I remember. What were you doing there?"

"I used to play a lot. Not much anymore. But I still have a rank in the Red Silk Guild. When I saw you I was trying to use my position to learn more about what China was up to. I was locked in my apartment, after all."

"You helped us find Archer. We found you after you made a public announcement that you had information about me. We waited until Archer came."

"Glad it was of some use. I figured there was no downside. Thanks for the BitStone."

Jackson smiled. "Never underestimate a BitStone. Tracking the money is always a good plan, especially when you don't have a double agent on the inside, like Hina."

Lily could not believe what she'd just heard. "Hina was a double agent?"

"Yes, we believe so. The Chinese were paying her to get close to Ambassador Tanaka from Japan, and our own Ambassador Blair. She was supposed to gather information. Her legal job was a cover. I think she learned something from Blair, or somewhere else, that she was not supposed to know. So they killed her, and held it over

Blair as blackmail. Two birds with one stone."

Lily's hand covered her mouth. Her mind raced through her memories with Hina. She had no way of expecting this. It changed everything, like a picture suddenly taking on a new dimension. Every word Hina had said could have meant something different. Lily thought of what Hina had said the one time they'd played Camelot together. *I can't believe you're in the Red Silk Guild. They own their players. I come here to be free for a while.* At the time it had sounded odd, but unimportant. Now it seemed like a key.

"I need to access Camelot," Lily said. "I think Hina could have left a clue there."

Jackson turned toward the cockpit. "Vin!" he shouted. "Vin!"

The man looked back. "What?"

"You have a headset in here?"

"Always, but...it looks like you still have your hands full."

"It's not for me," Jackson said. "It's for Lily."

Vin's brow raised, but he didn't ask more questions. He pulled out a headset from a drawer in the front. He handed it back to Lily and said, "You can use my hotspot."

Lily didn't waste time. She logged in as Sunbolt and found herself alone in the same shadowy forest where she'd seen Raven and Archer fight. She glanced through her inventory, but didn't see anything unusual.

Then she checked her messages. She'd ignored these last time because it was usually spam. Scrolling through dozens of them, she saw one from a character named Nusylil.

Nusylil. Lily smiled. A palindrome—Lily Sun spelled backwards.

When she went to open the message, she saw it was secured. That meant it could be opened only if she passed the retina scan. No wonder Hina had chosen this platform, right under the Chinese government's nose. She proceeded through the scan by the headset and opened the message. It was a video. A pale-skinned elf started speaking. The words came fast.

"Hey Lily. It's me, Hina. I'm sorry I couldn't tell you this in person. I'm worried I won't get a chance. Anyway, I didn't tell you everything. Blair invited me to dinner, like I said, but it *was* a big deal. We had lots of sake at this nice Japanese place and we ended up back at my hotel room and I don't know how it happened but I felt like I wasn't in control of myself, maybe drugged, and then he started to kiss me, I said no, but he kept going and didn't stop and then said it had been a lovely night that we should keep this secret, only I had recorded it because…well, I just did, and the next day I listened and heard Blair on his phone, soon after it happened, talking to someone about building a tunnel to Taiwan."

Hina's avatar paused. "I thought it was absurd, but I looked into it and it's true. There's a tunnel. Blair's company helped build it and move all the dirt. He made a fortune. It's finished now and the Chinese military has been sending troops through it. Look, here's the blueprint." An image filled Lily's vision, showing exactly what Hina described. "We have to try to stop this. My grandparents are there, in Taiwan. The Party told me they wouldn't use me like this, but they did and so I took this, and they might kill me for it. They're just waiting for the right time to attack. You know the treaty term we changed? I think the Americans had some kind of secret deal with the Chinese, to let them take the Senkakus, only the PLA isn't satisfied with that. They're going to move when the Americans have their guard down. Then it will be too late. Taiwan will be theirs. It'll be only the beginning. If I'm not around when you get this, tell the right people in your government." The avatar waved a slender elven hand. "Bye, Lily."

Lily was breathing fast. This was so much. She jerked off the headset.

Jackson was studying her. "Tell me."

Lily told him everything, saying as much word-for-word as she could.

Jackson was quiet. Eventually, with his eyes on Kathy, he said, "We have to tell the President. Reagan should be able to get us a meeting." He looked to Lily. "We may need to show him Hina's video. But don't tell him about me. Raven stays between us, okay?"

Lily nodded. "Your secret's safe."

64

REAGAN HAD READ half the President's morning briefing papers when Jackson called. Seeing his number sent too many emotions spinning. She focused on what needed to be done. One step at a time. She went to the door and closed it before answering.

"Hey Jackson."

"Reagan, I need to talk to the President."

His voice was urgent and exhilarated. The rush of background noise, like wind whirring, made Reagan imagine Jackson had just jumped off a cliff and called her.

"Where are you?" she asked.

"On my way to DC. Should be there in an hour. Can you get me a meeting?"

"Today?"

"Yes, as soon as possible."

"I might be able to get you a short phone call."

"No, it has to be in person."

"Why?"

After a slight pause, Jackson said, "Ambassador Blair is dead. So is an agent. Another one is alive and with me, but wounded badly. We rescued Lily Sun."

"Oh God." Reagan sat in her chair. They must have found her Chinese contact, Zhang. They must have fought their way out. This was not good. This was very bad. She started thinking of how they'd spin this. They couldn't just cover it up. They couldn't...

"Listen," Jackson said. "A lot more people are going to die if the President doesn't change his plans for the islands."

"I told you, Jackson. It's not going to be a fight. They'll have the island in a few hours, and then it will be over. There will be peace in the East China Sea."

"Reagan, for once just trust me, I need a meeting with the President. Can you do that?"

Reagan looked down at the President's schedule. He had an internal briefing with the national security team, including her, in an hour. Could she really trust Jackson? He was in a position to ruin her. "What are you going to tell him that you can't tell me?" she asked.

"I will tell him what China is *really* doing. He has the red button, Reagan, so right now he's the only one who can stop a war. Ten minutes. That's all I need."

She sighed. "I'll see what I can do. Can you get to the West Wing entrance by 11:30 am?"

"I'll be there."

65

ONLY ONE HELICOPTER could land on the South Lawn of the White House, and that was Marine One, not Vin's Sikorsky. So the helicopter instead landed at Georgetown Hospital. It made a perfect backup to the South Lawn—about as close as you could land to the White House, and where Kathy needed to go immediately. Jackson had kept her wounds from hemorrhaging, but they were bad. Not necessarily fatal. Likely fatal. The shot to her shoulder wasn't much worse than Jackson's. The one to her gut was. It all depended on which organ had been hit. She could spare a kidney. Not a liver, or a stomach. Internal bleeding was a hard way to go.

Vin had made arrangements for the emergency landing. A landing crew and ER staff were waiting when they touched down. They whisked Kathy's body away on a gurney. Jackson didn't mention his shoulder. Lily had helped him tend the wound, only vomiting once, on the flight down. It was wrapped tight and cleaned. The blood barely showed on the black coat he'd stolen from the room service guy. He felt pretty sure he could make it at least another hour without passing out from blood loss.

They said quick goodbyes to Vin. He protested at first about wanting to join them, but Jackson wasn't going to let Vin anywhere near the President, especially now. He told Vin to focus on getting the helicopter scrubbed of evidence and out of sight, and then log into Camelot and track any major activity.

As Jackson and Lily rushed through the hospital and rode an elevator down, Jackson felt grateful all over that they had survived. He'd done everything in his power to save Lily, to keep her from getting hurt like his sister Julia had years before. But somewhere along the way Jackson had realized that Lily was not like a sister. She was more than that. And now she was safe.

Zhang had been the surprise that saved them. There was no way they could have gotten out if he hadn't fired the first shot, causing mass confusion. Kathy and Grant had been an even match for five semi-automatics after that. The world might never learn about it, but the CIA would give them the honor they deserved.

Still, Jackson knew a larger danger loomed: war.

A black SUV was waiting in front of the hospital, as Reagan had promised. A man in a black suit and sunglasses opened the door when he saw them. Jackson and Lily hurried in and were barreling towards the White House moments later.

At the sixth red light of backed up cars, Jackson turned to Lily. Her shoulders were bunched up, her breathing shallow, as she stared out the window. Her past day was more than enough to cause a nervous breakdown. "Know the worst thing about DC?" he asked.

Lily turned to him. "The politicians?"

Jackson smiled. "Okay, how about the second worst?"

"The lawyers?"

"You win. But all those politicians and lawyers cause another problem: traffic." It was late morning on a Monday. They should have been moving fast. Government bureaucrats were probably leaving for a long lunch, oblivious to the geopolitical guillotine hanging above their necks.

"How do you think the President is going to react?" Lily asked.

"He'll doubt it at first, until we show him the message. Then he'll have to understand. At worst, he's a rational politician, with an election coming."

"Let's hope so."

They talked over the message more, and confirmed they had all the evidence properly backed up. They had the snapshot of the blueprint from Hina, uploaded onto Lily's phone. Jackson felt ready by the time they arrived at the West Wing gate. The driver showed a badge and spoke with the guard. The gate swung open and they rode inside.

The Secret Service agent who had welcomed them into the SUV led them without a word into the West Wing lobby. He didn't even frisk them.

When they entered, Reagan was pacing in front of a large

antique clock. "About time," she said, then looked at the agent. "You can go."

He nodded and left. Reagan studied Jackson, then Lily. "Looks like you two have been in a fight."

Jackson shrugged. "Yeah, we survived."

Reagan glanced at Lily and smiled. "Sorry he dragged you along for that. He's trouble. Here." She pulled a mirror and comb from her bag and handed them to Lily. "Take a few seconds. It's not every day you meet the President."

"Thanks," Lily said, nodding and then turning her back to look in the mirror.

"What about me?" Jackson asked.

"You're hopeless." Reagan stepped closer and wiped a fleck of imaginary dust off Jackson's shoulder. He winced, and Reagan's smile suddenly turned to concern. She spoke softly, meeting his eyes, "You're hurt."

"I'll be fine." Jackson held her gaze, but it wasn't easy seeing her concern. It brought back the old arguments, the old emotions. She hadn't wanted him to go off on secret missions, risking his life, maybe because she had loved him. Once they could have had a chance, but too much had happened. They'd both changed. Their past was no water under the bridge; it was water behind a dam.

He looked away from her green eyes, to the antique clock ticking towards 11:30.

"Okay," Lily said, turning back to them. Jackson could not help but find her stunning. Even after being kidnapped and almost killed, she had twice the warmth of Reagan.

"Follow me." Reagan spun and led them toward the Oval Office.

66

THE PRESIDENT DID not stand from his mammoth oak desk when Reagan, Jackson, and Lily entered the Oval Office. Reagan led them to three chairs that had been set up in front of the desk and motioned for them to sit. They did.

"Ready when you are, Mr. President," Reagan said.

His head was still down, finger on the page in front of him. When he finally glanced up, wire-rimmed glasses on the tip of his nose, he did not look pleased as he met Jackson's eyes. He looked like a principal dealing with a troublemaker.

"I remember you," he said. "Reagan convinced me to give you five minutes. Go ahead."

Jackson took a deep breath. He needed to keep this polite and professional. "You have heard what happened at the Waldorf?"

"I am aware."

"It's because of what you did, with the treaty."

"We changed a term," the President said. "We brought peace."

"Not that treaty." Jackson leaned forward. "The secret one."

The President glanced to Reagan, who nodded.

"You removed our protection from the Senkaku Islands," Jackson said. "And you knew what the Chinese were planning. You secretly agreed to let them have it, and all you got in return was a hollow promise that they'd stop there and stay quiet for five years." Jackson felt sure he was antagonizing the most powerful man in the world enough, so he didn't add that those five years happened to coincide perfectly with the President's re-election and next four-year term. He cut to the point. "Mr. President, the Chinese have been playing us all along. Their main target is not the Senkakus. It's Taiwan. And they're invading today."

"That's ridiculous." The President laughed in disbelief. "You expect me to believe *you*, instead of the President of China? He wouldn't dare. He knows we protect the Taiwan Strait."

"They're not using the Strait. Here, see for yourself." Jackson glanced to Lily, who handed her phone to the President. The screen showed the blueprint that Hina had stolen, with the tunnel design and the numbers of soldiers moving toward Taiwan.

The President turned slowly to the screen, and as he reviewed it, his face became unnaturally serene. He slid the phone back across the massive desk, but kept his eyes on it. "Why should I trust this?"

"We received it directly from Hina Himura," Jackson said, "the woman who was killed in the Treaty Room. I also learned some supporting evidence from a contact in Beijing."

"What were you doing in Beijing?" the President demanded.

Jackson didn't answer. "I don't expect you to trust me," he said. "But I do expect that you, as our commander in chief, will take this information seriously."

"What do you recommend?" he asked.

Jackson turned to Lily. It was her idea. She deserved the credit. "This is Lily Sun, from my office. She'll tell you."

The President turned to her.

Lily met his gaze, but then glanced briefly at Reagan. "I was in the Blair House, talking with Reagan, when it came to me. It's still spring, months before you are up for re-election, and China is flexing its muscles. The exact thing has happened before."

"When?" the President asked.

"March 1996. I was visiting family in Taiwan at the time. The Chinese started firing missiles. People were terrified, but President Clinton stopped the fight before it started. He sent the largest American fleet into the Pacific since the Vietnam War. And guess what happened?" She put on her most convincing smile. "China backed off. War was averted. And President Clinton was re-elected."

"Okay," the President said. "But if this image of the tunnel is right, sending in our navy won't help."

"It could help some," Reagan chimed in. "I'm just learning this, too, Mr. President, but I think they're right. We need a show of force to deter them. We can't let them take Taiwan. Can you imagine how that would look?"

Jackson ignored the political calculus, which meant nothing to him compared to war breaking out, but he was grateful for Reagan's support. He added, "We can deter them, but time is running short. If they try to take the Senkakus after dawn, that gives us about one hour, maybe two. You need to get the Chinese President on the phone. You have to tell him what you know, that you're prepared to stop it by any means necessary, and that the secret agreement about the islands is no longer in effect."

The President's eyes were on Reagan. "And if we don't deter them?"

"We can still back down," Reagan said, "without anyone knowing. But it's worth a try. At worst it's a bluff."

The President leaned back and sighed. "Thank you for the information. Reagan, please see them out. Then gather the team in the Situation Room."

"Yes, sir." Reagan stood quickly and motioned for Jackson and Lily to come.

They stood and began to follow her out, but Jackson stopped by the door. "Mr. President," he said across the Oval Office, "I know China's power is growing. But we're still stronger. *You* still command the greatest military force the world has ever seen. So when you say stop, and you mean it, they will back down, sir."

"Very well, Mr. Crow. Thank you."

"You're welcome, Mr. President."

67

DONGHAI MARVELED AT how this sunrise, while identical to the day before with brilliant light glinting off the steel rails of his aircraft carrier and the water beyond, could leave such a foul taste in his mouth. The order had come from his father, General Li, thirty minutes ago. It had been a simple message. A terrible message.

Mission aborted. Fall back to port immediately. Appear weak.

Appear weak was another of Father's favorites from Sun Tzu. *Appear weak when you are strong, and strong when you are weak.*

It meant Father still believed in their strength. It meant that their day would come to take back the Diaoyu Islands, and Taiwan, and much, much more.

But this would not be that day.

Donghai forced himself to look at the news, to find the reasons why this had happened. He would learn the full truth when he returned, but he could not help but discover what he could. He found a statement issued by the U.S. President just an hour earlier:

Today I have agreed with President Liu Wei of the People's Republic of China to a cessation of all acts of aggression and territorial claims in the East China Sea and the South China Sea for a period of five years. The United States remains committed to the peaceful resolution of territorial disputes in these waters, and to its allies and enduring prosperity and peace in the region. - PRESIDENT MICHAEL WALLACE

The statement answered none of Donghai's questions. He searched further for any reporting involving China in the United States. It did not take long before he pieced together a few answers. There had been a shooting at the Waldorf in New York City. The U.S. Ambassador to Japan, who was believed to have been a guest at the hotel, was assassinated in an apparent murder-suicide involving a Chinese reporter named Patrick Li. The investigation was ongoing, now in combination with the continuing investigation of the murder in the Treaty Room seven days earlier.

Zhang, my brother...

Donghai might grieve in time, but now he felt only fury. His brother had always been the weak link. He had never respected Father as Donghai had. Zhang had never maintained the honor, courage, and discipline needed to serve his people. Father still did. They would fight again, when the Americans' resistance had no option but to crumble away.

They had already laid a foundation under the waters of the Taiwan Strait—an 80-mile tunnel connecting mainland China to Taiwan. It remained hidden for now, but soon enough it would be known as a world wonder. The dirt and rock from the tunnel had proven useful in building up their island bases in the South China Sea. That secured China's perimeter. Now Father needed only wait for the right time to order their soldiers march on the defiant island. Taiwan's people had been softened. Their young generations would gladly choose China's wise governance over war, as long as the Americans did not rush to their defense.

The roar of combustion heralded a formation of fighter jets passing over Donghai's carrier. They were low enough for him to see the stars and stripes on their wings. They circled back and cruised high above, as if escorting the ship back to the mainland. Donghai gripped the rails of his ship with clenched fists.

He would not act. He knew the art of war. *Supreme excellence consists of breaking the enemy's resistance without fighting.*

This was a long game, and in time, America's resistance would break.

68

JACKSON LEANED BACK in his office chair, propped his wingtips up on the desk, and marveled that he was alive. It had been too close in Beijing, and even closer at the Waldorf. The fifty stitches on his shoulder attested to that. Other than a hospital visit to sew up the wound and confirm that Kathy had stabilized, Jackson's day had been quiet since the meeting with the President. A secret treaty of war had been ripped up. The two most powerful men in the world had reached a new, public deal. And China had backed down.

The office suddenly brightened as a young woman entered and sat across from Jackson. Her face radiated light, with no trace of fear, no quivering lip. She held a strange sort of power over him. Like kryptonite, he thought with a smile.

"Well you look pleased with yourself," Lily said.

"Hey, we survived another day," he said. "And not a bad day's work. How does it feel to stop a war?"

"Just doing my job."

"Oh? You expected to uncover critical intelligence about China's plans and brief the President in the Oval Office and save the world?"

She laughed. "Something like that."

"You never cease to amaze me. See anything else interesting in the news this afternoon?"

"Not really. The press keeps singing the President's praises after his statement. Still not a peep from Taiwan or the Senkaku Islands. You were right about deterrence."

"For today at least. No news is good news. By the way, I talked to Vin. He says all's quiet in Camelot. He also invited us to fly with him to Mauritius. He has a place there on the beach."

"Sounds nice. Your friend is very…interesting. But work has piled up since I've been away."

"Don't worry about the work. I'm giving us the week off."

"Us?"

"We both earned it." He swung his feet off the desk and stood. "Can I walk you home?"

"You still think I'm at risk?"

"Maybe. We need to let the dust settle after today. I was thinking we'd pick up sushi and eat up on your rooftop."

"Are you asking me out on a date?"

Jackson shrugged. "Just a—"

"Yes," she interrupted. "I'd like that."

A few minutes later they exited the State Department together. No reporters tried to stop them. No agents trailed them. No one paid them any attention at all. They looked like two lawyers in navy suits leaving after a routine day at the office.

They picked up sushi and sake and went to Lily's apartment building. It was a glorious spring evening, and they had the rooftop to themselves. They toasted as the sun set in long rays burning brilliant orange through the pink-and-purple clouds. The sushi couldn't compare to Tokyo's, but it was a fair trade for the peace and quiet.

Lily sipped her sake and said, "You know what would make this even better than our first date?"

Jackson's brow raised. "We had a first date?"

"In Tokyo, remember? You took me out for sushi and held my hand…"

"While we tried to evade surveillance."

"Yes, and our second date was here."

"While you were under surveillance."

"Yes, and now I'm not. Third date's a charm. And what would make it better is a little swim."

Jackson eyed the pool, glowing with enticement in the twilight.

"Come on, the water's heated."

Jackson's phone buzzed. He glanced at it and saw the text.

We have an urgent situation. Call now. – R

"What is it?" Lily asked.

Jackson tossed the phone aside, even as it buzzed again. "Just an old friend. It can wait."

Lily gazed up at the evening's first stars. Her hand found Jackson's. "Wait until after Mauritius?"

Jackson let his head fall to the side so that he could study the fine lines of her face and neck, her smooth black hair. "Yes. Maybe we'll stay there a while. Vin won't mind."

"Neither will I." She met his eyes with a mischievous grin. "You know, when we get back I'm thinking about applying to the Department of Justice."

"Oh?"

"Maybe I'll prosecute some normal thugs. Or track down money launderers in Camelot."

"You're tough enough for the job."

"Thanks," she said, her fingers going gently to the wound at Jackson's shoulder. "That means something coming from you."

He flashed a wry smile. "It's been an unusual week. We might as well cap it off with a swim. In neutral waters?"

"Au contraire. This is my territorial sea."

JAY BRADFORD is the pen name of a #1 Amazon bestselling author who knows too much. To learn more about the author and his work, visit www.jaybradfordbooks.com.

Made in the USA
Monee, IL
25 October 2022